SAVING SARKIS

Barbara!
Enjoy the ride!
Mary Gulaserian
2017

SAVING SARKIS

MARY GULESERIAN

GABRIEL PRESS

SAVING SARKIS
Copyright © 2016 by Mary Guleserian. All rights reserved.

No part of this publication may be reproduced, distributed or transmitted in any form or by any means, including photocopying, recording, or other electronic or mechanical methods, without the prior written permission of the publisher, except in the case of brief quotations embodied in critical reviews and certain other noncommercial uses permitted by copyright law.

Gabriel Press
377 Carolet Lane
Orange, CA 92869

Publisher's Note: This is a work of fiction. Names, characters, places, and incidents are a product of the author's imagination. Locales and public names are sometimes used for atmospheric purposes. Any resemblance to actual people, living or dead, or to businesses, companies, events, institutions, or locales is completely coincidental.

Saving Sarkis/Mary Guleserian. — 1st ed.

ISBN 978-0-9975151-0-7

This book is dedicated with love to my husband,
Armen Guleserian
Whose love, encouragement and support
never wavered.

"I am confident that the whole history of the human race contains no such horrible episode as this. The great massacres and persecutions of the past seem almost insignificant when compared to the sufferings of the Armenian race in 1915."

Henry Morgenthau, Senior US Ambassador to the Ottoman Empire

When Hitler first proposed his Final Solution, he was told that the world would never permit such a mass murder. Hitler silenced his advisers by asking, "Who, after all, speaks today of the annihilation of the Armenians?"

PROLOGUE

Constantinople, 1915
Armen Begosian woke to the sounds of his wife's weeping in the nursery and the soft whimpering of his infant son, Sarkis. For a few seconds, he wondered how he'd been able to sleep the last two hours. He shot out of bed, stumbled to the window, and stared through a slit in the heavy velvet drapes to the street below.

Terror gripped him. The gendarmes were still there; they'd been tailing him for the last week.

He left the bedroom, walked down the hall and entered the nursery. Varteni had placed a brown felt bonnet on their son's head, and tied the bow under his chin. She picked up the sleepy infant and held him close, shooting an accusatory glare at her husband. "We could have done something. Anything! I can't do this. I won't."

He gazed at his sleeping son and, for a moment, Armen didn't trust himself to speak. Instead, he leaned into his wife, putting his hand on the dozing newborn, kissing his cheeks, breathing in his baby scent. He brushed a shaky hand over Varteni's hair. "If we bring Sarkis with us, we condemn him to all those rumors of an uncertain fate." He fought to quiet the helpless raging inside. "If Sarkis goes with the Alexakis family, there's hope. If we take him, who knows? We have an idea what awaits us. We have no control. We've made a plan. Let's keep to it."

He turned and made his way to the stairs. His hands trembled as he reached for the banister; he felt his heart would certainly fail.

The authorities expected them at the dock at ten o'clock. It was now nine. He had no idea what to expect, or where they'd be taken.

The stairs behind him creaked. He knew Varteni followed. Bright sunlight streamed into the living room, giving the space a rosy hue. He felt the strange juxtaposition of his seething fury and the glorious brilliance of the morning.

Armen started at the soft knock at the door, catching his breath. Varteni came into the foyer with baby Sarkis. His gaze locked with hers, and she nodded. She walked into the living room and sat on the divan. He opened the door.

Theodore and Neoma Alexakis struggled with a baby carriage as they came into the foyer.

"Good morning!" Theo almost shouted. "Fine day, isn't it?"

Theo shut the door, passed in front of his friend, and whispered. "They're still out there, Armen."

"Yes, I saw them."

Neoma spotted Varteni in the living room and rushed to her. Varteni reached out with one arm and embraced her friend. The two women sat and watched the sleeping baby.

Armen crossed to the front window of his home.

Theo followed, and stood next to his friend, staring through the crack in the drapes. "Did you talk to a lawyer?"

"I went to the authorities, but they don't listen," Armen whispered. "I tried to secure legal representation, but was told there was no recourse." He peered over Theo's shoulder at the two men on the corner. "Our priest advised us to go along with their demands."

"What?"

"Because the authorities promise this is a temporary action for the protection of Turkish citizens." Armen turned away from the window. "I also took that summons to three men in my church. They're established businessmen like me. Not one of them had received the notice! Only me!"

Stunned, Theo looked at his friend. "What do you think it means?"

"We're being ordered out of Constantinople to be relocated. There's no question as to the consequences of disobeying! You know what's happened to Armenians over the last twenty years," he hissed. "The massacres, kidnappings... ."

"But why you and not all of the Armenians living here?"

"It's my store, that's what it boils down to, Theo. They want the store." He shook his head and fumed. "This is my fault. I've endangered my son and my wife, because I cared more for my business. Why did I put off leaving? I saw trouble coming, but I never thought it would come to this, ever!"

His lucrative jewelry shop, *Treasures of the Golden Horn*, was located in the Grand Bazaar, the fashionable tourist shopping area in Constantinople. The small showroom, well known and respected for the high quality of gems Armen Begosian bought and sold to other jewelers, had earned the respect of his peers.

Neoma rose. "I, I think it's time."

The parents of ten-day-old Sarkis held each other and kissed their son goodbye. Now it was Armen who pulled away gasping for air, struggling to regain his composure.

Theo followed him into the foyer. He passed his wife and they exchanged a worried glance.

Neoma reached out to Varteni, stroking her arm. "Varteni, tell me what you've packed for Sarkis."

Varteni stood and placed her son into the baby

carriage. "You have all his clothes, his blankets." She lifted the small mattress of the buggy to reveal a small bundle. "And here is our family Bible, and a collection of some family photographs."

Neoma smoothed the top of the baby's head with a soft pat. "I found a wet nurse, like I promised. Angeliki Pappas."

"It breaks my heart to think of another woman... ."

"Another woman who will feed your child, and nourish him," Neoma soothed, stroking the back of her neck.

Varteni nodded miserably. "You're right, you're right." The two women gazed at the sleeping baby.

With worried strokes to his mustache, Theo reassured his friend. "Don't worry. Little Sarkis will want for nothing."

Armen leaned close to his friend. "You're moving back to Crete? That's the plan?"

"Yes, we'll stay with my cousins. We leave in less than a week. You have the address."

"Your brothers have all moved to the United States... ."

"That's true. I told you we'd join them there eventually. They've been sending money for my parents' move."

Armen's eyes clouded over. "The United States!"

"I'll wait to hear from you at the address I gave you. We'll leave for the United States as soon as we can get the money together. It might take a few years."

Armen was silent for a moment, the corners of his mouth turned down. He took a steadying breath. "If we don't return, if you don't get a letter from us in the years while you're in Crete... you go on."

"I'll leave a forwarding address with my cousins when we leave for America."

Armen gripped Theo by the shoulders. "You'll raise my son as your own?"

Theo nodded, his eyes misting over. "I'll raise Sarkis as my own."

"Thank you, Theo. We've been so worried; I've heard nothing from my family in over six months. It frightens me, but it helps knowing that you and Neoma will protect our boy."

Theo clasped his friend's neck, leaned in, and whispered, "You'll be the one protecting him. You'll be the one to love him. You'll be the one to teach him! Don't think the worst!"

"The worst?" Armen shook his head. "We have no idea what the worst is. That's why we chose you and Neoma to watch over Sarkis."

"Just while you are away," Theo reminded him.

"Yes." A huge sigh escaped Armen. "Just while we're away."

Armen and Varteni gave their son a final kiss. Standing with stoic resolve, they waved goodbye from the window. They held their breath as they watched their Greek neighbors and their precious son pass with ease under the watchful eye of the Turkish police stationed at the corner.

Varteni fled upstairs. Armen would wait a few minutes, collect his wife, and then they'd leave to report to the officials.

Sighing, he gazed down at the tiled entryway. He knelt, and tapped on the floor, listening. No hollow sounds.

He stood, and walked up the carpeted stairs three feet from the bottom step. Turning, he looked down at the tile. No one would ever know. No one would ever guess.

ONE

Orange, California, Present Day
I've always considered the disappearance of my fiancé, Jayson Carpenter, and my decision to give up our infant son for adoption the two worst things that could ever happen to me.

I was wrong.

The morning of the kidnapping started normally enough, and then it all went to hell.

I'd come into the office early, made coffee, perused the morning paper, and was about to tackle a stack of files on my desk when my partner, Ralph, walked in.

"Hey, Jen."

"You look like you've had a rough night," I said.

"Didn't sleep much."

"How's Lynne?" I knew his wife had been suffering a persistent sore throat for nearly three months. A few days earlier, Ralph finally had insisted she see a doctor.

"A couple of her tests came back positive. We had an appointment today, but the doctor was called out on an emergency. We rescheduled for Friday."

"Positive for what?" I steeled myself. Please, not the word that elbowed into my mind.

"Lynne says she'll wait for the doctor's diagnosis, no sense in giving energy to what it could be." Ralph plunged both hands into his pockets and gave me a searching look. "I've been reading up on her symptoms. It doesn't look good."

My voice caught. "I... I don't know what to say, Ralph. Can I do anything? Anything at all?"

"Nope. Just be patient like the rest of us."

The silence between us lingered a minute.

My phone rang. With a quick wave Ralph ducked into his office.

"Jenna Paletto." I swiveled to face the window.

"This is Jenna Paletto the investigator?"

"That's me."

"My name is Sophie Alexakis. I, I uh, I need help. My husband's been kidnapped." The woman on the phone sounded shaky.

I wrote down her name. "Are you sure? Have you contacted the police?"

"You helped my friend, Helen Fincher, with her divorce. She said for a private investigator you were honest and fair."

"Have you notified the police?" I asked again.

"Wait, there's more. This morning I found the body of a man on my front lawn."

I straightened. "There's a dead man on your front lawn and your husband's been kidnapped?"

The woman's voice quivered. "I thought he'd had a heart attack! He was just lying there when I went out to get my paper. Then, I found out from the police that he'd been shot. He died right on the lawn."

"Did..."

"Then, at about eight thirty, the college called," she continued. "They told me my husband never showed up to teach his class. I tried calling him a dozen times, but he doesn't answer his cell phone."

"Have you..."

"You have to understand. My husband never misses his classes. Not ever!"

"That may be, but..."

"Then I received a call from some men. They spoke with an accent I didn't recognize. What English they did speak was garbled, but they made it plain they have my husband, Sarkis! I'm scared!"

"Have you informed the police?!" I demanded.

"No! Because the man who called said not to contact the authorities. And the police have been right outside my home all morning because of the murdered man on my front lawn. The kidnappers said they're watching me."

"Do you know what these men want from your husband?"

"Well..." she hesitated. "I think it might be our family Bible."

I closed my eyes. Oh. Please.

"He didn't call it a Bible; he called it the 'book,'" Sophie Alexakis went on. "Why they want this Bible is a mystery to me, but Professor Takmaz at Chapman College had an appointment with Sarkis between classes this morning and my husband didn't show up."

"Okay, okay, stop." Already confused, I needed a face-to-face. "Where do you live?"

"No! You can't come here. I think it stands to reason that the police might know you. If you just show up out of the blue, they'll wonder why. And they'll suspect something's up, right? And so far, the police have no idea my husband's been kidnapped."

At last, she paused. I could tell she was holding her breath. She had a point. A lot of the local cops know me, and they'd put Mrs. Alexakis on the top of their list of murder suspects if I just happened to show up at their crime scene. Who was I kidding? With a dead body on her front lawn, she was their number one suspect.

"Where's your car?" I asked.

"In the driveway, and they're still doing all their forensics. Miss Paletto, I need to meet Professor Takmaz at the Starbucks at Beckman Hall at Chapman College in an hour. He has an eleven o'clock lunch date with his wife, so I have to be on time. He has the Bible. I obviously can't walk all the way to the college." Her voice broke.

"Tell you what, I want you to try to find a way to leave the house in, say, ten minutes. Meet me two blocks from your house. Where do you live?"

"Orange Park Acres. How about Palm Reed Court? That's two blocks away." She gave me directions.

"I'm leaving now, Mrs. Alexakis. I'll be driving a black Toyota Forerunner."

"Call me Sophie, please."

"See you in two shakes, Sophie."

As I passed by Ralph's door, he glanced up. I was about to tell him where I was going when I heard the front door open and the sound of footsteps. It was nine forty-five. Appointments always started after ten.

"You expecting someone?" Ralph asked. I shook my head 'no.'

"Jenna Paletto?" a voice called out. "Is Jenna Paletto here?"

Wary, I took a few steps into the small reception area. Ralph followed me.

A young man stood in the semi-dark reception room, his face shaded. In one hand, he gripped a small duffel bag and in the other the strap of his backpack. He wore a black t-shirt with the words, 'Quit Staring At Me,' in bold, white type across the chest.

His stance seemed oddly familiar. I inched forward for a better look. "May I help you?"

He stepped into the light, the corner of his mouth sliding into an uncertain half-grin. "I probably should've called first."

"Oh, my God..." My voice caught as I tried to take a breath.

Ralph, standing beside me, asked, "You know him?"

"Yeah ... I know who he is." I grabbed Ralph's arm for support while a mirror image of the man I would always love stared back at me.

The kid straightened. "My name is Isaac Carpenter. They call me Zach."

Ralph's eyes widened. "Are you sayin' you're Jayson Carpenter's kid?"

"That's what the birth certificate says." Zach kept his eyes fixed on me.

"You're my Isaac." My heartbeat thrummed in my ears.

Ralph, for once, was as stunned as I was. "I'll be damned."

"This is my partner, Ralph."

Zach stepped forward and shook his hand. "Pleased to meet you."

"Your ... your father disappeared twenty years ago." I dared to move even closer, taking in every inch of him, devouring the shades of white blond in his hair, the deep blue of his eyes, and the hard angles of his face. Handsome. And, oh so familiar.

He leaned close, obviously searching for words. Sweat

beaded his upper lip. "As soon as I found out about you, I wanted to meet you." His chin lifted.

There was something defiant, perhaps even angry, about him.

"Found out? Found out what? I don't understand," I said. But I began to suspect what I'd always feared.

"That I was adopted!" He hurled the words at me. "I found my adoption papers last week."

I blinked back surprise. "They never told you that you were adopted?" Deep regret stabbed at my heart, even though I'd always known that my wishes hadn't been a priority with his parents.

Ralph leaned against the doorframe. "Hell of a way to find out something that important, kid."

"I Googled your name and found you. Cop, ex-cop, detective, private investigator, and all around bad ass." He took a deep breath, and then exhaled a gust of air. "Now, I'd like some answers. I'm sure not getting any from my parents."

I bit back a smile. From my years as a police officer and working with teens, I recognized Zach's impatient vulnerability for what it was. Fear.

"Look, Zach, more than anything I want to sit down and talk to you every minute of the next twenty-four hours. But, I've just been called out for an important appointment." I wavered over not telling Ralph someone wanted my help without police involvement. "I have to leave. Do you have a cell phone?"

For a split second, his face fell. Then, he recovered.

My heart broke as I took in his obvious fatigue and disappointment.

"Well, then... Can I come with you? Please? I'm a good listener. I just want to talk, to get to know you."

"Zach, it's not that simple." I dug through my purse for my keys. Abruptly, I stopped. What in the world was I doing? After nineteen years, my son had finally found me, and I was about to walk out the door? I couldn't leave him to wait for me in my office. Everything in me said it was wrong. Here he was in the flesh. I pushed the alarm bells ringing in my head away. Ah, the consequences be damned. My son wanted to know me. I mentally added a grudging justification: I had a strong suspicion I might be calling the police in on this case anyway.

Planting myself in front of him, I folded my arms. "Can you keep quiet and be inconspicuous?"

His blue eyes widened. "My lips are sealed."

I studied him. "Okay. You listen to everything I say. Anything I tell you to do, you do. Got that?"

"Are you kidding me? I'm going to work on a case with you?"

"You're not working on anything. One false move and I pull over and haul you out of the car. Leave your stuff here, but bring your jacket. Let's go." I turned and opened the door.

Zach nodded goodbye to Ralph, who shook his head at me. I read his glare: You and I are definitely going to have a talk.

TWO

We bolted for my Forerunner, jumped in and soon we were sailing up Chapman Avenue to the high-rent district known as Orange Park Acres. It was ten in the morning.

As I guided my car up the hill, I couldn't help stealing a quick glance here and there at Zach in the passenger seat, his long eyelashes, and that jaw line. My son. My son was actually sitting next to me.

"I'm sorry I didn't call ahead, but I've got a million questions."

"I understand. I've always wanted answers, too. I still want them. Your father's case was never closed. I was pregnant with you. We were happy, we planned to get married, and then, Jayson just…evaporated into thin air."

I stopped. A little information at a time would have to do. When Jayson disappeared, my life changed. My former self crumbled away; the new Jenna Paletto became hard, resolved.

I felt his gaze as he studied me.

"You loved him?"

"Oh, yes." The memory made me smile.

He gave me a pointed look. "You're prettier than I thought you'd be."

"Thanks." Heat crept up my neck.

"I'm really surprised you don't have blond hair. And you wear your hair kinda short. For some reason I thought you'd have longer hair. Do people ask you if you're a model, or something?"

I stared out my windshield, and gave a short laugh. "Nope. Nothing like that." I do have my mother's good looks and am thankful for it. But it's so far from important. I dress casually, jeans and tee shirts with a jacket or long shirt. I probably rotate two dozen ball caps most of the time.

"So, listen up." I gave him the facts on Sophie Alexakis' phone call. "And the kidnappers said no police, or else."

Zach frowned. "What do they want?"

"The Alexakis family Bible, apparently." I sighed. "Don't ask, I don't know too many details. And then she gets another call from a professor at the college, and he says her husband missed their appointment this morning. And surprise, surprise, he tells her he has the Bible."

"So now we're gonna do what?"

"We pick up Sophie, and then meet the professor."

"This is awesome!"

"Settle down. When we meet Sophie, you sit in the back and stay quiet." I opened the console and handed him a notepad. "Take notes, be invisible, and remember our client is going to be really stressed. We've got a dead guy, a missing husband, and she won't tell the cops."

"She's gotta be totally freaked."

"Exactly. So keep still, and be sympathetic."

A serious expression settled on his face. "I understand."

We drove by Sophie's cross street.

"Check it out. Police are still there, the Fire Department, ambulance, and, of course, news vans," Zach reported.

I noted the usual onlookers were present, restrained by yellow crime-scene tape. I wondered if Sophie Alexakis had made it past the police to Palm Reed Court.

I saw Palm Reed up ahead and turned into the cul-de-sac, where a woman was pacing on the sidewalk.

She signaled me. The designer sweat suit she wore let me know we came from different fashion police. I pulled up to the curb and lowered my window. "Sophie?"

Sophie nodded as she dabbed at her eyes with a tissue. "Thank you so much for meeting me. I'm desperate."

Sliding my aviators up on my head, I clambered out of the car, and reached out to shake her hand. "Think nothing of it. Why don't you get in, and we'll go meet that professor? What'd you say his name was?"

"Professor Takmaz. He's the dean of Arts at the college. He and his wife collect art and antiquities from all over the world. We've known them for years."

Zach got out of the front seat and moved to the middle seats. "This is Zach Carpenter, my... assistant."

Sophie extended her hand. "Hi, Zach."

"Hi." They shook hands.

"We've got thirty minutes or so. We can talk in the car on our way."

I pulled away from the curb and headed back down Chapman toward the college.

I drummed my fingers on the steering wheel. "Well, let's start at the beginning. Tell me everything."

The woman beside me took a deep breath. She was in her early thirties, maybe five-six, a-hundred-and-fifteen pounds. Her black curly hair was piled high in a loose-clipped bundle, and little black ringlets framed her pale complexion. Some women pay a lot of money to get that look. She didn't really need makeup, but she wore blush, lipstick, and had a little eye shadow on, although her lower lids were smudged from crying.

Sophie exhaled. "Well, first I need to let you know that Sarkis and I had a terrible fight last night! I know this isn't going to look good with the police."

Crap. I wondered if the police knew about their fight. "Anyone mention the fight to the cops?"

"Apparently my neighbor heard us. One of the detectives already asked me about it."

Terrific. "Your husband ever hit you?"

Sophie reared back as if *I'd* just struck her. She looked shocked. "Never!"

"You ever hit him?" I stopped at a red light and gave her a pointed look.

She swiveled her gaze right back at me. "Absolutely not!"

"Okay, that's good, good. What was the fight about?" I hit my horn to get the idiot on his cell phone in front of me to move.

She sat erect, leaning forward a bit in her seat, and pursed her lips. She seemed to grope for words. "The fight was about, it was about..." She gave her head a quick shake and took a breath. "My husband has two sons by a former marriage. Grant is a very successful businessman. The youngest son, Tyler, has had a lot of great ideas and made many attempts at starting up businesses, but has failed often. And to tell you the truth I think he drinks too much. Over the years, my husband has bent over backwards to help him. Tyler is married with two children, and has a lot of responsibilities. His wife is a nurse, and works constantly. But Tyler has used his father's good will and generous nature just once too often in my book. His dad has given him loan after loan."

"Has Tyler ever repaid a loan?"

Sophie shook her head. "Not in the ten years we've been married. I found out last night that Sarkis wrote him a check for over $30,000 without telling me. I mean, it has to stop! I'm so done with Sarkis enabling him and Tyler's incessant inflated stories of how this 'new venture' is the real deal."

"Thirty thousand dollars?" I whistled. "That's a nice chunk of change for a college professor."

"Besides teaching, Sarkis is also a businessman and his investments are lucrative. But teaching is his first love."

"So, how did you find out about this loan?

She shot me a sheepish look. "I opened the bank statement when it came yesterday. I know I shouldn't have but I had my suspicions. I was right."

"And so when you saw him last night?"

"I let him have it with both barrels." She fought for composure.

"And he just yelled at you, didn't touch you?" In my rearview, I saw Zach lean in to hear her answer.

"No! Sarkis doesn't yell. I yelled because he was silent and guilty. He didn't have much to say. But he'd broken a firm promise to me, and I felt our trust had been violated." Gazing out the front windshield, Sophie pursed her lips, and shook her head. "Wait. I don't want to give you the wrong impression of Sarkis. He's really a decent man, good and kind, and generous like I said." She shugged. "He's just weak when it comes to Tyler."

"So, what was the upshot? You two make up?"

"He left me standing in the kitchen and went to bed. I didn't go up until much later. By then, he was asleep.

When I woke this morning, he was standing by the bed saying goodbye. He told me he'd call me later, but he never did."

Zach leaned forward again. "Ma'am, did you say anything to him?"

I caught my breath. He wasn't exactly staying invisible, but it was a good question.

"No, I was still mad. I pretended to be asleep." She twisted around to face Zach. "He said, 'I love you, Sophie C.' Those were his last words to me."

THREE

I felt sorry for the lady, which surprised me. I'd denied myself the luxury of emotional release for years. Now, I questioned my feelings. When I was young, I'd hurled myself headlong into police work. Yet Jayson's unsolved case is the one that haunts me the most to this day. Police work had been far off my radar before Jayson's disappearance. But when it happened, I worked his case with everything I had.

Why had we failed to find him? I'd followed directions of the police, and campus authorities. We'd canvassed neighborhoods, passed out fliers. Had I tossed aside or ignored the one piece of evidence necessary to find him? I would never know. With Jayson gone, I'd learned the hard way not to overlook evidence, not even the bits and pieces that seem insignificant.

When I did decide to become a police officer, I excelled at it. Yet the mistakes I'd made early in my career, those embarrassing leaps to conclusions that were dead wrong, taught me to rein myself in. I no longer opened my mouth to offer unsolicited opinions. I studied my instructors and the sergeants I admired. I behaved with such caution my fellow officers thought me cold and aloof. I rather liked that façade, the cool police officer who had her act together.

So while I drove, I checked myself, and although I felt for Sophie, who sat in my car fearful and jittery, my job was to extract information, absorb her persona, and judge her until I felt I knew her to the core. I like to think I'm pretty good at it.

I saw real regret and sadness in the woman seated beside me. In these few moments, I was close to believing she'd had nothing to do with her husband's disappearance.

Husbands and wives fight in as many ways as they love. Some stoke the coals of anger for a season; others do a dance of bitterness and resentment for years. Many spend a lifetime tiptoeing around the elephant in the room. Sophie's marriage sounded healthy, except for Sarkis blowing this very important promise to his wife.

She sat there, wound up, fighting back tears.

"Sophie C. C stands for...?"

"Catherine, Sophia Catherine." She shut her eyes against the reflected glint of sun from the car ahead.

I glanced at her. "Honestly, you know, I don't know one couple that doesn't fight. It's not the end of the world."

"But we never fight. I'm serious!" She declared. "But yes, he went behind my back, that's why this hurts so much."

I beeped my horn to signal a car in a driveway to go ahead of me. "You have any trouble getting out of your neighborhood?"

"Well, I wanted to appear like I was... you know, very obliging. I'd already brought out a couple carafes of coffee for the police, and I opened up my house so they could use the bathroom. So I figured they'd know I wasn't going anywhere, right?" Her words seemed to give her new strength.

I gave her a halfhearted shrug.

"I went outside and asked them how much longer they'd be. Then I got a CSI lecture from this detective on how every little thing is examined." With a pinched thumb and forefinger, she punched the air on *'every little thing.'*

"So, you got out of your neighborhood with no problem."

She nodded. "No problem. I just walked over to neighbors I hardly know. Chatted it up with them for a minute or two." Sophie twirled an escaped tendril of hair around an index finger. "And reporters were interviewing people! I don't think half of them even live in my neighborhood. I was careful walking by those people, I even wondered if any of them might be the kidnappers!"

Suddenly, she put a hand to her mouth and turned to me. "The kidnappers said they'd call tonight, did I mention that? Oh, Lord, I hope they're still planning on calling. They have to call. They have to!"

I smiled to myself. She was exhausting but it was hard not to sympathize. "The kidnappers want something from you. Trust me, they'll call."

We hit a clump of traffic due to road construction. Traffic condensed into one slow, miserable lane.

I gave my steering wheel an impatient slap. "So, let's focus. You came outside this morning, found this guy's body, and you called the police?"

"No, my neighbor Deirdre called the police. She was about to go on her five-miler with her baby. She saw me across the street, standing over that poor guy. I asked her to call."

"When did you learn your husband never made it to his class?"

"The college secretary said half a dozen students had come into Administration, wondering what had happened to Mr. A. So she gave me a call. Talk about shocked! I mean my husband never, ever misses a class." She made a single nod with her chin. "It's a known fact."

"And you think the kidnappers want what book?"

"The kidnappers, oh! I can't even believe I'm saying that word." Sophie bent forward, fingertips pressed to her temples. "Kidnapped!" She straightened and turned to me. "They called right after the secretary did. They said, 'We have your husband.' They sounded foreign. Did I mention that?"

I gave her a nod. "Where do you think they're from?"

Sophie shook her head, shrugging. "I couldn't place the accent."

"Foreign. French? German? Russian?"

She thought a moment. "No. It wasn't any of those accents, and it wasn't Asian... I don't know."

"Again, what book is it you think they want?"

"Okay. I've been thinking about this one." Turning to include Zach, she leaned closer. "About five months ago... is that five? Let me see—" she counted off on her fingers "December, January, February, and March. No, four months ago, at the faculty Christmas party Professor Takmaz and his wife were talking with Sarkis and a bunch of other professors. At the time, I wasn't paying too much attention because they were talking about a cancer gene fingerprint. It was a bit over my head." She stopped for a deep breath; the sheer act of explaining herself seemed to visibly lift her worry.

"Later, I heard Sarkis mention his family Bible. He told Professor Takmaz there were some handwritten pages in Greek in the front of his family Bible. Professor Takmaz offered to translate the pages."

Sophie dug through her small backpack, pulled out a tissue, and blew her nose.

"Then, this morning, Professor Takmaz called. Sarkis was supposed to meet with him at nine, but he didn't show. The professor said he had finished the translation, and was Sarkis ever in for a surprise. I didn't even know Sarkis had taken him up on the offer to translate!" She shook her head. "I don't even know when he gave him the Bible."

"So, he never got to hear what the professor found out, because he was kidnapped."

"Yes. Who could've done this? Why would they want that Bible?"

"Not so fast," I countered, "maybe it's not the Bible. Maybe it's a different book." I searched for a more reasonable answer.

"Well, it all sounds pretty suspicious to me. Not only did the kidnappers call it 'the book,' so did Professor Takmaz. He didn't call it 'the Bible.'" She bit her lower lip, falling silent for a blessed three seconds. "I can't believe this is happening!"

I patted her shoulder. "It's a lot to take in."

Zach reached out and stroked her arm. "We'll try to get to the bottom of this. Hang in there. You'll see."

Sophie sniffed, and nodded.

Zach leaned back and settled into his seat.

I glanced in the rearview and caught his reflection looking slightly grim, gazing out the window. And then he turned and began to glance over the notes he'd taken. I wanted to pinch myself. He's sitting here in the flesh, he said he wants to get to know me; he's earnest and kind. I know I'm rushing headlong into intense infatuation and I don't care.

FOUR

We arrived at Chapman College, and I found an empty guest parking spot. My lucky day.

"We're here. You all right?"

Sophie's hands trembled, and her face looked drawn. "As much as I can't believe this is happening, yes."

"Let's go find out what Professor Takmaz has to say."

Sophie nodded, and brought out her compact. She dusted her nose and cheeks, and then applied a little lipstick. "Do I look like I've been crying?" she asked.

I gave her a quick once over. "Hardly."

Zach slid out of the back seat and opened her door. He stood in front of her, and took a good look. "Ah, maybe like you've had a touch of allergies. Nothing more."

"Okay." She slid out of the car.

I turned to Sophie. "Where exactly are we meeting the professor?"

"At Beckman Hall." We headed onto the campus.

I sought to lighten Sophie's mood as we walked across campus. "You know, I've been in this business for a long time, and people rarely commit felonies over works of nonfiction. I don't care what the title is. You've got a murder and a kidnapping over what?" I gave a short laugh. "A family Bible? It's either got gold pages, or the name of John F. Kennedy's real killer is in there."

Sophie slowed her walking. She gave me a quizzical look that bordered on a smile. Then her focus shifted. "There's Professor Takmaz. Professor!"

Standing outside the imposing five-story Argyros School of Business, and grinning from ear to ear, the professor approached us. He waved the Bible over his head like a trophy.

I have to admit, Professor Takmaz, for an old guy, was very engaging. Nattily dressed, despite his navy blue sweater being sugared with dandruff.

After introductions, the professor led the way to the ground level Starbucks at Beckman Hall. This was a cozy little place with lots of tables and forest green Starbucks umbrellas outside. We chose a table outdoors. The professor and Sophie began to discuss the last time they'd seen each other at the Christmas party and a colleague's sudden plans for divorce. Zach and I took drink orders and went inside while Sophie stayed with the professor.

"Tell me, Zach. Do your parents know where you are?" I knew what it was like to worry about the missing.

He looked guilty. "I'm pretty sure my parents are calling out the National Guard or something, and I'm sorry about that, but finding you was too important."

I leaned forward. "I think you owe them a phone call to let them know where you are. And by the way, where are you staying?"

He stared off for a minute, and then shrugged. "Please don't think of me as a stupid, impulsive kid. By and large I'm not. I have a 4.8 GPA, and I've won physics scholarships to Berkeley, Stanford, Irvine, to name a few. I graduated high school last December and have been taking courses online until the fall quarter starts at Berkeley."

Zach reddened. "I know better than this, and my mother did teach me manners." His eyes settled on me. "But is it a terrible imposition to stay with you? I know this is sudden." He shifted his stance, "I know my coming here has been a shock," he said, his voice tremulous. "But, it's like all my life I've gone down a dark hallway and every door's been locked. And now I have one door open. I have one answer."

Maybe it was the dark hallway analogy. I could relate to that. Zach was endearing, young, smart, and brash. I relished the idea of spending time with him, to find out what he thought, what his ideas were. This was a gift, a dream come true.

I made the decision. "You can stay with me, I have a spare bedroom you'll have to share with an ironing board. But first, I'd like you to call home and let me talk to your mom. I won't sleep tonight if I know your parents are worried about you."

He grinned. "Great! Thank you."

We brought back hot cups of tea. The professor and Sophie wrapped up their discussion of the new president at the college.

Zach sat opposite me, and Sophie and the professor faced each other.

Sophie apologized to the professor for Sarkis' absence.

"He's suffering from a bout of diverticulitis, " she lied.

The professor frowned in concern. "Oh, dear. No fun. I know how painful that is."

"May I ask where you're from?" I asked.

"I'm Lebanese." He gave me a wide smile. "I think I've been doing a good job over all these years of speaking to my classes with only a little accent."

"It's nice. Intriguing." And foreign, I thought.

Sophie sat ramrod straight while her left leg under the table did a lonely jitter. She clasped her hands so tightly her knuckles turned white.

Pushing his glasses up onto the bridge of his nose, Professor Takmaz removed a file from his briefcase. He then opened to the handwritten pages of the worn black leather Bible, positioned on top of the table. "Well, let me tell you what I've discovered, and then you have Sarkis call me tonight."

"Sounds good." Sophie's voice trembled.

"What's so fascinating," the professor began, "is that Sarkis thought these handwritten pages in the front were written in Greek. But it's not Greek. It's Armenian! In fact, the entire Bible is written in the Armenian language."

Sophie frowned, leaning forward. "Armenian? No, this Bible is an Alexakis family heirloom. Sarkis is Greek, not Armenian. Trust me!"

"That may well be, my dear, but this Bible is written in Armenian." He produced two printed sheets with a flourish. "I have some examples of each. Look here, the languages are hardly alike."

We all leaned forward to study the sets of pages. I saw a distinct difference in the two.

Taking one of the pages from the professor, Zach also examined the writing, his eyebrows furrowed in concentration.

Professor Takmaz's aged hands brushed the pages of the Bible as he spoke. "See? Why Sarkis thought the Bible was in Greek is a mystery."

I had to agree. "You know, perhaps Sarkis had been told all his life it was Greek. And apparently no one even opened the Bible." Zach handed me the Greek page, and I compared it to the Armenian font sample.

Sophie tenderly fingered the leaves of the old Bible,

gazing down at the foreign words. "Well, they were Christians, but why wouldn't they open this Bible? It's hard to imagine isn't it?

"Well, think about it." I leaned in. "When a family immigrates to America the old ways of thinking change. It's a new country, and the parents have to learn English. Their children become Americanized. This thing probably sat on a bookshelf and collected dust."

Nodding in agreement, Sophie's eyes lit up. "Sarkis' grandfather and grandmother emigrated from Crete. Most of the family was already here and living in Chicago. They sent for the last of the family in the late 1920's, I think."

Professor Takmaz brought out several stapled sheets. "So, here are the translations in English from the Armenian. I managed as much as I could on my own, though I had help from the Hambarian's at our church."

I smiled to encourage him along.

"Now," he said gleefully as he pointed to the Bible. "These handwritten pages are written by the original owner of this book." He gave the Bible an affectionate pat. "The author's name is Armen Begosian. He and his wife, Varteni, had just had a child." He held up a finger, signaling us to wait a moment. "Oh, yes. The year is nineteen fifteen. They lived in Constantinople, Turkey." Professor Takmaz peered at us over his bifocal glasses. "Does that mean anything to you?"

We shook our heads.

The professor nodded as if he'd expected that response. "Constantinople is now called Istanbul. A man named Ataturk became president of Turkey in... hmm... I think it was 1922 or 1923. He made tremendous changes in Turkey that brought the nation right into the twentieth century."

I wished he would just cut to the chase without the history lesson.

"But, in 1915, before any of what Ataturk did took place, a terrible war raged around the Christian Armenians who lived in Turkey. A group called The Young Turks forced them to leave their businesses and their homes. Armen Begosian owned a jewelry business in the Grand Bazaar in Constantinople. His shop was called..." The professor paused and peered through his bifocals to read the translation. *"Treasures of the Golden Horn.* Now, because he feared for their lives, Begosian was especially concerned for his only child, a son he named Sarkis."

FIVE

Sophie's hand flew to her mouth. "What?!"

And from Zach, "No way!"

My response was to lean back in my chair and frown at the professor. "That would make that tiny baby Sarkis's father?"

Sophie looked bewildered. "Wait, let me get this straight. The baby is named Sarkis, he emigrates to the States, he grows up, has a son he names after himself. That man is my husband. Good grief!"

"Anything is possible!" Takmaz went on, knowing he now had a captive audience. "The author, the jeweler Armen Begosian, has written that he and his wife have turned their son over to their Greek neighbors for safe keeping. Do you know anything about the Armenian Genocide in 1915?"

Again, we shook our heads.

Professor Takmaz took off his bifocals and wiped them clean with his napkin. "This group, the Young Turks, came like a plague into almost all the cities across Turkey. Large and small towns alike. They rooted out the Christian Armenians."

I almost choked in a mixture of surprise and outrage. "Did anyone try to stop this?"

The professor shook his head. "No one with any authority did much. People who voiced opposition were shot on the spot as examples to the rest. Of course, the murders created instant fear. Terrible things occurred, kidnappings and rapes of young daughters and wives, appalling brutality. Well," he said on a sigh, "the crimes of war."

"I've never heard of this. This is history? This is fact?" Sophie questioned.

"Read Henry Morganthau. He was the United States ambassador to Turkey at the time. Over one and a half million Christian Armenians lost their lives. Perhaps as many as eight hundred thousand Greeks were slaughtered also.

"And other Christian sects were killed as well. The Turks today say these people were 'relocated,' out of their homes and businesses. For those who remember, it remains a bitter, shameful, and atrocious treatment of humanity. A prelude to what Hitler did to the Jews!"

Taking furious notes, Zach froze, his brow furrowed, deep in thought. He looked up at the professor. "Pardon me, but does that translation give the names of the Greek neighbors?"

"Indeed they do." The professor handed the translated page to Zach.

Zach scanned the page and then blinked rapidly. He gazed at me then at Sophie.

"What?" she asked.

"Their names were Theodore and Neoma Alexakis."

"Alexakis!" A broad look of surprise swept across Sophie's face. "Oh, my gosh. This is unbelievable! You were right, Professor, you did have some incredible news for Sarkis."

Albeit we had just changed his heritage in one afternoon. I had an unfamiliar feeling of apprehension juxtaposed with discovery. Yet a flash of indignation overwhelmed me because of what I was hearing. I silently rebuked myself for my lack of knowledge.

The excited professor slapped his wrinkled hands together. "But this is where it gets so intriguing! Before Armen Begosian and his wife, Varteni, hid their precious son Sarkis with their Greek neighbors, they also hid a large…" He paused, searching for the right word, "reserve, if you will, of jewels and diamonds from his shop in the Grand Bazaar. This last page contains the written directions to the exact location of the hidden treasure!"

"Whaaat?!" Zach wore a look of disbelief.

The professor had us, hook, line and sinker. "Buried it all right in the entryway of his home."

Energized, I shot forward in my seat. "Are you kidding me? Wow! Bet you it's gone now, though, after all these years. I mean, 1915? That was a hundred years ago." I gave a decisive nod. "Someone got lucky!"

Professor Takmaz chuckled. "You never know! That's what I spend my whole life doing, studying ancient artifacts, discovering ancient treasures, from all around the world. Including Turkey and the old Ottoman Empire." He turned to each of us, brimming with excitement. "Wonderful things do turn up!"

Smiling, he continued, "In fact, I took the liberty of calling a few dealers I know in the Grand Bazaar in Istanbul. I asked them if there had been a jeweler's shop called *Treasures of the Golden Horn*, in the bazaar around 1915. You see some of the families have owned several of these shops for generations. However, it didn't ring a bell with any of my contacts."

Sophie straightened in her seat and shot me a look of astonished disbelief.

I sat there stunned. "You... you called them and told them you were in possession of a treasure map?"

Sophie studied Takmaz with a solemn gaze.

SIX

Professor Takmaz raised his hand. "No, no. Well, yes, but these are my trusted friends. We go back thirty or more years. I told them about the book and the possibility of the book having some directions, a map if you will, to the location of a treasure."

He widened his eyes, as if trying to convince us. "I didn't tell him the location, of course, but I just wanted to know if this Begosian had a jeweler's shop in the bazaar in 1915."

"What did they say?" Zach asked.

"Offhand, they didn't know anything." The professor tapped his fingers together. "So many years have passed since that time, but they did promise to get back to me."

I felt Zach and Sophie's gazes boring into me. I gave Professor Takmaz a long look. Forcing a lilt to my voice, I asked, "By any chance, did you mention Sarkis by name?"

The professor beamed. "No. I told them he was a colleague of mine, a Greek professor of Biology at Chapman, but that was all." He began to chuckle. "Oh, and about his mistake that the writing was Greek, when it was really Armenian. It's kind of comical." His eyes twinkled as he spoke.

The professor had no idea what he'd done.

Leaning forward, Sophie cupped her hands over her mouth, staring down at the pages Professor Takmaz had given her.

I gave Sophie a couple of pats on the back. "Well, this is exciting, isn't it, Sophie? Wait'll Sarkis finds out!" I turned and smiled at the professor. "So, have you heard from anyone yet? When did you make that call?"

"I called about a week ago. Let's see, no it was a week ago last Friday. Ten days, so far! They still haven't gotten back to me yet. Well, maybe they won't." He struggled to his feet. "Maybe they can't be bothered. But I think it's a wonderful, personal, historical document."

Sophie gathered the translated pages together. She caught on, following my lead. "Sarkis will be surprised, that's for sure! Thank you so much for your hard work, Professor." She glanced at her watch. "We've got to run, and I know you're joining your wife for lunch. If you hear from Istanbul, let us know!"

Zach leaned over and handed the professor his briefcase.

"You can be sure I will! Tell that husband of yours to get well and to give me a call, he owes me a lunch." Professor Takmaz left us with a cheery wave.

We watched him walk away. I caught Sophie's gaze, and we exchanged a knowing glance. "I'm going to run after him and get the name of that contact in Istanbul," I said.

Sophie pulled her jacket close to her and shivered, watching the professor cross the quad. "No. What's done is done. We can always contact the professor if things don't work out tonight. I'm taking his age into consideration, and his naiveté. He wouldn't have done this on purpose."

We stood and wove our way past tables of students studying or chatting. As we walked to the car, Zach asked, "Don't you think we should have told the professor Sarkis has been kidnapped? Is the professor in danger?"

Sophie stopped next to the car, wide eyed. "Zach has a point, Jenna. Could the professor be in any trouble?"

I slid into my seat and sighed, staring straight ahead. "We take a risk not telling him," I admitted, once they climbed into the car. "But if all goes well, Sarkis will be home tonight. That poor guy would have a heart attack if he knew he'd caused Sarkis any kind of grief."

Sophie settled into her seat, and then leaned her back against the passenger door, folding her arms over her chest. "Now this entire thing makes sense and it's the professor's doing." She frowned and stared out the windshield. "But, he's only guilty of trying to help his friend. I can't believe this. My stomach's in a knot." She held both hands under her rib cage.

"Are you feeling sick?"

Sophie stared off in resignation. "Sort of. I'm just confused. I don't know what I should do."

I started the car, and then turned to Sophie. "We'd better get clear about something. Are you sure you're willing to forego any help from the police? Or from the FBI?"

I could see the wheels turning. She realized the implication of what I was putting forward. I was, in effect, offering her a way out of hiring me.

I persisted. "The proper authorities can get all sorts of surveillance equipment. More than I have access to. Not to mention they're very experienced with kidnappings." I took a deep breath and exhaled. "I should also tell you that the closest thing to a kidnapping I've been involved in is a missing persons case about twenty years ago."

I turned to gaze at Zach. Our eyes locked for a moment, staring at one another in understanding. He leaned forward, waiting to hear Sophie's answer.

She turned to me, shaking her head. "And did you get the kidnapped person back?"

"No, I'm sorry to say. He vanished from the face of the earth. They never found him. He was twenty years old."

Sophie stayed completely still and thought while she

stared ahead. "I'm not taking any chances! They said no police. I won't involve them. I know in my heart I'm doing the right thing. You're hired and that's it. I don't want that treasure. If someone wants it, they can have it! I just want Sarkis back!"

SEVEN

Sophie didn't know me, but I appreciated her trust. This case meant more to me than she realized.

When Zach's father had gone missing, I'd worked tirelessly with many good people, but we'd never found Jayson. Sophie's declaration of faith in me prompted a determination to locate her husband. I vowed to do for her what I had failed to do for myself.

Sophie closed her eyes and shuddered. "Ugh. I feel sick."

I glanced at her, worried that she might be in shock after the events of the morning.

"You know, I'm kinda hungry. Can you eat something?"

"I could eat!" Zach said.

"Good. We'll go to Watson's."

"That might help." Sophie leaned her head against the door window and grew quiet.

I drove a few blocks south to the plaza circle in the historic Old Towne district. I parked a half a block from Watson's Drug, my favorite place for comfort food.

Zach scrambled out of the car and slammed the door. I slid out of the Toyota, and motioned Sophie to follow.

We waited while she dug through her purse for her sunglasses, and checked her phone for messages.

Without warning, a quiver of unease hit me as I walked behind the car. I scanned the storefronts and the center of the Plaza, a beautiful park-like area with a fountain that was surrounded by evergreens and palms. My sense of foreboding lingered.

Zach meandered over to me. "What's wrong?"

I stared at my son. Could he read me that well? I smiled and patted him on the shoulder. "Nada." I opened Sophie's door.

"Come on, I'm buyin'."

As we walked toward Watson's I kept my eyes peeled for trouble. Sophie paused on the sidewalk, her fingertips to her temples.

"Soph, you okay?"

"I feel like I'm wading through mud. What's wrong with me? Do you think it's from hearing what Professor Takmaz did?"

"Could be that, or you finding that guy fertilizing your lawn this morning. Or your husband gone missing. Cut yourself some slack. Can you eat something?"

"I dunno." She hugged herself around the waist. "You're right, I haven't eaten since lunch yesterday."

Sophie chose a table on the patio. Zach sat down across from her and handed her a menu.

Watson's, a landmark restaurant in Orange, was touristy. At the cashier's counter, frazzled parents dealt with children begging for wax lips, candy cigarettes, and Necco wafers.

While we waited for a waitress, I inspected our surroundings. Traffic passed by in a steady stream. From my vantage point, I saw nothing out of the ordinary, yet my jittery feeling persisted.

I trusted my instincts, though, and stayed alert. The waitress appeared with three glasses of water. Zach ordered a double cheeseburger, onion rings, and a chocolate shake. Ah, youth. Sophie asked for a big bowl of vegetable soup, and half an egg salad sandwich. I ordered my usual, a grilled vegetable, three egg-white omelet with dry wheat toast. I'd allow myself a half slice. No need to undo the torture of my six a.m. workouts.

As we ate, I kept my back to the restaurant. I could scan in three different directions, and ate with my head up, unable to shake my growing feeling of unease.

I devoured my omelet as I studied the woman beside me. The strain showed in fine lines around her mouth, her pale cheeks, and the perpetual furrow between her eyebrows. Sophie finished her soup and nibbled at her sandwich. Sipping from her water bottle, she watched me finish off my omelet. "I've never seen anyone eat as fast as you just did."

Zach gave me a pointed stare, complete with raised eyebrows.

Can't deny the truth, so I didn't bother. I smiled at Zach. "Zach, you'll need to contact the Carpenters and find out what's up."

He nodded and wolfed down the last of his onion rings. He picked up his phone and walked a few steps away.

Sophie sat quietly, watching the busy waitresses. "I feel a little better now. Thank you for breakfast, Jenna."

I glanced at my watch. "No problem. Look, it's probably still crazy on your block. Why don't I take you back to my office for an hour or so?" I signaled our waitress for the bill. "It's just up the street."

"Will the police mind, do you think? I've been gone awhile, I don't want to get into trouble."

"We can go through these translations the professor gave us. And then we can check out what the Internet has to say on that genocide thing. Then we can head up to your house."

Sophie yawned. "I'm exhausted."

"That's the downside of stress." I kept scanning the area. The niggling feeling still nagged at me. "We need to plan our next move. They said they'd call, right?"

Sophie nodded. "Tonight, they just said they'd call tonight. No specific time."

Zach approached our table. He looked angry. "Just a minute," he said, and raised the phone at me. I stood and took the phone from him. "She wants to talk to you."

"I'll be right back," I said to Sophie. I had to make this quick. And with Lizabeth... well, I knew she'd be difficult.

I put the receiver to my ear. "Hello, Lizabeth, it's been a long time."

"Jenna. I apologize for Zach's intrusion into your life. This was a shock to both Kent and me. I can well imagine your surprise." Her voice seethed with control.

"Surprise is an understatement. I hate to do this to you, but I have a client waiting for me, and it's urgent. How about we continue this later? I wanted Isaac to let you know he was okay." For nineteen years I'd thought of him as Isaac in my head.

"We're so sorry. And he won't be bothering you; Kent is on his way down now. He'll collect Zach and again, we apologize for any imposition that you've experienced."

Heat flushed up my neck. "Kent's coming here? Zach's a big boy, Lizabeth."

Her voice steeled even more. "I appreciate your concern about what our son should know and understand. Our family doesn't share our stories with everyone. We keep to ourselves."

"Judging by the way Zach walked in here wanting

answers, I'm figuring you should have told the truth and not kept him in the dark."

She ignored me. "Jenna, I also want to ask a favor. Please don't discuss Jayson. I don't want Zach knowing how peculiar he was."

Frowning, I shook my head at my cell phone. What in the devil was she talking about? "As far as I'm concerned, you're the peculiar one. And to talk ill of the dead, after all these years is so unfair. I've got to go. I guess I'll talk to Kent later." I hung up.

Zach met me a dozen feet away from our table.

"Well. That didn't go over too well. And your father is on his way to take you home."

Zach clenched his teeth, and gave a quick shake to his head. "I'm not going back home."

"Let's talk about this later, I don't want to leave Sophie by herself." He nodded and we walked back to the table.

I thought about my conversation with Zach's adoptive mother. Lizabeth sounded like she'd had liquid starch on her oatmeal this morning. What did she mean, Jayson was peculiar? We'd dated for almost eighteen months; in all that time Jayson had been nothing but captivating, and we'd been madly in love. I shook off my irritation and took my seat across from Sophie.

A man with a drink in his hand walked by and sat down at the table next to us.

With a casual glance, I gave him a once-over.

Oh. My.

Adrenaline surged. It was all I could do to reach for my water, and take a sip.

What gave the guy away was the way he wore his baseball cap. The cap, pulled low over his forehead, forced him to tilt his head up to see where he was going. At the café at Beckman Hall, his cap had been black, with a small white Nike logo on the back. Now, it was pale green with a mountain emblem. He wore the same plaid flannel shirt, and the same-mirrored sunglasses as before. I hate those things. You can't see their souls when you can't see their eyes. And sometimes these damned perps have no souls.

Was he working alone? If he had a partner, the two of them should've traded places to eliminate recognition. Amateurs.

He'd arrived a few minutes after we'd sat down with the professor. He'd bought a coffee and read the newspaper. He'd had no books or backpack. Sherlock had changed his ball cap; that was it. Who did he think he was tailing, a couple of Orange County housewives? What an idiot!

I said nothing to Sophie. She was already freaked out enough.

Zach gave me a puzzled glance.

I winked at him.

First things first. Sherlock's car and his partner. After a minute or two, I casually checked him out. I caught him glancing across the street before he shifted his attention to two elderly women coming in for breakfast.

I glanced down the street. *Ha! Got him.*

The car parked beside the Wells Fargo Bank was a white 2012 Chevy Malibu. A single occupant sat in the front seat, staring straight ahead. *Bingo.*

Who were they? Certainly not the kidnappers. I doubted it. Would kidnappers nab the husband, demand a ransom of the wife, then turn around and follow the wife the day of the kidnapping? I hate it when things get all convoluted and muddy. So, who were these guys? Definitely not the police. I'd made them too easily. I had to get them off my tail. How?

Sherlock seemed fascinated by the concrete. He was handsome by my standards, dark hair, olive skin, around five-foot-six, and probably twenty-five or thirty years old.

I sipped from my soda. My goal was to prevent this amateur sleuth from overhearing anything. "Did you have enough to eat, Zach?"

He gave me a studious nod. "I'm good, thanks."

Sophie played with her sandwich, moving it around the plate with her fork. Exasperated, she sighed. "I can't believe the professor. Can you imagine someone who traipses all over the world doing something so... so irresponsible!"

I almost choked on my water. Time to change the subject. "Well, let's chalk it up to his age. Hey, you know,

I meant to ask you, how long have you and Sarkis been married?"

"Going on ten years."

"Yeah? How long's he been at the college?"

"I dunno, a long time." Giving me an irritated shrug, she appeared distracted, and fretful.

Zach searched my face with a worried, probing look.

I leaned in to Sophie, speaking in a low tone. "Okay, it's time to leave. I'm losing you to exhaustion."

"Two more bites, and I'm done." She reached for her sandwich.

At that moment, an old, faded aqua blue sixty-six Mustang clattered into view. The vehicle stalled as the driver began to park behind the white Malibu. The driver started up the car again. It coughed and shuddered as it rolled to a stop.

The kid behind the wheel got out and slammed the car door. He loped across the street toward the restaurant.

I was struck with sudden inspiration. I love when that happens. "I'm going inside to pay the bill, and then we'll take off."

EIGHT

I ducked into the diner and waited for the kid. He was picking up a to-go order. It wasn't quite ready yet. He wandered over to the candy and gum in front of the cashier, pausing to study the selections.

Tapping him on the shoulder, I said, "Hey. That car of yours takes me back in time, I'll tell ya." As I nodded toward his car, I placed three bottles of water on the counter and slipped the cashier my receipt and two twenties.

Grinning, the kid turned. "Yeah, but she needs a lot of work. Got her from my uncle in Redlands. She needs a lot of engine work. There's some bodywork, she has a little rust, but at least she gets me around." He smirked. "Well, almost."

"Well, hey. Maybe I can help you out." I reached into my wallet and brought out a fifty-dollar bill.

The kid's head reared back, his eyes widening in surprise.

"I want to play a little joke on my brother. See the car in front of yours? The white Chevy Malibu?"

The kid swiveled and found the car. "Yeah."

"The guy sitting shotgun is my brother, Gary. He's waiting for his friend Shorty outside that bank." I leaned nearer, confiding, "Last week, they played a practical joke on me." Chuckling, I shook my head. "Those two lame brains called Pizza Hut and ordered five large any-way-you-want-it cheese and anchovy pizzas, and had em' delivered to my house."

The kid grinned. "Seriously? Did you have to pay for em'? What'd you do?"

I shrugged and laughed. "Yeah, I paid for them, gave 'em away to any neighbors who were willing to eat them. It would be so cool to get those clowns back when they least expect it. Wanna play?" I nodded toward his car. "I saw how your car stalled when you parked, and it gave me an idea. All you need to do is stall your car right next to his so he can't move forward or back. I have my camera with me. I'll get a good shot of you blocking them. Stay there for, say, two minutes, if that."

His eyes focused on the fifty in my hand. "Hell, yes, I'll do it!"

"Outstanding! Give me enough time to get far enough

away to take a shot of those two all ticked off. That will remind them who rules!"

"You mean, right now?"

"Right now. What's your name?

"TJ."

"Okay, TJ, I'm countin' on you."

"You got it." We shook hands and I slipped him the fifty. I'd add it to my expense account.

He pocketed the bill and walked out of Watson's with a smile on his face.

I tucked the bottles of water under one arm, and sauntered outside. "Let's get over to my office. It's just down the street, then we can head up to your place."

Sighing, she stood up quickly. Zach followed. We walked toward my Forerunner.

TJ paused for traffic and then jaywalked across two lanes to his car. He started it up, and it gasped to life.

I fought back a smile when Sherlock stood uncertainly at his table. He looked at the cold root beer the waitress had just served him, then gazed at the Chevy, threw down some dollar bills, and bolted toward the car.

We climbed into my car. I reached past Sophie to my glove box and pulled out a pack of bubblegum.

"Want some?" I waved the pack in front of her nose.

Sophie shook her head. Zach took one.

I unwrapped a stick and started chewing, keeping one eye on my new accomplice.

TJ maneuvered his Mustang beside the Chevy, stalled

it, and created a mini traffic jam of a dozen cars. Chuckling, I threw my car into reverse, found a break in the traffic, and then tooled off up Chapman Avenue. The last thing I saw in my rearview was both men getting out of the Chevy while TJ lifted the hood on his Mustang.

TJ earned his fifty bucks, and I gave myself a pat on the back for ditching those two.

NINE

Two questions remained. Who were they? Why were they following us?

To be on the safe side, I took a circuitous route to my office. I cracked my gum, took an arbitrary right, and glided through a neighborhood filled with Victorians, Craftsman bungalows, and Hip Roof cottages. I loved the quaintness of this town.

All the while, I kept an eye out for the white Chevy. No sign of it. I smiled.

"So, hey, you were telling me you've been married for ten years? How'd you two meet?" I asked Sophie.

"At church. This is my second marriage." As she adjusted the strap of her seat belt, Sophie looked wistfully at a group of children playing on a front lawn. "I married at twenty-one but it only lasted about fifteen months. He left."

I shot her a look of surprise. "Idiot."

In the rearview, Zach nodded his head.

Sophie pursed her lips. "Sounds like you've been there."

I shrugged.

"Some friends of mine kept pressing me to try their singles group, but I wasn't interested. I was angry back then, and bitter. My friends persisted and invited me to their church beach party, a baptism."

I cringed at the mention of church and baptism, but kept my mouth shut. Religious dogma had been rammed down my throat during my childhood, so I had a hard time listening to church people, idealistic doctrine, and Christians in general. You wanna see my skin crawl? Start talking Bible.

"So, there I was, watching this line of people in their bathing suits go, one by one, into the surf and this handsome Greek guy..." She froze, her eyes widening. "Gosh, it's this handsome Armenian now!" She turned and smiled at Zach, who remained an attentive listener. "Well, anyway, Sarkis was baptized and quite thrilled with his new commitment to God. I had no idea who Sarkis was. I just enjoyed listening to him. He has quite a sense of humor."

I kept my eyes on the road, checking my rearview every five seconds. I wanted to make sure the Chevy stayed lost.

I paused at another red light. "So, you guys just hit it off and started dating, huh?"

"At first, he was just a friend, someone I could confide in. Then, one day, I realized he meant everything to me. I cared about what he thought, his opinions, his health. I loved him. But he was worried about our age difference."

"How much older is he?" Zach asked.

She swiveled to face him. "Fifteen years."

I gave a short laugh. "Ah, that's not too much."

"When you've gone through a lot in life, it doesn't make any difference," Sophie observed.

"So, when you say you've been through a lot, are you referring to the jerk from your first marriage?"

She nodded. "Brett and I met in our junior year of college. We were crazy about each other." She twisted the napkin from Watson's she still held, growing silent.

Time to head to the office.

The March sun shone in the sky, despite being surrounded by incoming dark clouds, reflecting off the cars positioned in front of us.

Sophie put on her sunglasses. "You know, Brett was a great guy. For a couple of years, anyway." She took off the shades, squinting as she gazed through them, and wiped the lenses with her napkin.

"I'd had Non-Hodgkin's Lymphoma when I was a teenager. I was in remission all through college, but I can't have children."

"You can't? Because of Hodgkin's?" I frowned as I glanced sideways at Sophie.

"Uh, huh. After all the treatment you go through, it's impossible to have kids. Brett had always said it wouldn't bother him, that it didn't matter if we couldn't have children, and we were in this together." She twisted the napkin so tight, it resembled a long thick rope. "But after we married, the disease became active, my markers increased, and it came back with a vengeance. It didn't take long for the reality to hit that, not only could I not function as a wife, because of all the chemo and drugs, I really couldn't give him the son he wanted. When Brett suddenly decided that adoption was out of the question, things just fell apart."

"I'm sorry, Sophie." What else could I say?

"It wasn't his fault, really. He was young, inexperienced and—"

"An idiot," I reminded her.

We arrived at my office a few minutes later. Like dozens of others in Old Town Orange, my Victorian-style house had been remodeled. Even if I do say so myself it looked quite tasteful. A large home, I'd had it painted in a warm taupe with accent colors in black, white, and burgundy.

Sophie looked at the building as we approached the driveway.

"We're back," Zach said.

"This is nice, Jenna. I love these converted homes."

"Thanks, I like it too." I'd worked like a damned fool to restore it.

I'd refinanced only once, spending a small fortune on landscaping, interior plumbing, and new electrical. My savings paid for the remodel of the kitchen and removing a few walls to expand my office.

By renting the two upstairs offices, I made a nice bit of change on the side.

This was my pride and joy, my only property, a little buy-off from my ex-husband, who'd wanted to unload the house and me in one fell swoop.

"Welcome to my world." I pulled around to the small parking lot behind the house. I stopped the car and turned to Sophie. "So. Whatever became of your genius donkey of an ex-husband?"

Sophie's jaw clenched twice before she spoke. "Brett's married with two sons now. They're eight and ten." Sophie looked at me, her eyes bright with unshed tears. "Brett Junior and Kyle."

My caustic retort was muffled when I slammed my shoulder against the car door to push it open.

Zach scooted out when Sophie pushed against her door, holding it open for her. Sweet kid.

I stood and stretched a bit, then opened the back passenger door and retrieved one of the storage boxes I keep in my car.

As we walked from the side of the house to the back door, I turned to Sophie. "You know, I never asked if you worked or not."

She shrugged. The wind blew her curls across her

face, and she tossed her head to move them aside. "I work with an established philanthropic corporation."

"I don't come cheap, Sophie, and we haven't talked money yet."

She inclined her head to one side. "What and how much do you charge? By the day? Week?"

Pausing at the back door, I answered, "Five hundred a day, not including a two thousand dollar retainer."

Zach, my experienced assistant, yelped, "Wow!"

I gave him a 'careful' look, then took the gum from my mouth and placed it into a wadded-up Kleenex from my pocket. "You get your money's worth. I have a list of satisfied clients you can call. Most of my clients do check my references. I'll give you the list."

I held the storage box against my chest while I reached for the brass doorknob.

"I don't need a list. I'll write you a check today."

I gave her a satisfied nod. "I'm not your usual cloak and dagger P.I. I've never worked a kidnapping, I did work with the FBI on that missing person's case about twenty years ago."

Sophie studied me. "I trust you, Jenna. You're the right person for Sarkis and me. I go with my instincts. I don't want to endanger my husband's life, and I insist that we keep the authorities out of this.

"You got it. And once the kidnappers call, we'll go from there."

Sophie shuddered. "I'm scared to death, and I'm terrified for Sarkis."

"You're holding up remarkably well, so keep it up, okay?"

She nodded as I pushed open the back door, and we proceeded through the rear of the house to the kitchen.

I loved my kitchen. I'd remodeled it with dark granite countertops, and new antique-glazed cabinets. A modern desk and large dinner table fit in the old dining room, along with my fax and copy machines. The built-in china cabinet stored office supplies.

I kept a basket full of various flavored teas, hot cocoa mixes, and a small bowl filled with sugar packets and artificial sweeteners on the countertop for guests and clients.

"You want anything to drink?"

"No, thanks."

"Okay." I waved her toward the reception area. "Why don't you write that check while I tell my partner we're here?" I gave her a direct look. "You sure you can cough up two thousand dollars?"

Sophie lived in a neighborhood that said she could. But in my line of work, I've encountered folks who live far beyond their means. Trouble with a capital 'T.'

Sophie absently twirled a long corkscrew strand of hair around her index finger. "Money isn't a problem." She spoke with an air of casual sincerity that made me want believe her. "I want to turn the Bible over to those men as soon as possible and get my husband back."

So, she really isn't interested in that treasure in Istanbul, because she's already loaded, I speculated. Nice.

I said nothing, but I decided to do a background check on Sophie Alexakis. She sounded almost too good to be true.

I led her into the reception area. Ralph stuck his head out of his office and waved me over. Sophie sank onto a nearby sofa.

I motioned for Zach to follow me. Assistants don't loiter in reception.

Ralph tilted his head toward the reception area. "Hey, kid," he said to Zach as I closed Ralph's office door. "So, who is she?"

"Her name is Sophie Alexakis. Here, let me use your computer to Google her name." I scooted around to his computer and typed in the information I needed. "Her professor husband was kidnapped this morning by some men she thinks are foreigners."

"Kidnapped! What do they want?"

Zach answered, "They want this old family Bible that gives the exact location of a treasure that was buried under the entryway of a home in Istanbul almost a hundred years ago."

Ralph whistled. "Istanbul? Hello Indiana Jones. Damn."

"I know." I straightened, folded my arms over my chest, and looked him in the eye. "There's a dead man who bled out on her front lawn. He'd been shot, and her husband never made it to class at the college."

"Then the kidnappers called her and told her they had him," Zach added.

Ralph nodded at me. "Homicide will put Levine or MacGinnis on it."

I shook my head. "Client doesn't want the proper authorities! She refuses to engage the police with her husband's kidnapping or involve the FBI. Trust me, I tried. She's insisting on meeting the kidnapper's demands, and they're supposed to call her tonight."

"I don't like not involving the proper authorities. This thing goes south, and it'll be our butts on the line." Ralph looked at his watch. "Crap. Patterson called, and he wants me to assist on the Delaney case."

"Why don't you put Henry Brazel on it? He'd love the work, and I need your help with Sophie." I glanced at the screen and blinked in surprise. All I could do was sit down. There were thousands of hits attached to Sophie's name.

TEN

Ralph and Zach joined me at the computer.

Ralph read aloud, "Sophie Alexakis, aka Sophia Catherine St. James, daughter of trillionaire George St. James!"

Zach sucked in a sharp breath at the word trillionaire.

I clicked on another link. Up popped a *Time* magazine article dated over fifteen years ago. The headline read, "Profiles of Endurance and Courage: The St. James Family Heartbreak Continues." A subtitle read, "All the money in the world couldn't save Catherine St. James." The story told of George St. James losing his wife to heart disease. There was a photo of a much younger Sophie, a sad-looking waif, standing next to her powerful father at her mother's funeral. A paragraph described Sophie as full of spunk and mentioned her ongoing battle against Hodgkin's.

"*She's* your client?" Ralph's voice rose.

"That's her!" Zach nodded. "Amazing!"

"Shhh! She's in reception. Oh, my God!" I hissed, staring at the computer screen. "Sophie C. She told us her middle name was Catherine." I glanced over my shoulder to look at Ralph. "She has more money than Bill Gates."

"Who referred you?"

I thought back. "Helen Fincher. Can you believe it?"

"No kidding." Ralph paused and then said, "I'm worried for you, Jen-kins."

"Why?"

"Think about it. You've got the only daughter of one of the richest men in the nation asking for your help with the kidnapping of her husband. If her father knew anything about this, every FBI agent within a thousand miles would be at his beck and call. Did she say why she won't contact the power she has at her disposal?"

I thought back. Nothing in her history, or what she'd told me stood out. "The only thing I can come up with is she means to absolutely follow the instructions of the kidnappers to save her husband." I stood and faced my partner. "I'm doing this, Ralph. Besides, it's not against the law to work a case on your own. We do it all the time."

"But..."

"Are you intimidated because of her father and his gazillions?"

Ralph, clearly furious with me, spat, "You're so full of it, Jenna. You know what's at stake here."

My blood boiled. I wondered about Ralph's attitude. Was it because of Lynne's illness, or because he sensed a real threat to our business? I didn't have time to argue.

"I gotta check on her." I got up, walked out of the office, and stuck my head in the reception area.

"Come on back to my office, Sophie."

Sophie slowly got to her feet.

"You're looking real comfortable on that couch," I commented.

"I'm exhausted, but I'll sleep later... after we find Sarkis. Here." Sophie extended a check. "Two thousand."

I took the check and folded it in half. "Thanks. Come on back to my office, and let's see what we can dig up on the Internet."

Zach followed us, wandered over to my couch, and sat. He brought out his iPad began to charge it. Turning it on, he stared at the screen.

I turned on my PC, beginning my search on the history of Armenians in Turkey. My phone rang. It was a freelance private detective who sporadically worked for me.

"Hey, Paletto. I need the name of the contact you promised me on the Montgomery case," said Don Spaulding.

"Hold on, I have it here somewhere." I thumbed through my files.

Meanwhile, Sophie strolled around my office. She stood in front of the built-in bookcase that took up an entire wall. It was filled with current best sellers, and numerous classics. Most of the books I owned, even the fiction ones, dealt with forensics and crime.

The office walls, painted a light linen shade, provided a soft backdrop for the entire room. The room, done in chocolate, green, raspberry, and wheat, was designed, according to my decorator, to make my clients feel comfortable. I'd added a brown leather sofa, two chairs, a small table, and reading lamp. It was my favorite place to read, study and think.

I motioned Sophie over to my desk.

The information on the Armenian Genocide appeared on the computer screen. Sophie sat down and began to read while Zach inspected a Facebook page. I found the file I needed, excused myself with my phone, and left to complete Don's call.

When I returned fifteen minutes later, Sophie inclined her head toward me, turning her attention to the screen. "Who do you think we're dealing with? As far as I can see, the kidnappers appear to be from a country with a history of treachery and murder."

"They've abducted your husband for a treasure that may or may not exist!" I was blunt, but it was the truth.

Zach looked up from his iPad. "I've been scanning Ambassador Morganthau's story, the one the professor recommended. It's pretty gross."

Sophie looked even more pale and gaunt now.

"Sophie, you look beat." I stood, motioning to the sofa. "Take a little nap. We'll work in the kitchen office."

"Oh, that sounds good, but I wonder if I can sleep. I am exhausted."

Zach stood up, holding the iPad he was using. "We'll be right in the next room if you need us. Can I get anything for you now?" He bent over and took the charger off the outlet.

I smiled at him.

Sophie made her way to the sofa. "Thanks, Zach. I'm fine."

I left the office with an armload of files, glanced back at Zach and saw him leave the door ajar. He hesitated, frowning with concentration and listened.

I suddenly heard Sophie's muffled weeping, followed by her plea, "Oh, God, help me!"

Zach looked up, emotion glimmering in his eyes. He returned to the room and firmly shut the door.

Intrigued, I moved to the door, pressing my ear against the smooth panel. I too, wanted to offer Sophie some kind of comfort, but then I heard her murmur something about taking away her fear and giving her strength. I strained to hear more. Zach spoke to her in a soothing tone. I marveled at him. He'd been raised right, I had to admit that. What a sweet, sensitive young man. How could he be such a wonderful person with such flawed parents?

Ralph strolled into the open dining room. "Hey, I

forgot. While you were out, Lizabeth Carpenter called and said to please tell Zach to turn on his phone. His father is trying to reach him. She's not happy."

A rush of alarm swept over me. Lizabeth had mentioned that Kent was on his way down to California to get Zach. I looked at the clock. Almost one thirty. How much time did I have with Zach? I needed to talk to him about what he'd do when his father arrived. The idea of a confrontation with Kent held zero appeal.

Zach arrived in the kitchen with his iPad fifteen minutes later. "She's sleeping now."

"Zach, that was very sweet of you to go back and comfort Sophie."

He shrugged, embarrassed. He leaned over and plugged his charger into the outlet in the dining room.

I smiled. "Your mom called and asked Ralph to have you turn on your phone. Your Dad's been trying to reach you."

"I told you, I'm not going back. I've been thinking. Maybe I'll go to UC Irvine, or USC. I like it here, and I want to get to know you."

"Look, I can understand you're thinking I have an exciting life. Truth is, I don't. This is the most excitement we've had around here since we opened. My days are boring. I sit in my car and watch a car or a home for hours, I take a few pictures and I do hours and hours of research and detecting on the Internet. Whoopee. You need to be in college."

He smiled at me and nodded. "I am going to go to college, but I just found you. I'm not leaving until we get to know one another." He took a deep breath. "I have a question for you."

"Shoot."

"What do you want me to call you?"

The question didn't exactly surprise me. Yet. Hmmm, what should he call me? Mom? Out of the question. I wasn't his mom. I liked 'Mom,' but it felt forced.

"How about Jenna?" I smiled. "Ms. Paletto seems kind of silly, doesn't it?"

"Jenna, then. Since I'm your new associate, it stands to reason I'd call you Jenna." He grinned back at me as he stood. "I'll call my dad."

Ten minutes later, Zach sank into the chair beside me. "I couldn't talk any sense into him. He'll probably be here in the morning."

"He's driving down?" I probably looked like I felt. Stunned.

"Yeah, well. My folks are thrifty. What can I say? They don't fly anywhere. In fact, I've flown more with my water polo team than they have in a lifetime. And that's not a lot." He laughed and threw me a look that was exactly like his father's.

Zach's presence was confounding. The shocking likeness of Zach to his father Jayson was truly unbelievable. As we sat across from one another, I still couldn't believe Zach was here. Yet, I wanted to cook for him, walk on the beach with him, introduce him to my crazy family, take him to Big Bear Lake and go fishing. We had a lifetime to catch up on. "I can't get over how much you look like Jayson."

"Would you tell me about him? My parents won't tell me anything. You should know they were dead set against me ever meeting you."

"Did your parents explain why they didn't tell you that you were adopted?"

"Mom said it was their choice."

Not a revelation, I realized, especially after the way Kent and Lizabeth had departed for Boise. They'd moved, unpacked the china, probably landscaped, and had several barbecues before they'd revealed their location change. Lovely way for me to learn that they'd left the state: a change of address card. And I'd read between the lines. Their message had been clear: we prefer our new life not to include any reminders from the past.

"What do you remember about my birth father?" Zach asked.

I smiled. "Ask me anything about him, I remember it all."

Jayson had been the brains of his family, that's for sure. Sheer intellectual genius. Kent was smart, but nothing like his brother. Jayson's passions had been astronomy, physics, and math. His idea of a great date was to go out to Joshua Tree Monument with the Astronomy Club. He'd been wild, impulsive, and funny.

He'd never had a dark day. Though, to be sure, there had been strange days if I was honest. But I wasn't about to let Lizabeth remind me...

I met my son's eyes. "He loved physics, and astronomy, all those heavens out there in the universe."

A smile appeared on Zach's face. "Astronomy! I love astronomy!"

I recalled those times in the desert, seeing Jayson's dark profile against the starlit sky, hunched over a telescope examining the heavens till the dawn approached. I'd spent many nights wrapped in a sleeping bag on the desert floor, studying post Civil War history by flashlight, while he scanned the universe.

"And Kent, your adopted dad, was the serious one. He and Lizabeth lived a ... very structured life."

Zach laughed out loud. "Structured? More like control freaks."

I ignored his remark. "You know, back then, your dad and mom had been trying for years to have a baby. And then Jayson and I announced to the family that we were expecting our first child and would be getting married. That didn't go over too well. I underestimated the impact it had on them."

"Was Jayson excited about me? He wasn't mad that you'd gotten pregnant?"

"On the contrary! He was wild about becoming a father. And he loved the idea of marriage! He even named you after Isaac Newton. That was the only thing

I asked Kent and Lizabeth to promise if our baby was a son, that they'd name you Issac, because it was what Jayson wanted. And I love your nickname, Zach."

He shook his head. "I never knew any of this."

"Now, you know some of it," I said quietly, wondering where we'd go from here. I knew what I wished for, but I'd keep it to myself.

ELEVEN

Zach glanced over my shoulder at the computer screen. "So, what did you find out?"

Intermittently, we checked on Sophie, sleeping soundly on the couch. We spent the next few hours researching the information provided by Professor Takmaz. One particular website about Ambassador Henry Morgenthau and his book, *Ambassador Morgenthau's Story*, recounted the history of what had happened in Turkey during Morgenthau's tenure as United States ambassador there between 1913 and 1916.

It was awful stuff, a first hand account of the henchmen who controlled Turkey, not to mention a laundry list of the vile acts committed by the gendarmes with the full cooperation of the Turkish government.

To neutralize thousands of Armenian soldiers in the Turkish Army, government agents removed their firearms, and then forced them to work as laborers, without food or water. After digging their own graves, their fellow Turks stole their clothing and slaughtered them. Again, with the backing of Turkish officials, the Christian Armenians who populated entire cities and towns were marched at gunpoint into the Syrian desert, where they were stripped naked, and forced to walk across the wastelands. Without provisions, hundreds of thousands of women, children, and old people had perished. Had Armen and Varteni Begosian died in the blistering sands of the Syrian desert?

After an hour and a half of investigating, we needed a break. I had to hand it to Zach. He knew how to research.

I finally said, "So, baby Sarkis' new family immigrated to Chicago, where he grew up believing he was Greek."

Zach nodded. "Our Sarkis' father was the little baby in Constantinople."

"Right. He married, had a son he named after himself, who then grew up to become a professor in Orange County, California, and Sophie's husband."

Zach looked up at me and said, "Listen to this. We're in 2015. The Armenians are calling attention to the 100th anniversary of the genocide of 1.5 million Christian Armenians. Articles are flooding the Internet. This is from *The New York Times*, titled: *Armenian Genocide of 1915: An Overview*."

"Are you really going to read me the entire article?" I moaned.

"No." He took a swig of water. "Just this paragraph: 'But to Turks, what happened in 1915 was, at most, just one more messy piece of a very messy war that spelled the end of a once powerful empire. They reject the conclusions of historians and the term genocide, saying there was no premeditation in the deaths, no systematic attempt to destroy a people. Indeed, in Turkey today it remains a crime—insulting Turkishness—to even raise the issue of what happened to the Armenians.'"

"Yeah. What country would want to admit to annihilating a million and a half of their people?"

Sick of reading or hearing the debates and sicker still from the history of one atrocity after another, I reached for a bottle of Advil and took two tablets.

Ralph lumbered out of his office and plopped down next to us at the table. He picked up one of the translated sheets from Professor Takmaz, held it up, and squinted.

"Hey, Ralph." I felt encouraged as he leaned forward, seemingly captivated by the story. I needed his involvement.

I put my elbows on the table. "The man who wrote this, Armen Begosian, was a jeweler who owned his own shop. He apparently buried a treasure trove of jewels under the entryway of his home in Istanbul."

His expression pensive, he shook his head. "Jenna, what are you getting yourself into?

"We have an accurate address, and he left a map showing exactly where."

"How long's it been since this genocide thing happened?"

"A hundred years exactly. But hear me out. In over a week's time, Begosian took the inventory from his jewelry store and hid it from the Turkish officials and other jewelers on Gold Street in the Grand Bazaar."

Zach stood and walked into the kitchen, keeping a close eye on Ralph and me. He opened a hot cocoa packet.

"Wait a minute. You're doing an awful lot of concluding based on ancient history."

"No, Ralph. Research."

"And what are the odds of that loot still being there after a hundred years?" He stroked his stubble covered chin.

I straightened. "It's not ancient history. Do you realize the Turks slaughtered a million and a half Armenians? Those people were their friends and neighbors."

Zach stirred hot water into his mug. "That would be like us killing a million and a half Mexicans to get their property and businesses, with the blessing of our government! And to this day the Turks still deny it happened. Even the Pope talked about it. He used the term 'genocide' and pissed off Turkey so much they recalled their ambassador to the Vatican. But it wasn't just Armenians the Turks butchered. They slaughtered Catholics, Orthodox Syrians, Assyrians, Chaldeans and Greeks. Actually, between five and eight hundred thousand or more Greeks."

Score one, Zach. I lifted my gaze to Ralph.

Ralph stood, went into the kitchen and poured himself a cup of coffee. He leaned against the island next to Zach. "The kidnapping of Sophie's husband is the most important thing here, Jenna. We should go to the proper authorities. What's your gut telling you?"

"My gut?" I rifled through some papers and held one up. "Someone questioned Adolph Hitler about the 'Jewish Problem,' and he answered, 'Who still talks of the extermination of the Armenians?'" I shoved the printout back in the folder. "That was twenty six years after the Armenian genocide."

Ralph sighed. "Okay, I didn't know that. But you sure as sugar aren't going to fly to Turkey, right? In fact, you wouldn't be able to get that treasure out of the country. It would be impossible! What's it matter to you, anyway?"

"What's it matter?" I shook my head. "I guess I don't want those thieving Turks to get one more thing. I believe someone sent criminals over here to try to steal that Bible, to get to that buried treasure. Why would they kidnap Sophie's husband if not to get to that fortune?"

"Fortune! And you won't involve the police or the FBI? This is dangerous stuff." He held my gaze with his narrowed gray-brown eyes.

"My client refuses to involve the authorities," I corrected him.

"And who the hell is the dead guy?" He moved forward and leaned against the doorway.

"I have no idea." I straightened and looked him in the eye. "And I guess this is the perfect time to tell you that we were tailed by a couple of men from the college to Watson's, but I did manage to lose them."

Zach gave me a stunned look. "We were?"

I nodded, watching Ralph stare at the light fixture for a ten count.

Ralph shook his head and sighed. "What can I do to help? Watch your back?"

"I told you, my client insists no police and no authorities be involved. The kidnappers threatened to kill Sarkis if she does. She's firm on this, Ralph."

"When's the trade-off?"

"Tonight," I said. "They're calling tonight."

"May I remind you this isn't infidelity or some blockhead messing with bank deposits. This is deadly serious stuff. The Udall case? Remember what the kidnappers did to their son? That P. I. firm lost everything."

"I remember." Just hearing Ralph mention it made me cringe.

Ralph gave me a long searching look. "All right. I want you to call me the minute the kidnappers lay it out, and I'll try to get there before you."

Relieved, I sighed. "Thank you, Ralph." His

involvement would cost him time with Lynne. That bothered me. I'd make it up to him.

Nodding once, he made his way down the hall. "I got calls to make." He stopped and turned jerking his head toward Zach. "And keep him out of it."

Zach sped to the table and stood in front of me. "Were we really tailed by two men?"

"I didn't catch it until we were finishing lunch at Watson's. Guy wearing a ball cap sat down at a table next to us. The same guy was at the Starbucks at Chapman."

His eyes grew bright. "You're kidding me! I completely missed that! I wish you would've told us."

Shaking my head, I smiled. "No. Think how Sophie would have taken it if she'd known."

Zach's forehead smoothed out. "Oh, right. She'd have lost it."

"Good call."

TWELVE

While Zach continued to read Morganthau's account of the genocide of Armenians, I searched for information about Sarkis Alexakis, locating his family in the Chicago area. Names and dates checked out, and his family history proved easy to follow.

I caught the time on my computer. Four forty-five! "We have to go! Let's wake Sophie." Zach and I walked back to my office to find her still sound asleep.

"Time to wake up, Sophie. We need to get you home."

Her eyes opened, and she stared at the brown leather sofa in front of her nose. Frowning, she jerked back, trying to focus.

"Sophie, it's Jenna. Time to rise and shine."

She sat up. "It's not just a nightmare. Oh, Sarkis." She swiped at the tears on her cheeks.

Zach joined her on the sofa. He placed a hand on her shoulder while I placed a pack of tissues into her hand.

"We're going to get Sarkis back, I promise you, but you've got to suck it up and help us. Now, we need to get back to your house for that phone call."

Sophie nodded, mopping her face and blowing her nose. "You're right." She glanced at her watch. "I slept that long!"

"You needed the rest, and we've been busy. Now, give me two minutes, and we'll take off. Zach, bring your iPad, your jacket and backpack."

After I grabbed my keys, I knocked on Ralph's office. "We're leaving."

He nodded, closed the file on his desk, and got up.

***

I unlocked my old champagne-colored Corolla, and placed our research in the trunk.

"Why are we switching cars?" Sophie had followed me outside.

"Generally, I never take my Forerunner out when I work. I use the old Corolla, because it blends in with thousands of others on the road."

Ralph emerged from the house. He stuck a hand out to Sophie. "I'm Jenna's partner, Ralph Liebrandt. It's a pleasure to meet you."

Zach stood to one side, observing.

Sophie shook his hand. "My pleasure, Ralph. You have a nice partner. I trust her, and I think Zach is wonderful. You're blessed."

Ralph nodded. "You doing okay? Jenna gave me most of the particulars on your case."

I didn't mind Ralph's intrusion. It was typical. He needed to evaluate our client for himself. His way to verify what I'd told him. Ralph's intuition was hard at work. As I joined them, I heard him ask, "You're willing to let us handle the whole thing?"

Sophie paused and gave him a thoughtful look. For a moment, I thought she'd changed her mind. "That's exactly right, Ralph. No police. Jenna has given me a great deal of confidence that I'm doing the right thing, and I believe she'll get Sarkis back."

Ralph nodded, his eyes flicking from Sophie to me.

"Time to go." I met his gaze. "I'll be in touch."

"I understand." He bit the inside of his lower lip, a trademark pensive look.

"See you, Ralph." A brief wave from Zach.

"Stay loose, kid."

We climbed into the old Corolla and headed out. Rolling down the passenger window, Sophie waved to Ralph, who stood with his arms folded on his chest.

After a quick run to Farmer's Ranch market, we drove by Sophie's empty cul-de-sac. Plastic yellow crime-scene tape outlined her driveway and the parkway where the corpse had been found. I pulled over and parked just outside the cul-de-sac.

The sun had settled in the west. Orange rays shot out from behind a canopy of gray clouds as they spread across the darkening sky.

"We'll walk from here," I said. "That yellow tape means the police aren't through with their investigation."

Zach took both grocery bags.

"Okay, you two, we go in fast and quiet."

A few minutes later, we stood at the front door. Black clouds tumbled overhead and a cold wind began to blow. I shivered.

"What's this?" Sophie lifted a business card that had been folded into the lock. On the back, a handwritten note asked Sophie to call the police department a.s.a.p. Detective Thomas Berhmann had signed the card.

"Well, well, well… Tommy Berhmann," I muttered, arching an eyebrow at Sophie. "Plot thickens."

"What do you mean?" Sophie asked.

"Thomas Berhmann is a real bulldog. Once he gets his teeth into a case, he doesn't let go. He's as tenacious as they come."

"You two have a history?" She unlocked the door, entering into a foyer bigger than my living room.

"He's the best detective in the city. He's hard-nosed,

a guy that doesn't miss a beat. If you don't want the police to know about Sarkis, we'd better come up with some kind of explanation for his absence."

On my way up a short flight of stairs to the kitchen, I checked out the large, circular entryway. The place was filled with fresh flowers, and expensive looking art. Everything shouted sophisticated taste and money. Lots and lots of money.

"I'm going to check my voicemail for messages. I'll be in my office." Sophie went upstairs with a heavy tread.

Zach and I moved to the kitchen French doors to look out on an impressive backyard. Subtle lighting revealed a cascading waterfall that tumbled into a pool with a dark gray bottom giving the water a dark-blue hue.

"Cha-ching!" Zach stood beside me, his nose pressed against the glass.

"Impressive." I scanned a raised barbecue area that contained outdoor tables and chairs, all protected by a wood canopy. I couldn't help but admire the view.

Sophie returned to the kitchen. "There was only one message, from Detective Berhmann. He asked me to call." She picked up his card again and studied it. "What else could he want to discuss that we didn't talk about this morning?"

"No doubt the police found out Sarkis didn't show up at work, today. They'd have questions."

Sophie tapped the card against the palm of her hand. "More questions? Wonderful."

I leaned against the island. "Sophie, they're trying to put the puzzle together. You've got a dead guy on your front lawn, so they focus first on the person or persons at the crime scene."

"Me?" She yelped. "They really think I had something to do with the dead man?"

"They don't just think you had something to do with him, they're probably assuming that either you or Sarkis killed the guy."

"This cannot be happening. What should I tell them? I won't lie." A crease appeared between her brows. She began putting the groceries away. Zach stepped up to help unpack her bags.

I brought the kettle to the sink and began to fill it. "Tell as much of the truth as possible. You didn't realize Sarkis wasn't at school today until the secretary called. That part's true. Tell them Sarkis planned to meet a business acquaintance, and you don't know where he took them for dinner."

Sophie frowned. "Business acquaintance?"

"This is about money, right? And money is associated with business, so it's not a total lie." I reasoned as I placed the kettle on the range.

"Oh, for heaven's sake, Jenna. That's really stretching it."

Zach leaned forward and parked his elbows on the granite. "You actually think the cops'll buy that?"

"You have to return Berhmann's call, and you have

to explain Sarkis' absence." I surveyed the kitchen. "You got any teabags around here?"

Sophie reached into the pantry and took out a cherrywood tea box.

Nice. I chose Earl Grey.

Sophie placed a crystal dish full of sugar packets and sweeteners on the counter. "Should I call him now?"

I nodded. "Yeah, go for it."

"Okay, then, here goes." Sophie dialed the number on the card.

"Detective Berhmann? This is Sophie Alexakis. I'm sorry I didn't get to... Um..."

I watched her, mentally crossing my fingers.

Sophie's eyes widened in surprise. "Yes, yes, I am... Oh..." She hung up and stared at me. "He's coming over right now!"

Adrenaline surged. "I thought he'd interview you on the phone! Listen, either we get the hell out of here now and go to my place, which means we miss the kidnapper's call, or you deal with Berhmann alone."

Sophie stood there, a stunned look on her face.

I returned the mug to the cupboard, and then shoved the cherrywood tea box and the bowl of sweeteners into the pantry.

"What! Face Berhmann alone? Wait." Sophie followed me around the kitchen as I swiftly moved through it.

Alarmed, Zach asked. "What are you doing?"

I scanned the room for any other evidence of my

existence. Grabbing my coat, I slipped it on. "We're leaving."

Panicked, Sophie grabbed my arm. "Please, don't leave! Can't you and Zach wait upstairs? I'll answer all Berhmann's questions as best I can."

I slapped my coat pockets, pulling out my car keys. "Zach, get your things. If Berhmann knows I'm involved on any level in a homicide or a kidnapping, and I've concealed that involvement, my license is at risk. I could be charged with obstructing the investigation of two felonies." I pointed my finger in her face. "And remember, you don't want the police to know Sarkis has been kidnapped!"

"I don't think we should leave like this..." Zach began.

"Quiet, Zach." I snapped as I headed to the front door. Sophie trailed after me, making small protesting sounds.

"We have to leave. Now." I turned to her. "Do you think you can do this? You will have to lie, Sophie. Can you lie to protect your husband?"

"Lie? I'm not a good liar. People always know..."

I cut her off. "Listen to me. If you don't want the police involved, this is vital. This is major. You must lie." I watched her face register my words. She looked as though I'd gut punched her.

"Couldn't you wait up in the attic? It's the first door right off the hall upstairs." Sophie stood with her hands pressed together in front of her.

I glanced upstairs and saw the door. It looked like a closet. I kept walking.

"Pay attention, Sophie." I went down to the entryway. "Act as normally as you can. Begin to cook dinner for yourself. Start a fire in that fireplace. Bring out your knitting, turn on the news. Anything. Just act like you expect Sarkis home soon. Come on, Sophie, move!" I grabbed a pen on the massive desk in the entrance and wrote my cell number on a piece of paper.

Zach touched my sleeve. "Jenna. The attic is a good idea. It would give her security."

A cold jolt shot through me. My son had just used my name for the very first time.

Sophie's voice shook with fear. "What if the kidnappers call when the detective's here?"

"If that happens, call me on my cell no matter what. Excuse yourself, take the call upstairs, then call me." I crammed the piece of paper with my cell number scribbled on it into Sophie's palm.

"Please, don't leave."

"You can do this!" I flew out the door with a backward glance at Sophie. "Let's go, Zach! We won't be far!"

THIRTEEN

Zach stayed with me as we bolted in the direction of the car. "I thought the attic was a good idea. Why didn't you even consider it?" Zach argued. "She's been through so much. We can't leave her alone."

Anxiety flooded me. "Berhmann is a first rate investigator. He'll put her through the freakin' wringer."

"All the more reason for us to be close by."

We approached the front of my car. I paused, weighing all the options. The attic? I groaned, "You are so going to regret this, Paletto."

Zach beamed. "No, you won't, you'll see."

We raced on foot back to Sophie's street, tore up the driveway and rang the front doorbell.

A few seconds later, Sophie answered, her eyes brimming with unshed tears.

I pushed past her. "The attic. Let's make it quick." I took the stairs two at a time. Sophie and Zach followed.

"Oh, thank you, thank you! You're my only security." She ran up the stairs and hugged us both.

I opened the door to the attic and faced her on the landing. "Thank Zach. Your security is out of her ever-loving mind."

"I turned on the fireplace." She waved in the direction of the living room.

"Yeah, saw that."

"I put a lasagna in the microwave. We'll eat it later. A normal routine, just like you said."

"Nice touch." I glanced into the living room. There was paperwork on the ottoman, and a glass of red wine on the table.

"I put my Bible study out. Convincing?" She sounded breathless, nervous.

Zach followed my gaze. "Very."

Tension lines across her forehead revealed her stress. I didn't want her obsessing about Berhmann, so I smiled. "Yeah, that oughtta convince him."

Her eyes wide with worry, she nodded.

"Go on. It's time to give the performance of a lifetime. We'll settle in." I waved her off and shut the door. Her footsteps faded away.

Zach whistled under his breath. "Check it out."

I followed his gaze to the well-lighted attic a few steps above us. It contained an orderly array of dozens of boxes labeled in distinct bold print.

"It's so organized. Christmas. Fourth of July. Bird Day. Ha!" Zach grinned.

I frowned. "Bird Day?"

"Thanksgiving."

"Shh." I sat on the stairs. Zach joined me. We concentrated on the sounds filtering through the walls. Sophie rushed down the hall. Not three minutes later, a couple of knocks from the entryway door resounded up the stairs. Then, the doorbell chimed.

I leapt to my feet, and pressed my ear against the smooth wood. Zach did the same.

The attic door suddenly flew open. Startled, Zach and I jumped back. Sophie, clad now in navy blue sweats and matching tennis shoes, trembled. "What if I blow this?" she whispered.

"You're gonna do fine. Sarkis'll be okay. You'll see," I promised, hoping I wasn't lying.

She mouthed the words; "I'm so thankful you're here!"

"Go on now!" I shut the door with a quiet click.

I listened again at the attic door. Because Sophie had turned the fountain off, the travertine tiles and vaulted ceilings made every sound distinctive.

"Oh! It's raining!" Sophie said. "I never believe them anymore when they say it's going to rain! When did this start?"

Berhmann sounded disarmed, perhaps surprised. "Uh, maybe five minutes ago."

"Well, come on in. The home fires are burning. Can I take your coat?"

Silence. I pictured Sophie taking the detective's coat. Below me, the sound of the opening and closing alcove closet door confirmed my guess.

"Come on upstairs. You caught me in a struggle between watching Access Hollywood, Jeopardy or doing my Bible study. The study of Daniel, or the latest on who's divorcing whom in Hollywood."

No reply from Berhmann.

"Have a seat, please." Sophie sounded calm.

Berhmann replied, but I couldn't make out his words.

"Can I offer you a cup of tea? Or a soft drink?"

"No."

"Okay, then. What additional questions do you have for me, Detective?"

"You were asked not to leave your home, until we gave you permission. Where'd you go?"

I held my breath, afraid of what she'd say.

"I visited with a friend, and we had lunch at Watson's Drugs. Later, I had a nap at her office. I was so stressed finding that man on my lawn, I just needed to be with a friend."

Whaddya know? The truth fit perfectly within the blurred confines of her white lie. For what seemed like an entire minute, I felt the weight of silence between Berhmann and Sophie.

"Mrs. Alexakis, I'd like to speak to your husband."

"I'm sorry, I don't know where he is. Probably having drinks with those businessmen from Hong Kong."

My jaw sagged in shock. Zach looked just as stunned as me. Hong Kong? If *we* thought that was crazy, what would Berhmann think?

"Hong Kong," Berhmann echoed.

"That's right."

She was killing me.

"I understand your husband has never missed teaching a class."

"Well, you can't say *never*. I mean people do get sick at least once a year."

"But not your husband."

"You know, this is not his fault. He called Jeff two days ago, and he asked him to cover his classes. This morning when I told Sarkis that Jeff had forgotten, he was furious."

"What's Jeff's last name?"

I cringed. For someone who hated lying, Sophie excelled. Zach looked terrified.

"I don't know. I met him once about two years ago at some faculty thing."

"And your husband is meeting who?"

"Businessmen. From Hong Kong. You see, two years ago Sarkis invented a lounge chair that supports your lower back and your neck while you're lying face down. He was awarded a patent on it."

I clenched my teeth and shook my head.

"I'm listening."

"Well, this attorney from the gym where Sarkis works out saw the chair, and to make a long story short, they sent it off to Hong Kong for design improvements."

An edgy quiet filled me with dread.

"Go on," said Berhmann, his tone tense.

"The Hong Kong group is here to finalize their agreement with Sarkis. I know they met in Anaheim this morning for breakfast, but I have no idea where. I think a couple of them wanted to see the sights. If Sarkis had remembered to charge his phone, I'd be able to talk with him. But charging his cell phone was the last thing on his mind last night. If you recall, we had that fight."

Even Zach cringed at that remark.

"Yes, I remember. What was your fight with your husband about?"

"My husband broke a promise to me. He had promised not to lend his son any more money. I opened his mail and found out he'd given his son, Tyler, thirty thousand dollars."

"Ah, right."

"That's what the fight was about. And to tell you the truth, I'm still upset with him. I spoke to Sarkis only once this morning. That was when I told him what had happened on the front lawn."

Again, Berhmann was silent.

I gnawed on my knuckles waiting for her next comment.

"Do you want to see the chair?"

Zach and I glanced at each other, eyebrows raised.

What the hell is she talking about?

Sophie obviously surprised Berhmann, too. "You have it here?"

"Oh, sure, we have several prototypes. Come on, I'll show you. You can even try it out."

They moved out of the living room and took the stairs to the garage. Below me, I heard their footsteps fade off.

My instincts screamed at me to stay put. But my curiosity made me crack open the door and look down the steps. Turning, I whispered to Zach, "Don't move until I come back. Got it?"

"Are you crazy?" he hissed.

"I'll be back. Don't. Move."

With movements I hoped were hushed and muted, I moved down to the entryway and into the hall that led to the garage.

I heard Sophie explaining the chair Sarkis had built to Berhmann. "... And he teaches anatomy, physiology, biology. He has for years now. He really knows the human body. And then one day he got sick and tired of not being able to lie face down and read a book while tanning his back, at least not without some serious neck and lower back problems."

The garage was off a short hallway to the right. To

my left, I spotted a beautiful room with rich paneling, and filled with books. Ah ha, the library.

Sophie laughed, "You'll excuse me if I sound like a commercial! I'm very proud of my husband."

"So, the business acquaintances from Hong Kong are going to produce these?" Berhmann at least sounded interested.

Sophie's voice took on a winsome quality. "He's put his heart and soul into this. I'd love nothing more than to see it become a success."

"Why don't you manufacture it for him?" Berhmann had done his homework. He knew she had money and where it came from.

"My husband's his own man, Detective Berhmann." Sophie sounded firm. "Sure, I could have done it for him. But trust me, Sarkis gets his own projects done in his own way, his own time." She gave a soft laugh. "That's one of the most appealing things about him. I may be rich, but I'm even richer for marrying a man like Sarkis."

I applauded Sophie in my heart. Good for her.

"See, this is how it works. Sit here, and I'll show you." She sounded confident.

"It's pretty comfortable, I'll say that."

I couldn't believe she'd gotten him to sit in the thing.

"And look, when you lie face down... see these cutouts here for the shoulders? You can read a book, eat something, even sip a drink, and you won't tweak your neck or lower back."

"Okay. So that's the Zakis-Chair." Berhmann's humorless voice echoed off the garage walls. I heard him grunt as he got off the chair.

"It certainly is, Detective."

The garage door closed. The light switched off. They moved upstairs. I waited a moment and crept along, hugging the wall across from the library.

"Okay. Just a few more questions." Berhmann sounded weary.

Suddenly, Sophie blurted, "Detective, who was the dead man in my front yard? Do you know his name?" She sounded concerned.

I thought, nice touch.

"Haven't got anything on him... ."

"Gosh, I keep wondering about his family. They're probably very worried about him. It's so sad."

"Sad. Huh." Berhmann paused. "I gotta speak to your husband, Mrs. Alexakis. I need to know what he saw."

"Let me say this, Detective Berhmann. Sarkis would never drive off and leave someone hurt or dying on our front lawn."

"When do you expect him home?"

"He said late tonight. This morning, he told me he'd be glad to talk to the police. He mentioned it would have to be tomorrow though, because of his schedule."

"Tomorrow, then."

"Yes, but after his classes. He gets out at noon from his last class." Sophie cleared her throat. "Would you mind if he had lunch first? Then, we'll both come down to the station, or, if you want, you can come here. Say, 1:00 or 1:30?"

Don't push it, Sophie!

"One-thirty at the station, Mrs. Alexakis. You and Sarkis, one-thirty sharp."

"Thank you. We'll be there."

The detective thanked her for her time. I heard them walk down the stairs, followed by the click of the entryway closet.

"Good night, Mrs. Alexakis."

"See you tomorrow, Detective Berhmann."

FOURTEEN

I waited for the proverbial clear coast. Finally, I moved out from the hall into the entryway.

Sophie had turned off the lights. She sat on the arm of the sofa in the dark living room, looking out to the street.

I walked into the room. She jumped. "Oh, good heavens! You scared me to death. He just this second drove off. Did you hear everything?"

"Almost." I called up the stairs, "Zach, you can come out, now! Sophie, you did great. I gotta hand it to you."

"I didn't do too badly, and he liked the chair."

"So I heard. I'd like to see the Zakis-Chair. Is it true what you said?"

Zach came down the stairs.

"Most of it. The design team from Hong Kong visited last week." She smiled. "Sarkis is brilliant, and the investors are very real."

"No kidding."

"Honest, cross my heart." She stood abruptly. "I'm hungry. I'll bet you are, too."

As though fueled by the tension of Berhmann's visit, Sophie chattered as she put out plates. "I really didn't outright lie. Although, I did stretch the truth."

"You were great." I checked my watch, 7:30. "Now, we wait for the kidnapper's call."

Zach set the table without being asked, and he poured glasses of water for each of us.

Sophie brought her wine into the kitchen and dumped it down the sink. "I need my wits about me. I'll have a glass later."

While Sophie prepared dinner, I began to give her a short run down of what we learned about the Armenian genocide by the Turks. She threw a simple salad together of feta, cucumber, tomatoes, and Greek olives, with Zach chopping up the cucumber and tomato. He seemed to make a place for himself, no matter where he was.

Zach and I shared the stories we'd read; the mini-history lesson brought us together as we brought the one hundred years of denial and blame to an unsatisfactory close. Sophie asked us questions while directing Zach and me as we set the table. She expressed her extreme distaste of this sad history and wondered how, through all the drama, God had guided this little baby Sarkis' upbringing and new life.

She sprinkled on a bit of homemade olive oil and lemon dressing. A nice addition to the lasagna she'd heated. Sophie ate with a hearty appetite, a big change from this morning. Perhaps the shock had worn off.

After supper, we settled in the living room near the phone. Zach asked for permission to do a load of laundry and to take a quick shower. While I waited, I stared up at a black and white photograph of Sophie and Sarkis surrounded by a sea of friends.

"Here's some reading for you." I handed Sophie the printed pages I'd copied that afternoon.

She tossed the pages onto the coffee table and picked up her cell phone. "First, I'm gonna take a two minute shower, and put on clean clothes."

"Wait. What if the kidnapper's call? Leave me your phone, and I'll answer."

Sophie handed me her phone. "I promise you, I'll be back down inside of five minutes." She glanced at the clock on the mantle. "It's 8:30. I'll read this later." She took the stairs two at a time.

Exhausted, I stretched out on the sofa, grabbed a soft pillow, and crammed it under my head. I heard Zach rummaging around in the downstairs guest room. Sophie's and my cell phone were within arm's reach. I gazed at the fire in the fireplace.

In a haze of sleep, I registered Sophie's return to the living room, and then I was out cold.

My cell rang. I popped up, grabbed my phone, squinted at the number, and then groaned in frustration. My brother, Luke. It was late, and it meant only one thing. No other sucker would accept his calls. I hit the talk button.

"Hey, Luke," I whispered. Three feet away, Zach slept soundly in front of the fire.

I listened to my brother's stutter as I stared at the fire.

"Hos-hospital. I have to go to the hospital. Pain—my, my, my, my hip is killing me. Hos-hospital. It's a ee- emergency."

The familiar blend of extreme annoyance and empathy flooded me. "Okay, Luke, what's wrong? I can't help you; I'm eighty miles away. What time is it?" I glanced at my watch. "Eleven forty-five? Luke!" I struggled for calm. "Did you call Mom?"

"I, I tried to call Mom, but Dad wou-wou-wouldn't answer."

"Yeah, not after eleven o'clock, pal." My thirty–three year old brother never worried about inconvenience. In fact, he possessed a remarkable sense of entitlement.

"I nee-need to see a doctor. Excruciating pain, Jenna. Excruciating."

"Listen to me, Luke. Do you have pain pills?"

"I do-don't like those pills, Jenna! They make me sick."

"Well, you have to eat food when you take them, buddy."

"I know! I forgot that one time."

I yawned and scratched my head. "Hey, how's that neighbor of yours? Mr. Rodriguez? How's he doing?" I liked Rodriguez; he kept an eye on Luke for us.

"His dog had puppies! He's giving me one! Free!"

"That's really nice of him." I glanced at my watch again. "You want a boy or a girl?"

"I, I don't care if it's a boy or a girl. His name is MacGyver."

"Wow. That's an impressive name. You always think of the coolest names."

"I know."

"So, listen. I hate to sound like a commercial but why don't you take two aspirin and call me in the morning?"

Luke exploded in laughter. "You. You crack me up."

"Yeah, well, you crack me up, too. You get a good night's sleep, and I'll talk to you later, okay?"

"Okay, bye."

Sweet relief washed over me. I'd dodged the bullet. And not having to call my father was icing on the cake.

I set down my phone and stared out the window at the rain. Lightning illuminated the living room and thunder rumbled in the distance, both unusual in southern California. Had I really slept through thunder?

Sophie came in from the kitchen, holding the copies I'd given her in one hand, and Zach's folded laundry in the other. "Feel like a cup of something hot?"

I nodded. "Love it." I excused myself to use the

downstairs bathroom. I grimaced when I saw my reflection in the mirror. The fine lines around my eyes and mouth seemed deeper. I touched the skin under my eyes. My short dark hair was flying in all directions. Yikes. I ran water over my hand and tried to tamp down the fly a ways strands. I knew it was useless and the hair would dry any which way. Feeble attempt, but who cared?

A few minutes later, I wandered into Sophie's spectacular kitchen. "Oh, good, kettle's on." I stood at the counter, stretching my neck from side to side.

"Hot cocoa, tea?"

"Oh, cocoa, for sure," I said. "Got any marshmallows?" I hadn't had the latte I'd promised myself earlier in the day, so I could make up for it now.

"Of course."

Soon, the kettle whistled. Sophie poured steaming water into the mugs.

I stirred my cocoa, clanging the spoon against the cup. I added a fistful of mini-marshmallows. All this coziness seemed a bit bizarre under the circumstances.

I took a sip. "Let's sit down."

We sat at the dining table and stared out into the backyard. The tall camellias, illuminated by amber highlights, danced as wind and rain lashed the garden.

I took a cautious sip of the hot cocoa. "Mmm, marshmallows."

"Sarkis loves them, too." Sophie leveled her gaze at me. "So, who called you so late? Was it work-related?"

I stared out at the rain swirling in the muted light. "My brother, Luke. He's convinced he has a tumor growing in his hip."

"Good heavens! How terrible!"

I hunched forward, warming my hands on the mug. "There's nothing growing in his hip. The doctors are sure, but he says they're wrong, and he's gonna sue them. He didn't have a brain tumor last year, or cancer of the stomach six months before that."

"Oh, dear. I see."

"Yeah." I shrugged. "So, how are you holding up?"

Sophie glanced at the phone, her expression worried. "I'm all right, but I'm terrified for Sarkis. What is he going through?" She closed her eyes. "Why haven't they called?"

"Anyone in your situation would be scared to death. The kidnappers expect to get the Bible, we'll just hand it over."

"From your mouth to God's ear."

The quiet grew between us. We both turned our attention to the rain outside.

"How old is Luke?" asked Sophie, a few moments later.

I pressed my lips together, counting back. "He's the youngest of four, thirty-three now."

"He's my age! Does he work?"

I faced Sophie, leaning back in my chair and drawing my knees to my chest. "Luke is cognitively challenged. He can't earn a living. His dipstick doesn't touch oil, if you get my drift."

"Oh."

"I'm not being unkind. It's just the truth."

"Down's syndrome?"

"His life would have been better if it had been." I refocused on the backyard, taking another sip of cocoa. Luke lived the nightmare of being rejected by our father. Dad hated him and what he represented: failure.

The phone rang, jolting us both. The wall clock read 12:10. I ran for the extension in the living room.

Zach lurched to his feet, looking dazed and disheveled.

"On a two count," I called out to Sophie. "One… two… now." We simultaneously lifted the receivers.

"Yes? Hello?" Sophie's voice sounded tremulous.

"You have book?" A man asked in an accented voice.

"Yes. I have the book."

"*Inchallah!* You know Town and Country Office Park in Orange?" The kidnapper spoke slowly, struggling with each word. "Building six. Go now."

I knew the location.

Sophie asked, "When?"

"Drive now. You wait."

Sophie sucked in a steadying breath. "I'll bring the book."

"We kill husband if police."

"No police," she promised as the man severed the connection.

I walked into the kitchen.

Sophie stared at the dead phone in her hand. Her face pale, she lifted her gaze to meet mine. "It's happening."

Immediately, I called Ralph and told him the location

of the meeting. He said he'd be close by. I didn't have to remind him to stay out of sight. It was a given.

Recradling the phone, I said to her, "I'm outta here. You stay put. I'll take the Bible and trade it for Sarkis, we'll be back before you know it."

She jumped to her feet. "I'm going with you, Jenna."

I shook my head. "No. Too dangerous."

"Of course, it's dangerous. Sarkis might be killed!"

"And some guy—probably one of the kidnappers—died on your front lawn. This isn't a debate. You stay here with Zach."

"I insist! Otherwise, you're fired." She glared at me.

Outraged, I shot back, "The hell you say! You fire me, I'll call Berhmann and tell him everything."

A defiant Sophie raised her chin. "What was that you said earlier? '*We'll* just hand them the Bible, and it should all work out?'"

"I was referring to Ralph and me."

I grabbed my raincoat, put it on, took the Bible from Sophie and headed for the door.

Sophie took the stairs two at a time as she called over her shoulder. "No! I'm going. I'm grabbing my jacket. One minute."

Turning to Zach, I said, "It's your job to stay here and keep her calm. I'll be back."

Zach waved me off, "Go, go. We'll stay."

"Thanks." I smiled at him and cuffed him lightly on the chin. "Tomorrow we'll have a good day."

"This has been a great day!" He leaned over and hugged me. "I love this!"

FIFTEEN

I left the house on the run. Rounding the corner of the cul-de-sac, I raced for my car. I fumed over Sophie, clueless about the potential danger. She reminded me of the typical spoiled, rich Orange County housewife used to getting her own way. Jeeze Louise.

I silently congratulated myself on winning that round, as I started the car and took off to meet the kidnappers.

The wind gusted and rain hammered the car. Street lighting cast wild shadows along the road. I cracked open a window to let in some of the cold air.

Santiago Park, on the south side of Parker, loomed dark and over-grown. Streetlights illuminated the area, the leaves of the oaks and sycamores shiny in the tawny, misty light.

Finding the correct office park, I drove past it to check out the lay of the land. I didn't see Ralph's car. I fished in my pocket for my cell and gave him a call.

"I'm in place... near building seven," he whispered.

I was relieved. "Thanks, Ralph."

Circling to the back of the office buildings, I saw a few parked vehicles. The business park itself appeared ghostly in the night. I backed into a parking place and cut the ignition.

It was a perfect spot for an exchange. I cranked my neck from side to side, stretching the muscles, not liking the isolation.

A few minutes passed. Then, a car slowly edged into the back parking lot. Holding the Bible to my chest, I swung open the door. I jumped out of my car, and then stepped forward until I reached the hood.

A black or dark blue Mitsubishi sedan crept toward me. It braked. There were four silhouettes in the car. I clutched the Bible against my pounding heart. The bright headlights prompted me to shield my eyes with one hand.

The driver sat, not moving. He appeared to be speaking to the man riding shotgun. The headlights died. My breath caught in my chest as the front passenger door opened and a tall, slim man emerged. He looked around, as though sniffing for any scent of trouble. He stood perhaps forty-five feet away from me. A black fisherman's cap sat low on his brow.

I nicknamed him The Skipper.

"That is book?" The same foreign voice I'd heard on the phone.

"Yes."

"Bravo. You good wife."

"Where is my husband? I want to see him!"

"*Ya-vash*! First, book."

"No! First, I see my husband, and then you get the book."

"Do not play games with husband's life!" he snarled.

"No games. Let me see my husband."

Even in the murk, his menacing stare challenged. He turned his head, his gaze still fixed on me as he issued a sharp command.

A flurry of activity ensued in the back seat.

With a gun held to his head by one of his captors, Sarkis Alexakis emerged from the car. He wore black sweatpants and a pale gray sweatshirt. His posture told me that Sarkis' hands were secured behind his back. He cocked his head. "Sophie?"

I called, "Sarkis, are you okay, honey?"

"I'm fine, just fine... matia moo. Give them the book, and then get back in the car. Everything will be all right." I heard iron control in his voice. Nothing more. Matia moo?

"You're really okay?" I asked, trying to sound wifely.

The Skipper waved his hand in a cutting motion. "Enough! Lady, you blind? No more talk! The book!"

"All right! Sarkis, come here."

Sarkis hesitated, then stepped forward about two inches, only to be restrained by a sharp warning from the man who held the gun to his head.

I sucked in a breath.

The Skipper pointed at Sarkis. "Asla!" he hissed. He glared at me. His eyes shifted to the Bible. "Lady! Book! Now!"

I finally exhaled. "Okay. Let's do this."

Suddenly, someone shouted. The kidnappers called out, "*Haydi! Haydi!*" The guy with the gun to Sarkis' head shoved him into the back seat of the car. The engine roared to life, the headlights blinked on.

The Skipper turned to me, his face contorted with rage. "I say no police!"

From the left, two black clad figures darted at the kidnapper's car, screaming in a foreign language.

Stunned, I tried to make sense of the situation.

A second later, a silenced handgun coughed and a bullet hit the ground in front of me. I dove to the pavement and rolled. The Bible flew from my hands, slapping against the wet pavement.

Pain shot through my knees. I groped for the gun tucked in my back holster. Extending it in front of me, I gripped the weapon with both hands. Bright headlights blazed, blinding me.

Another figure came at the car from the right—a tall, slender male with white blond hair. Zach!

I scrambled to my feet, screaming, "No! Zach, no!"

He'd reached the rear passenger door where Sarkis sat. As he pulled it open, I ran toward him. Another bullet thunked into the building behind me. I hit the ground and rolled again.

Two more shots rang out. A scrabbling sound. And man's loud curse of distress.

Off to the left, two more shots were fired in quick succession. As I climbed to my feet, the driver of the car hurled Zach atop Sarkis and slammed the car door. Bile flooded my throat.

More rounds were fired. They impacted right in front of me and to my side, pinging the metal of my car. My panic level soared even higher. My son! More shouted foreign words filled the air.

Car doors slammed. Tires screeched. Footsteps echoed as though in pursuit of the vehicle. Far ahead of me, I heard unintelligible commands. Then, silence.

I knelt on the ground, swinging my weapon from side to side, an impotent reflex that now seemed useless.

Jittery, I stood. "Zach!" I cried out.

Ralph ran up, out of breath, chest heaving. Beads of perspiration streamed down his face. "That was Zach?"

"Yes, my God, yes!"

He stopped dead in his tracks, looking past me.

"What the hell were they doing here? Are you out of your friggin' mind?"

I whirled around and saw Sophie standing about six feet away from us. Anger flooded me. I roared, "I told you this was dangerous! I told you to stay home!"

Ralph walked a quick, tight circle, his gaze roving around the dark parking lot.

Sophie burst into tears. "It was me. I insisted on coming. Zach said he wouldn't let me come without him!"

"Now they have them both, Sophie. Do you realize what you've done?!"

"I didn't know!" she wailed.

Rage churned inside me. I scanned the parking lot. Nothing. Helpless, I stared down the road. *Now what?* My heart hammered.

"Who were those other men?" Sophie paced, her face ashen. "Did you call the police?"

The insinuation stung. I took her by the arm to stop her. "Do you see any police, Sophie?"

Still weeping, she jerked free of me. "They kept Sarkis?" She walked across the parking lot and stared off in the direction of the fleeing car.

Ralph put an arm around me.

"Why would Zach do something so stupid?" My voice broke.

Ralph shook his head. "Maybe he wanted to please his mother."

"Oh, my God."

"His mother?" Sophie asked.

He held me close. "Hang on. We'll get him back."

Sophie burst into tears again. "I threatened Zach. I forced him to come."

My God. They had my son. Pain, anger, ricocheted around inside me.

Limping over to the Bible, Ralph gathered up the soggy pages and handed the mess to Sophie. She held it to her chest as she hesitantly approached me. "I'm sorry, Jenna. I'm so sorry."

I hung onto my fury, letting it pour into every cell of my body. I felt overwhelmed by the burning desire for revenge. I straightened with the onslaught of rage.

A movement down the alley caught my eye. I roared to Ralph, "Behind you!"

He spun toward the alley.

I pulled out my gun, stepping in front of Sophie. "Do not move, do you hear me?"

SIXTEEN

Sophie managed a strangled, "Yes."

Two men dressed in black ran up the alleyway. One of them held up his hand. "We need to talk."

"Stop right there!" bellowed Ralph, waving his gun at both men. "Put down your weapons, and step away from them!"

The two immediately complied. One of them spoke. "Hey, we weren't the ones shooting at you."

"On your knees!" Ralph ordered. Keeping his gun trained on them, he walked behind them and frisked them for weapons. He tossed two revolvers onto the pavement.

I collected the guns, emptied them of bullets, and

placed the ammo in my jacket pocket. I sniffed the business ends of both the barrels. "They haven't been fired."

I stood next to Ralph, signaling Sophie to join us. Rivulets of sweat streaked Ralph's face and soaked the collar of his fleece shirt. "Okay, on your feet, both of you," said Ralph, in cop mode.

Sophie shifted closer to Ralph.

Both men, clad in black turtlenecks, jeans, and jackets, moved carefully. The youngest wore the same baseball cap he'd worn when he'd followed us this morning, the one I'd nicknamed Sherlock.

"What did you see before their car took off?" I asked.

Sherlock spoke. "Some guy tried to pull the professor out of the car. Instead, he wound up in the back seat. They fired shots but they were wild. I think they tried to miss. Then, they took off. We followed them for a couple of blocks, but we lost them."

I looked at Ralph. "This is not happening."

"Who'd they pull into the back seat?" the older one asked.

"It's Zach, he's just a kid," said Sophie, wiping away tears.

"Zach is Jenna's son," Ralph corrected.

Shocked, Sophie turned to me. "Your son? Zach is your son?" Fresh tears flooded her eyes. "Oh, dear God! Oh dear God! Can you ever forgive me?"

It was all I could do to hold back the invective-filled rage churning within me. Sophie's insistence on being at the scene may have destroyed two lives. But I managed an angry, "Looks like we have something in common now, Sophie," in clipped tones. I pivoted and studied the two men standing in the rain.

They were short, five-foot-six or thereabouts; both had dark eyes, dense eyebrows, and curly brown hair. Sherlock also wore narrow wire-rimmed glasses and a diamond stud in his left earlobe.

Both sported a couple of day's beard growth, and they reeked of cigarette smoke and stale coffee.

"Who the hell are you?" I demanded. "Do you have any idea what you've just done?"

For a brief moment, the older of the two studied Ralph and me. Then, he turned to Sophie. "Mrs. Alexakis, my name is Monte Kazarian, and this is my brother, Eznik."

With an abrupt nod, Eznik's eyes darted between Ralph and me. The older man remained focused on Sophie.

"You talk to all of us, or we're outta here," I snarled.

He leveled his gaze at me. "Who are you?" he asked. "What are your names?"

"This is Jenna Paletto, and her partner, Ralph. They're private investigators I hired," Sophie offered.

Ralph's voice shook with anger, as he demanded, "Why'd ya interfere with this? It was none of your damned business!"

"We are members of AJA, the Armenian Justice Alliance." Monte raised his chin.

"The Armenian Justice Alliance?" I said, "You're kidding, right? How many members are there? Two?"

"We are members of AJA," Monte repeated. His gaze swept over Ralph and me for a split-second, then back to Sophie. "We have over fifty thousand supporters in the United States alone.

"One of our CIA contacts in Washington called us four days ago. They alerted us that four Turkish businessmen landed at JFK from Istanbul, two of whom are known criminals in Turkey."

Turkey! While I connected the dots, a niggling fear snaked its way around my heart.

Sophie blanched. "The CIA, Jenna!"

"You think that makes them legitimate?" I ground my teeth to keep my breathing even. I wanted to claw out someone's eyes. These two were likely candidates.

"We've been tailing them since they arrived in the U.S. Two days ago, they began watching your home."

Sophie's eyes widened.

"Mrs. Alexakis," Monte said, "We watched these men abduct your husband this morning."

Sophie gasped. "You saw it?"

"Yes. Their manner was aggressive." He nodded toward his brother. "We couldn't just watch it play out, so we intervened."

"Who shot the guy on the lawn?" Ralph asked.

"When they tried to force your husband into their car, he didn't go peacefully. They pulled a gun on him and us." Monte shook his head. "It was crazy. Lots of shoving. Your husband even managed to break away from them." He pointed at his brother. "Eznik tried to stop one of them. He grabbed his gun, but in the confusion, the man's own gun went off. The bullet hit him in the chest. It was an accident."

Sophie shivered. "I didn't hear anything."

"They used silencers."

"He died," she informed them.

Monte nodded. "We thought so. We tried to get to your husband, but they shoved him into the back seat of his SUV and took off."

"Their car followed your husband's SUV. They took alternate routes; we followed your husband's car, but we lost him in morning traffic."

"You tracked Sophie here?" Ralph asked.

"We figured they'd contact you. We waited until she left this evening, then followed. Simple." Monte said smugly.

I shook my head. "This mess could have been avoided if you'd made yourselves known to us or called the police immediately."

Monte nodded to Eznik. "We did wonder what they could want from a biology professor with a wealthy wife."

Sophie shook her head. "The kidnappers don't know I have money. That's not what they're... ."

I hissed, "It's none of their business what the kidnappers want." I turned and spoke to the brothers.

"You spoiled a planned exchange tonight. You acted like morons. Now, we have to deal with the consequences of your actions."

Monte Kazarian spoke quietly but with authority. "It was your son's choice to try to rescue Mr. Alexakis. We had nothing to do with that. Mrs. Alexakis, again, we're sorry to have ruined this chance. May we ask what was it they wanted? Your husband's life for what?" His voice resonated compassion. His head cocked to one side, he looked earnest.

"We're not telling you a thing. I don't trust strangers, pal, and I definitely don't trust you."

Monte gave Sophie a quizzical look, his intense brown eyes rimmed in red and bloodshot.

Uncertain, Sophie turned her gaze to me.

I took her by the arm and propelled her toward my car. "Come on, let's move. Ralph, meet us at Sophie's. We need to get back there and hope they call."

"Wait a minute." Monte swung in front of us, forcing us to stop. "You need information about the kidnappers."

Sophie stopped dead. He was right. If he had intelligence, we needed to hear it. My knees hurt after hitting the pavement twice in the melee. I'd have sold my soul for getting Zach back and four Advil.

Ralph and Eznik followed us. They stood opposite each other, facing off like gunslingers in a misty rain.

Monte took a deep breath. "These businessmen are ruthless. These Turks care nothing about your life, your home. They care only about what they want. These men have long criminal records in their own country."

I shot back, "We know. We've spent the day figuring out who these thugs are. And we've read about the 1915 history of Turkey. You can't tell us anything we don't already know."

Monte raised his eyebrows in surprise. "Why are you talking about the genocide of a million and a half Armenians in Turkey a century ago?"

I mentally kicked myself. Damnit! I'd helped them make a connection. A stupid blunder. Before I could say another word, a cell phone rang.

Sophie cried, "That's Sarkis!" She dove for her purse.

"Get in the car, you'll hear better!" I jerked open my car door and got out a pad and pen from the glove compartment. Sophie sat shotgun as she dug for her phone.

Without a word, Eznik and Monte drew close, hunched against the cold, and stood next to the car.

I sat in the driver's seat. "Give me the phone, Sophie. I can ask the right questions."

Sophie hesitated, glancing up at Ralph, who nodded. She handed me the phone on the fifth ring.

"Yes? Hello?"

"I said no police!" The Skipper's hysterical voice again.

"Those men were not police! They were just some Armenian... idiots... whatever, I never heard of them before. AJA or something."

Monte and Eznik freaked and motioned wildly.

I ignored them. "It was just two men. Not police. Please. Let's try this again, right now. Tell me where to meet you."

"Who this boy?"

"His name is Zach, and he's only nineteen years old! He was trying to help, that's all."

Rapid-fire Turkish went on for a long minute.

"Where AJA now?" the Skipper demanded.

"I told them to leave," I lied. "I was very angry. They left."

The yelling on the other end of the line sounded hostile. Then the line went dead.

I stared at the phone.

"What?" said Sophie. "What did they say?"

"They hung up."

"Give me that!" Sophie grabbed the phone and speed dialed Sarkis' number. We stood close by as she listened. "They turned it off." Sagging, she closed her phone.

Monte raised his hands and said, "Listen, we've got the make and number of their car. We'll work this out."

"Gee, let me think... nah, your work here is done." Reaching for the car door, I tried to shut it.

Eznik stood in my way.

"Nik, let's go." Monte turned away. The two began to walk down the alleyway.

Sophie hefted herself half out of the car. "Wait, please! Follow us back to my house, we need to talk."

Monte lifted a hand in acknowledgement.

She was right. We needed to talk.

Ralph shivered and tucked his hands under his armpits as light rain dripped off his eyelashes. "Gimme a lift to my car, will ya?"

"Of course."

"My car has to stay. Zach has the keys." Sophie took the backseat, lapsing into a pensive state.

Ralph hefted himself into the front. He blew into his cupped hands for warmth. "I can't believe how this went down."

"They've got Zach, Ralph." And he'd been right. We don't do kidnappings. I sighed and looked at Sophie in my rearview. "If they've been tailing those guys for four days straight, those two twits must be exhausted."

"That's the first half-way decent thing you've said about them, Jenna," Sophie remarked.

I stared intently at my dashboard trying to get a grip on myself. "What do you expect, Sophie? Look, if they hadn't interfered, Zach wouldn't have tried to rescue Sarkis. Now, there are two hostages thanks to you and them." I started the car. "Let's get back to the house."

We dropped Ralph at his car. "I'll follow," he said. "I want to hear what these two have to say, and I don't like the idea of you being alone with them."

SEVENTEEN

We arrived at Sophie's house at 1:00 a.m. Again, we parked outside the cul-de-sac.

Ralph pulled up behind us and got out of his car.

As we walked up to the house, Sophie brought out her keys, and then jumped back in alarm. "The door's open!" she said. "It was locked, I always lock it!"

Tension zinged through me, I pulled her aside and saw that the door was ajar. Adrenaline surged. Ralph put a finger to his lips and raised his other hand to signal Sophie, *Wait here*. I whispered to her. "Wait."

Sophie, too fearful to move, watched us make our way into the house.

Ralph and I took the lower part of the tri-level house first. Empty.

Upstairs. Clear.

In the office closet, the floor safe gaped open. Legal documents were scattered about. I called for Sophie to join us.

Breathless, she entered the room. She dropped to her knees on the floor, picking through the pages and folders. "Sarkis' passport is missing! He's been here!"

We crouched beside her and examined the papers.

Sophie said, "We keep about ten thousand cash in the safe. That's gone. Everything else seems to be here." She sat back with an anxious expression on her face.

"They're leaving the country," said Ralph.

I nodded. "Ralph's right. They intend to leave the country." I sucked in a sharp breath. "Zach's backpack! Did he take it with him to the exchange?"

"No!" said Sophie.

We raced downstairs to the guest bedroom.

"I folded his laundry, it was on the bed. The backpack's gone," Sophie checked the closet. "He wore his jacket because of the rain."

Ralph lumbered into view. "There are clothes all over the bed in your room, Sophie. Sarkis probably packed a bag."

She ran up to her bedroom; we followed. Sophie picked up a sweater from the pile of discarded clothing on her bed. She held it to her face, inhaling Sarkis' scent.

She turned to look at us. "That's good, isn't it, that he was allowed to pack warm clothes? It's a good sign isn't it?" She glanced into the walk-in closet. "I haven't a clue what shoes he took."

I searched my mind, but I couldn't remember Zach's shoes. The fact that he'd grown up in Boise meant he knew how to dress for cold weather. Right? Where would the kidnappers take Zach and Sarkis? And what kind of circumstances would they be forced to endure?

I leaned against the doorframe, exhausted.

When Sophie met my gaze, her face crumpled, and she began to weep. "I'm so sorry for what happened to Zach. I'm so scared for both of them!"

I pushed away from the wall. "I think Sarkis was probably very relieved not to find you here tonight." I took her by the arm and led her out of the bedroom. "Come on, let's go see what Ralph's doing."

Sophie swiped at her tears before giving me a brave smile. "You said Zach was your assistant. I wish I'd known he was your son."

We walked down the hall to the office.

Ralph knelt on the floor, returning all the documents to the floor safe. "Jenna. Did Zach have a passport with him?"

"I don't know if he even has one."

"Just asking," Ralph said. "They won't be able to take him anywhere without a passport."

My heart did a flip-flop. I'd have to ask Kent in the

morning about the passport. Definitely not a task for the faint of heart.

As Ralph spun the combination lock, Sophie asked, "Now what?"

He looked up. "It's just a matter of time, Sophie. Don't worry. They'll call."

Sophie swallowed, obviously fighting for her composure. "You sound sure of that. I hope to God you're right."

The doorbell rang.

"It's probably those AJA guys," Ralph said. He left us, eager to escape her anxiety.

Slumping into a chair, Sophie faced me. "How did Sarkis look, Jenna? Could you see?"

I sank into the desk chair opposite her. I thought for a moment. "He looked... tired." I smiled wanly. "He also seemed angry, but he stayed in control. He called me something like... matia moo? Is that an endearment he uses with you?"

A single tear slipped down her cheek. She blotted it away, taking a deep, tremulous breath. "Oh! Matia Mou! Yes, it's a Greek saying he's always used with me. It means 'my little eyes.' He was telling me that he loves me." She closed her eyes for a long moment. "That sounds just like him." Sophie exhaled heavily. "When Zach took off running for that car, I was terrified. And when the bullets started flying I curled into a little ball and prayed like I've never prayed before. I think Zach was trying to help."

"Zach's probably really angry with himself right about now."

We sat quietly for a moment, the ticking of the wall clock the only sound in the room.

Ralph called out. "You two coming down?"

We dragged ourselves out of our chairs and made our way downstairs.

Monte and Eznik Kazarian stood in the living room. They looked uncomfortable in Sophie's spacious and tastefully decorated home. I felt a little of the same. I appreciated good decorating, and I knew the cost of things. Hell, I couldn't afford Sophie's bath towels.

Motioning the men into the kitchen, Sophie walked over to the range. "Why don't we sit at the table?" They reeked of cigarettes, body odor, and soiled clothing. They hadn't shaved in days.

Sophie added water to the kettle and pulled out mugs. She opened a bakery box of cookies and put them on a plate, then heaped red and green grapes into a bowl. I marveled that she could play the gracious hostess under such circumstances.

My stomach ached, my heart was breaking, my knees were killing me, and I wanted to curl up in a corner with a blanket in the worst way. I searched for the strength to remain calm. Sophie had had a day to acclimate. I'd been without Zach for one hour. Not to mention the previous nineteen years.

Ralph and I prepared our tea. Sophie gave steaming mugs of hot chocolate to the two brothers, who dove at the tempting cookies.

"Monte, what do you think will happen now?" asked Sophie, taking a seat.

"They'll call again. Set up another exchange. More than likely, within the next few hours." He bit into a cookie and wiped his mouth with a napkin.

Sophie sat at the head of the table, holding her mug. Before I knew it, she leaned into Monte and Eznik. "They were here. Right before we arrived, they took my husband's passport and some cash. And they let Sarkis and Zach pack some clothes." I hid my surprise and annoyance at her revelation to two strangers.

Apparently stunned, the two men stared at her. Eznik said something in what I took to be Armenian to Monte, whose face blanched. He shook his head. "That's not a good sign."

"Why? Do you think they'll contact us again?" pressed Sophie.

"I think they will," I said.

Ralph murmured assent.

Monte shrugged. "Depends on what they want from you. How badly do they want it? They came a long way to steal from you. It seems unlikely they'd leave without whatever it is."

Despite my misgivings over Monte's earlier disdain for Ralph and me, I was determined to try acting decent and see where it got me. "Would you mind going over again what happened yesterday?"

Monte shifted in his seat, now including Ralph and me as he spoke. "We'd been following them for a couple of days. We were exhausted. Then things got interesting when we tailed them to Chapman University where Professor Takmaz has an office. The professor wasn't in, but his office partner was. They didn't stay but a few minutes."

Monte turned, nodding to his brother. "Around noon, we followed them to the professor's home. The kidnappers waited until the professor and his wife left in their car. We watched them break in. They were in the house for about fifteen minutes, then they took off."

He glanced at Eznik. "They spent twelve hours in a motel room in Tustin. We followed them when they left at five thirty in the morning. They'd been discreet at Professor Takmaz's home. But like I said, this morning they were brazen. We didn't have much time to think about it."

I felt a grudging admiration for Monte and Eznik. They were ignorant do-gooders, but their 'let's take 'em' on' mentality made me grind my teeth.

Sophie said, "I want to thank you for trying to help us. I'm sorry that man was killed. Death is a terrible price to pay for trying to steal... ."

"What? What is it?" Monte asked with irritation. "Money?"

Sophie leaned across the table. "It's a hidden..."

I shot to my feet. "Sophie! Not another word. We're

talking in private. Now!" I gave Ralph a 'watch these guys' look.

Sophie stood and faced me. "Sounds like something we need to do." She turned to the men. "We'll be back shortly."

Monte's gaze followed Sophie out of the room.

On my way out, I saw Ralph purse his lips. Not a good sign.

Sophie motioned me to follow her downstairs to the paneled library. When I arrived, I found her leaning against a desk, arms crossed, her head cocked to one side.

I shut the door and faced her. "Are you out of your mind?"

She answered my question with one of her own. "Why the cloak and dagger show?"

"These men are strangers, Sophie. Think about it. They appeared out of the shadows, messed up the exchange and we know *nothing* about them. And one man is dead because of them."

She nodded. "These men might have bungled things, but they tried to help Sarkis."

I cut to the chase. "Until I run a background check on their AJA organization and them, we tell them nothing. *Nothing!* We don't know anything at all about them. Even more important, we don't know what they're capable of."

"They've tried to protect Sarkis, and they don't even know him."

"Why?" I asked, "Think about their motivation. Why did they tail the kidnappers in the first place? We have no idea."

"They said..."

"*They said.*" I stabbed a finger at her. "You're making my point for me, Sophie. Did they protect Sarkis? No!" I paced the room. "Something is not right about these guys. Promise me you won't divulge any information—not about Sarkis and not about that Bible until I give you the go-ahead."

Sophie remained adamant. "They want to help us. They *have* helped us."

I swore. "What do I have to do, beg you? Don't say anything. They got a man killed this morning, and they blew the exchange tonight. Now, Zach is involved. How in the hell does all of that inspire your confidence? God, you're killing me."

"Would you mind watching your language? Your use of profanity offends me." She gave me a quick nod. "All right then, what do I say when we go back upstairs?"

I stood in front of her, hands on my hips. I slowed my speech down to deliberate. "You tell them I asked you to wait until the kidnappers call and they give us further instructions. Crap, *I'll* tell them. Will you cooperate?" I failed to mask my exasperation.

Sophie exhaled, and then said, "I'll continue to trust your instincts... for now."

"One more question. How do you know these guys

aren't in competition with the kidnappers? Maybe they already know what's written in that Bible."

"I still think we should tell them the whole story. I mean... they want to help us."

"Not a solitary word about that Bible. Are we clear?"

With a curt nod, she walked out of the room. I took a deep breath, shook my head, and followed the velvet steamroller.

EIGHTEEN

When we got upstairs, we discovered that the brothers had moved outside to smoke.

Ralph sat at the table, his head slumped forward. He snorted awake when I touched his shoulder.

When the brothers noticed our return, they put out their cigarettes and came back inside.

I met them at the slider and told them before we gave them any information we were waiting until the kidnappers contacted us again. They didn't say a word. Didn't even exchange a glance.

"Ralph, you look exhausted," said Sophie. "Why don't you take the upstairs guest room and have a nap until we get that call?"

"Good idea," I said.

Sophie turned to Monte and Eznik. "There's a guest bathroom downstairs you can use, a washer and a dryer, and a bedroom if you'd like a nap."

Irritation flooded me, but I gritted my teeth and said nothing.

The two chorused their thanks. Sophie led them downstairs to show them where the laundry detergent was located.

Ralph walked past me on his way upstairs. I rolled my eyes at him.

He chuckled and shook his head. "Let me know the minute you hear anything."

"Get some sleep." I gave him a pat on the back.

Crossing into the living room, I sank onto the sofa and stared at the fire. I yanked the paprika colored afghan over me, and then covered my eyes with my hand. Nothing could stop the tape in my mind as I evaluated the day's events. Sophie's voice filtered up from the laundry room. I thanked my lucky stars Ralph was with us, even if he was sound asleep. He always gave me a sense of security.

Rain started to fall again. The fireplace kept the room comfortable. Where was Zach? Was he warm and dry? Was he frightened? Angry with himself? Could he communicate with Sarkis?

Sophie re-entered the room. She dropped onto the sofa opposite mine. "You awake?"

I didn't reply. Opening my eyes, I stared into the flames.

"Are you going to tell Zach's father what's happened?"

I shook my head. "Zach's birth father is the man I was telling you about… the one who disappeared off the face of the earth, the one man I never found."

"Oh, my gosh. You're kidding! You raised your son by yourself? That's…"

"No." I shook my head again, and stared at the fire. "I gave up Zach for adoption. My fiancé's brother and his wife offered to adopt him. They took Zach and moved to Boise, Idaho. I never heard from them much after they moved."

"Well, I see a lot of resembleance and he's a lot like you. He's such a great kid."

"Sophie." I closed my eyes, suddenly done in. "We met this morning for the first time. He waltzed into my office, full of piss and vinegar and bursting with false bravado. It didn't take long for that to disappear." I stared at the flickering shadows on the ceiling. "And you're right; he is a great kid. He wanted answers. We didn't have time to share much, because you called. We've only had this one day together."

Sophie shook her head as she gazed at the fire. "That's unbelievable! You seemed like you knew each other so well. This is my fault. I never learn!"

I could tell she meant it. And now a few hours later, I too, was calmer, more reflective. "Look, you had no way of knowing that Zach would pull a stunt like that. Maybe Ralph's right, maybe he wanted to impress me. But it's done, and we go forward. From here on out, you and I are partners. We work together to get our men back, deal?"

"Deal. We work together. I like that. And I'll pray for the Lord's protection."

"You do that. Now, try to get some sleep."

"You, too."

Fat chance.

***

My eyes opened and slowly focused. I sat bolt upright with the realization there'd been no phone call during the night. Sophie lay on the sofa across from me. She was sound asleep, an arm thrown over her head. The clock on the television cable box read six-oh-four. Sinking back down, I pulled the comforter up under my chin.

The shrill of the phone cut through the quiet morning.

Jumping up off the sofa in one move, I called, "Sophie!"

She jolted awake with a small cry.

I bellowed up the stairs, "Ralph!"

In seconds, the bleary-eyed brothers appeared.

Turning to Sophie, I held up my hand. "Let me talk to them, okay?"

She nodded and stood close by.

I picked up the phone. "Yes? Hello?"

"This is Sarkis. Put Sophie on." Shock coursed through me. I handed the receiver to Sophie. "It's Sarkis!"

"Sarkis?" Sophie tore the phone from my grasp. "Sarkis! Where are you?"

Ralph hustled downstairs.

I placed a pen and pad of paper on the counter for Sophie. I dashed into the living room and picked up the other phone.

"... carefully. They won't give me much time, and my battery is almost dead. Honey, we're taking off. Write down the information I'm about to give you."

"Do you want me to call the police? The FBI?"

"No! Absolutely not. Take this address down, honey. Ready?"

I could hear short, quick breaths from Sophie. "How is Zach? Is he okay?"

Sarkis lowered his voice. "Zach's good."

There was a sharp command in what I assumed was Turkish.

"Okay. Okay!" Sarkis said. "Do you have a pen and paper?"

"Yes, give me the address."

"You need to come to Istanbul..."

"Istanbul, Turkey?" Her voice cracked.

"You have to go to the Hotel Citadel, Kennedy Caddesi, Sultanahamet." He carefully spelled out the address, and Sophie transcribed his words. "By Friday at 5:00."

My knees grew weak, my eyes filled with tears. I took the wireless phone, walked to the window, and stared outside. My son in Turkey?

I took a steadying breath.

"What about another exchange attempt here?"

"No, honey."

"You're flying to Istanbul this morning?"

Ralph glanced up at me with a look that could twist a pretzel. Not happy.

Sophie lowered her head, closed her eyes, and listened to Sarkis whisper into the phone. "These guys have contacts. One speaks pretty decent English. We're on our way to somewhere in South America in a cargo plane. My Spanish isn't great, but I think I heard them mention Venezuela. I think we fly to Turkey from there. It looks like we're leaving soon."

"Does Zach have a passport?"

"Yeah. It's in his backpack."

Sophie straightened. "Tell them I'll meet them by myself anywhere they want!"

"Honey, these guys are spooked. Zach's told me what's in the Bible, and what Professor Takmaz did. Who were the two guys who showed up last night?"

"They are the same two who tried to help you yesterday morning. They say they are members of the Armenian Justice Alliance. They followed the kidnappers to our home yesterday."

"All this for a buried treasure in Istanbul?"

"Yes. That's what the kidnappers want. Your great-grandfather buried it in his home in 1915."

Eznik and Monte exchanged a look.

I felt sick. Now the brothers knew the truth about something buried.

"I'm Armenian?" Sarkis mused.

"Looks that way."

"These guys are paranoid, and they're very pissed over the death of their friend. Sweetheart, bring the Bible to Istanbul."

Sophie raised her eyes at me. "I'll be there, but I'm not coming alone."

"Zach's mom, right?"

"Yes. We'll leave immediately." She glanced down at the paper she'd written on. "Hotel Citadel, Sultanahamet."

The kidnappers screamed, *"Haydi! Haydi!"*

Sarkis' voice softened. "Honey, I love you."

"Sarkis," she hurried, "watch over Zach! I love you. Be strong. Pray."

"Be careful. I will... ."

The call abruptly ended.

Sophie stared at the phone in her hand, and then gave us a wide-eyed look. "Istanbul! They're taking them to Istanbul."

The two brothers exchanged a look.

Ralph reached out to pat her on the back. "These characters know how tough American security is right now." He shook his head. "They wanna trade on their own playground, and they want you to play by their rules."

She nodded blankly at Ralph. "I need to borrow my father's jet." Sophie started to dial the phone, then checked herself. "Oh, it's not even six-thirty!" Her eyes shone with emotion. "Sarkis sounded good, didn't he?" She didn't wait for me to answer. Sophie shifted her attention to Monte and Eznik. "Do you speak Turkish?"

My hackles whiplashed to the upright position.

Monte nodded. "Yes, as a matter of fact."

Eznik also nodded. Did this guy ever talk?

I leaned against a counter top. "Why did you learn Turkish?"

He shrugged. "Our parents sent us, they wanted Eznik and I to live in Turkey, to learn all we could about the language and the culture. We were kids, right out of high school."

"Excuse us a moment, please. Let's talk." Sophie motioned for Ralph and me to follow her downstairs to the library. We gathered into the spacious room. "I want to hire them as translators. I think they'd be a big help."

Alarmed, I felt my stomach do a flip-flop. I shook my head. "Not a good idea. We don't know anything about them."

Ralph added, "I agree, it's not a good idea. We don't have time to do a complete background check on them."

"They're already involved," said Sophie.

"Sophie, we don't know their agenda." I countered.

Her jaw tightened. "The CIA wanted Monte and Eznik to help them, remember? And it's my prerogative to ask them. They risked their lives to try to help Sarkis, which speaks volumes to me."

I thought hard. With Sarkis and Zach headed for Istanbul, maybe her idea wasn't so off the wall. Monte and Eznik might be helpful, especially if they spoke the language and knew the lay of the land.

"Alright then, here are the ground rules," I said. "Operation, effective immediately. All decisions are mine. I'm in charge of this whole thing from here on out. No arguments, and absolutely no discussions about the treasure with those two. Agreed?"

Sophie nodded. "Agreed."

Monte and Eznik knew nothing about Armen Begosian or where he'd lived. I meant to keep it that way.

I looked at Ralph. "And, it wouldn't be totally awful if we found Armen Begosian's treasure."

Ralph gave me a hard look. "Not a priority, Jenna! It's not there, anyway. Not after a hundred years!"

I shrugged.

Ralph swore.

Sophie obviously agreed with Ralph. "Jenna, I just want my husband and Zach back, safe and sound. Let the kidnappers have the treasure, whatever it is."

Rescuing Zach and Sarkis was my goal, but screwing the kidnappers out of the treasure definitely appealed to me.

Ralph jerked his thumb in the general direction of the brothers. "Second thought, I like the idea of you taking a couple of guys along, especially since I can't go with you."

I shot him an incredulous look.

Ralph ignored my irritation. "Anyway, you need to run a quick background check on them, and get home and grab some clothes. I'll stay put and guard the fort."

"I nodded. "Do you want Henry Brazel onboard at the office for a few weeks to help out?"

"Good idea."

Wow. No arguments from Ralph. Henry, always available at a moment's notice, would be in seventh heaven.

We walked upstairs to the kitchen. The two men still sat at the table.

Sophie took the lead when I nodded at her. "We're flying to Istanbul to deliver the Bible. The kidnappers have instructed us to be at the Hotel Citadel by Friday 5:00."

Eznik frowned. "I don't know where that hotel is." He speaks!

Monte shot his brother a give-me-a-break look. "There are hundreds of hotels in the city."

Sophie ignored the exchange. "Would you come with us?"

I pointed out, "You've lived there and speak the language. That'd help us out."

"You'll be well paid," Sophie added.

"Istanbul's a huge, beautiful place." Beaming, Eznik nodded at us. "We would go, wouldn't we, Monte?"

Monte sent his brother a stern look.

"Yes or no?" I demanded.

Monte spoke with restraint. "Yes. Let us know when." Handsome and self-assured to the point of arrogance, I thought he acted way too cool. And I wondered why.

With a decisive nod, Sophie said, "Excellent. Thank you, gentlemen. We leave this morning by nine."

Shocked, I realized I was actually going to Istanbul. The thought of flying off to parts unknown made me feel both uneasy and curiously galvanized. I understood how Sophie felt; I wanted Zach home safe. With me.

A to-do list began to stack in my head.

I turned to the two brothers. "Passports?"

Eznik nodded. "We have them!"

I moved toward the sink to rinse out my cup. "Ralph, will you call Henry Brazel? Sophie, you'll take care of the plane?"

"Yes, I'll probably charter one. I'm certain Dad and his new wife took his to Costa Rica for their honeymoon."

Surprised, I turned to her. "He remarried?"

"Yes. Two weeks ago last Sunday, George St. James remarried. And now you know it before The Enquirer."

The power and prestige behind the St. James name made me fret over Sophie's vulnerability. Would that add more complications to an already complex situation?

"Don't you want to let your father know what's

going on in your life? This is serious stuff," I reminded Sophie.

"Jenna, I'm not interrupting my dad on his honeymoon! He's always been there for me, but not this time. I can handle this." Sophie turned to Monte and Eznik. "Get packed. We'll eat breakfast at the airport."

I turned to her. "I'll be back in ninety minutes."

Monte gave me a long look. "Dress for cold." He held my gaze.

Unsettled, I looked away, grabbed my keys, and headed for the door.

NINETEEN

At my place, I showered, packed warm clothes and my wool trench coat, grabbed my makeup bag and tooth brush, and threw it all in a small rolling duffel bag, and then hurried over to my office. I booted up both computers. On one, I started a background check for Monte and Eznik Kazarian, who claimed to be from Fresno.

Fifteen minutes later, I had the scoop on the two men now sipping coffee at Sophie's home. I crouched in my dinky office closet, rolled aside the carpet, and opened the floor safe. Removing my passport and five hundred dollars, I diligently recorded the withdrawal in the ledger.

Ralph called to say Henry was on board. Henry was thrilled to work with Ralph. Yay, team! I made a to-do list for Ralph and Henry.

A knock at the door interrupted me. A bolt of fear shot through me. Kent, or Detective Berhmann, I wondered. I tiptoed into the reception room and leaned out far enough to see Kent standing at the door. I glanced at my watch. Eight-ten. I remained still, watching to see if he would leave. Then he leaned up to the window and peered in, surprising me. Damn. He'd seen me.

"Jenna? It's me, Kent."

I swore under my breath before I opened the door. "Kent. It's been a long time."

He looked suspicious and uncertain. Any resemblance to Jayson, his long lost brother, had been erased by the years.

"Jenna. You've barely changed. Your hair's shorter." He drew a hand over his unshaven beard.

"It's been eighteen years since we've spoken, Kent."

"Yeah. I'm sorry about that, Jenna. It was... well... it was what Lizabeth wanted." He shrugged. "Moving away never felt right to me."

Really.

He stood stiffly. I could plumb a line with the rigidity of his spine.

"Is Zach here?" He peered past me.

"No. This is my office. All these rooms are offices. Zach stayed at my partner's house. He'll be in with

Ralph around ten this morning. I'm sorry, but I have an appointment with clients in about ten minutes."

"I'll wait." His steely blue eyes darted around the reception room.

"I'm sorry you can't. There are other tenants, so this is their private waiting room, too. Why don't you have breakfast at Watson's down the street? It's a great place." I stepped out onto the porch and pointed in the direction of the restaurant.

Reluctantly, Kent followed. "Zach's phone is turned off."

"I'll call my partner and have him ask Zach to turn on his phone. Let's have lunch or supper tonight." I suggested. "Lot's of years under the bridge."

"I'm not leaving without Zach." The crow's feet deepened around his eyes. His mouth narrowed into a mean line.

I felt a wave of nausea as I thought about Zach. "Look, he'll be here soon, you can duke it out with him." Shrugging noncommittally, I tried not to appear rushed. "By the way, I'm very impressed with how you've raised him. He's a great kid."

"He's a good one," Kent agreed.

"Kent, I'm really sorry, but I have to be at an appointment in five minutes. Have breakfast, read the paper, and wait for Zach's call."

"Fine, I'll get some breakfast."

"And dinner at my place, tonight?"

He studied my face. "Sure."

"Great. We'll talk later." I shut the door and locked it. I waited a beat to see if Kent drove off. He did. "You are a big, fat liar, and you do it so well," I whispered, as I picked up my keys, purse, passport, duffle and the cash. I ran for the back door.

***

Roaring into Sophie's cul-de-sac, I screeched to a halt in the driveway.

I popped open the trunk of the Corolla, grabbed a mini tool kit I rarely use, truth be known, and lifted out my duffel bag, and rolled it behind me to the house. Parking my luggage in the foyer, I sprinted upstairs.

Ralph was straightening his bed. "How'd it go?"

"Kent showed up about a half an hour after I got to the office. I told him Zach spent the night at your place."

"Crap."

"I know, I'm sorry. He wants his boy. He says he's not leaving without him. He still looks like someone rammed a steel rod down the entire length of his spine."

"What the hell am I supposed to tell him when he shows up at my door?"

"Zach was kidnapped by international terrorists and I went to save him?" I plopped down on the bed beside Ralph.

"Real helpful."

"Sorry. Tell him Zach is adamant about not going home for a while. He's of legal age, so he can do whatever he wants. He refuses to talk to his father right now, and he wants some space from the family for just a short time. Would that do it?"

"I can speak it, but will he buy it?"

"Just be your reasonable self. Explain Zach's need to find out the truth of who he is, and tell him I'm just trying to assimilate the whole thing. Give him some bull about my being really successful, and now I have this teenager wanting answers. I'm not too happy about it."

"Total bull."

"Yeah. Oh, God, I hope this all works out, Ralph."

"So, what'd you learn about the brothers?"

"They're clean."

Ralph raised an eyebrow.

I nodded. "As a whistle. No priors, no criminal histories. No arrests. Nothing." I leaned against the doorjamb. "And get this, they own six dry cleaning businesses."

"Dry cleaning? No kidding." He gave me a considering look, and then shook his head. "I can't see them asking anyone how much starch they want in their shirts."

"And the AJA is registered with Interpol, the FBI, and the CIA just like they said."

"I still don't feel good about this."

"Do you know what Sarkis said, while I was listening

on the phone this morning? He said to Sophie, 'She's Zach's mom, right?'"

He searched my eyes. "I don't get it."

"Zach told Sarkis I was his mom. I love that he said that. He called me his mom."

"Careful, Jen-kins."

"I know. I know." I stood. "Come on. We need to get moving."

We walked downstairs to the kitchen. Eznik sat with the morning paper. He wore a tailored shirt fitted to show off his torso and narrow waist. I wondered if he draped gold chains around his neck when he dated or bar hopped. *Eww.* He now wore boots that had thick heels, adding about three or more inches to his height.

"Hey, is your brother packed? Are you ready to go?" I asked.

"I'll check." He left the room.

Ralph let out a sigh. "So, you nervous about going?"

"Hmmm, I'm taking off to the other side of the world, looking for my missing son, and I've never been anywhere before."

Ralph glanced at me. Coming closer, he whispered, "Didn't Monte say a contact at the CIA called and gave them a head's up about those Turks entering the country?"

I matched his hushed tone. "Yeah. He said it was an Armenian contact at the CIA."

Ralph pursed his lips, and then gazed out the window

to the backyard. "Huh. You don't suppose those two are CIA? Or maybe FBI?"

I exhaled in a snort. "Those two? Ralph! They blew the entire exchange."

Ralph cocked his head. "I'm gonna look into it."

"Good. Call me in Istanbul and lemme know what year they flunked out of the FBI Academy."

"I'll do that."

His jaw flexed while he ground his teeth. He appeared deep in thought. "You said they came up clean, right?"

"Squeaky clean, not even a lousy parking ticket in the last ten years."

"Well, *I* haven't had a parking ticket in ten years."

"Yeah, me neither."

"I'm gonna dig deeper."

"You said you were okay with them coming along."

"Something's buggin' me, and I can't put my finger on it."

Sophie came downstairs with her suitcase.

Ralph said, "Oh, lemme get that for you."

"Thank you, Ralph, and I packed another one for Sarkis, it's upstairs."

"'I'll take care of it."

She crossed to the counter with her purse and set it down. "I called my dad's secretary and she told me that Dad and Gwen were using the jet. So I've chartered a plane with Pacific Moon Aviation. We've used them many times in the past. A plane is available, so we won't be delayed."

The brothers brought their gear into the foyer, and then took all of the luggage out to Sophie's SUV. We followed them.

I looked up, feeling the bite of the cold wind that whipped dark gray clouds across the sky. It would rain again, a California rarity. Normally, I'd hunker down and get cozy in this weather, maybe even read a novel.

Instead, I was going to Istanbul to rescue my son and Sarkis Alexakis.

TWENTY

Traffic was God-awful. No surprises there. My frustration spiked as we crawled at a snail's pace, ensnared with thousands of other cars making their way south on the 55 Freeway. Sophie navigated the car to a street west of the John Wayne Airport runway, which housed hundreds of businesses in glass and concrete buildings. Pacific Moon Aviation sat among them.

    I followed Sophie into the reception area. She made an immediate beeline for the women's bathroom. As soon as we stepped into Pacific Moon, it hit me; I was in the land of the rich and extremely prosperous. A huge four-story atrium overlooked the runway. Expensive bucket style leather chairs sat around eight glass tables.

A young woman worked behind a gleaming brass cart, serving coffees and cappuccinos. Businessmen waited for their flights, sipping coffee, reading newspapers, or working on their laptops. Another woman, dressed like a flight attendant, tended a second cart laden with fresh fruit, bagels, granola and yogurt.

People chatted in hushed tones with an occasional burst of boisterous laughter from a group of men in the corner.

A guy who looked like he belonged in an ad for Armani flight uniforms, sat behind the counter reading the newspaper.

Monte and Eznik remained outside to indulge their nicotine cravings. Rattled nerves from the traffic, no doubt.

I approached the counter. "Excuse me?"

The man appeared to be aware of my presence, but he didn't acknowledge me. Having been ignored by Monte the night before, I'd had enough attitude from the male species to last me a month.

"Hey, pal, I don't mean to interrupt you, but is your coffee break about over?" I leaned over the counter and arched an eyebrow. "We called earlier. For Sophie Alexakis?"

The most piercing, vibrant green eyes focused on me. He looked surprised. For the briefest moment, he seemed to hold back a smile. Then, he turned all business.

"Of course." He folded his newspaper, tossing it aside. His skin was lightly tanned, his crew cut hair prematurely gray. He had a straight nose and engaging smile. Not too hard on the eyes, either. And no wedding ring. I bit back a grin.

"You're off to Istanbul, correct? Not too many people want to leave for Istanbul at a moment's notice, but we aim to please." He crossed to the computer and started typing. He scanned the screen. "Departure is set for one o'clock. Four passengers going and six returning." He gave me a curious look. "Any changes?"

"No. Six returning. That's correct."

He extended his hand. "I'm Will Graham. You are?"

I shook his hand. Warm and firm. Good sign. "Jenna Paletto."

"Jenna," he said with surprising warmth. "Jenna, I'm going to need the passports of everyone boarding this flight."

I wondered about Sophie, who still hadn't come out of the bathroom. "I'll collect them."

He handed me several packets of forms. "Why don't you have the other passengers fill out their forms? Where's Sophie?"

"In the ladies room. I'll see what's keeping her."

Monte and Eznik sidled up to the counter. Monte's phone rang. He frowned, flipped it open, and checked the number. He shut the phone, shifting his focus to the bundle of forms I held.

I smiled. "Fill these out, okay? Then this gentleman here will need your passports. I'm going to check on Sophie."

I walked into the bathroom and found Sophie on a

small couch, a wet paper towel pressed against her neck. Her face looked pale, and beads of sweat dotted her upper lip and hairline.

Concern flooded me. "Sophie, what's wrong?"

"I should've had breakfast. I need to eat something."

"Hold on." I raced out of the bathroom, grabbed an orange juice and muffin from the cart, and threw a five-spot at the stewardess, or whatever she was.

Sophie sipped the orange juice and slowly ate the muffin.

"Listen, from now on, I want you to eat breakfast, lunch, and dinner." I sat on a chair. "I'll fill out this form for you."

Five minutes later, color bloomed in her cheeks. I stood up. "Just stay put and rest. I'll get these forms to Mr. Graham."

"Oh, Will's here?"

"You know him?"

"Yes, but I haven't seen him in awhile. He's a pilot, and part owner of Pacific Moon."

I made my way back to the reception area and gave the paperwork to Graham.

I kept an eye on the brothers, who roamed around the waiting area, watching small jets taxi to the runway.

Once again, Monte's phone rang. He ignored it. Eznik spoke to him in low whispers. Monte turned off the phone and shoved it into his trouser pocket. Both sauntered outside for another cigarette.

An old girlfriend? Another AJA agent, or whatever they called themselves? Something was up; my hackles were raised. I mentally kicked myself for agreeing to include these two.

The atrium had emptied of passengers. The woman I'd thrown the five dollars at approached us. She held a cordless phone. "Excuse me, is there a Monte or Eznik Kazarian in your party? There's an urgent message for them."

"What!" I shot a look at the brothers through the glass door. "Did they say who's calling?"

"No, they didn't. By the way…" She handed me my five dollars. "Breakfast at Pacific Moon is always complimentary."

"Keep it." A chill went through me. "The Kazarians are outside, smoking." As she went in search of Monte, I simmered. He'd obviously told someone about our flight to Istanbul. This did not sit well with me.

Sophie walked into the reception area looking 100 percent improved. Standing next to me at the counter, she wrinkled her nose. "Ugh, I can smell their cigarettes even at this distance."

A moment later, Will emerged from his office. "Sophie St. James! It's good to see you. What's it been, a year or so?"

"Will, nice to see you, too." She shook his hand. "And it's Alexakis, remember? Guess what? My dad just remarried. He's on his honeymoon."

Will snorted. "So your dad took the plunge, huh? She must be some kind of woman if she snagged your father."

"Gwen's a great lady. I like her a lot."

"Couldn't happen to a nicer guy. I've got great news! Your Challenger is coming in early, so your departure will be in less than an hour. Good thing you're all here. The caterers are on their way. Because this is an unexpected booking, we had them check your previous orders for lunch and dinner selections, so we'll have your favorites. Our pilots should be arriving any minute."

My cell phone rang. I glanced at the number. Maddie. More than likely, she wanted to discuss our brother, Luke. I thanked my lucky stars that she lived five miles from him. I ignored her call. I wasn't in the mood for complaints.

A caterer wheeled in a small cooler. The man began to remove the breakfast muffins from the reception area cart and load sandwiches and a variety of other packaged foods. Just in time. I was starved.

I helped myself to an apple and a cellophane wrapped package of carrots and celery.

My cell vibrated in my jacket pocket. I took out the phone and glanced at the screen. Maddie again. Dang. Hounding me wasn't her usual style. I conducted a brief debate with myself. For once, I decided, she could deal with Luke. I didn't answer.

I strolled to the doors and peered outside. Monte sat

on a wide planter. Eznik paced in front of him, talking on his cell. He whipped off his ball cap, twirling it as he spoke. Monte remained a quiet observer to his brother's drama.

I marched outside. The cold wind whipped grey clouds across the sky. I hunched against the blustery weather and handed Monte the car keys. "Would you guys bring in the luggage? We're leaving earlier than expected." I hesitated. "You had an emergency call. Is everything okay?"

Monte took the car keys. "Everything's fine."

"We're taking off soon? Great." Eznik nodded to me and strolled off to the parking lot with his brother.

I watched them for a moment before returning to the reception area. Damned if I knew what was going on with those two, and I hated it.

Will Graham smiled at me as I approached the reception counter. "So, what's taking you to Istanbul?"

Holy High School, Batman. The guy was flirting with me.

I gave him an abrupt shrug, a flush moving up my neck to my face. What was with me?

Sophie leaned in. "I'm on a buying spree. Art, actually."

Will seemed to accept the story, tugging absently at the tie that matched his eyes.

I turned to gaze off at the runway.

An overweight, middle-aged woman rushed in with

a bag from Office Depot. She placed everything on the desk behind Will and hurried to his side, looking flustered as she tucked a few blond wisps behind her ear. "Sorry, Mr. Graham, traffic was a mess. Here, I'll take over. Thanks for filling in."

"No problem." Just then his cell phone rang. "Excuse me." He tucked the newspaper under his arm, picked up his coffee, and strolled back to his office.

A minute later, Will returned to the reception area. He paused beside the desk.

"I'm short a pilot. Paul Venchisa's son just fractured his leg. I'm taking this one myself." He handed the receptionist a sheaf of papers.

Sophie smiled. "Oh, Will, you're taking us to Istanbul? That's wonderful news. Thank you."

The woman said, "I can contact another pilot. What about Victor?"

Will blushed scarlet. "Nope. I'm taking this one."

The secretary looked confused. "But... ."

He met my gaze, and then nodded at Sophie. "We'll leave shortly."

I didn't know what to think. Was he really short a pilot, or was he coming along because... Oh, don't even go there, Jenna. I shook my head and thought about Ralph having to deal with Kent. I glanced at my watch. I did not envy my partner.

Thirty minutes later, we boarded the plane after its refueling. Will and his copilot, a reserved, good-looking black man named Travis, welcomed us. After making sure we were buckled in, Will went into the cockpit.

As we lined up on the runway, my cell phone rang. I flipped my phone open. "Hey, Ralph. We're about to take off. How did it go with Kent…"

Ralph roared, "Wait! I gotta mess…" and the connection broke.

TWENTY-ONE

I tried several times to return his call, but failed.

Seated across from me, Sophie leafed through a thin green leather book. I leaned in and read the title, *New Testament, Psalms and Proverbs*. Whatever.

Behind us, Monte and Eznik gazed out the windows on either side of the jet. Monte caught my eye and arched his eyebrows. I nodded and looked away, awash in my own misgivings.

Travis took a forward seat and tucked in with a blanket and pillow.

***

Somewhere over Arizona, I started to relax. I felt dog-tired, lack of sleep taking its toll. Sophie had already fallen asleep. The butter yellow leather seats, extra wide and long, reclined with a push of a button.

I pushed the button, tucked a pillow under my head, and curled up beneath a blanket. The steady whine of the jet engines soon lulled me to sleep.

***

A hand on my shoulder shook me awake. I sat up to find Sophie smiling at me. Travis was back in the cockpit.

"We're landing in Bangor. We have to get our seats upright."

I turned and looked at the brothers. Seated with their backs to us, they were watching *Groundhog Day*. Bill Murray was running to catch a kid falling out of a tree. Did those two ever sleep?

Sophie lifted the shade on the window. "We slept the entire time."

I gazed down at the lights below. "I'm still tired." I stretched my arms above my head. The flight was almost six and a half hours to Maine. With the time difference, it was seven fifteen in the evening.

Sophie looked toward the galley. "Did you happen to notice what we have in the fridge?"

I nodded. "Lasagna, beef stroganoff, fruit, Caesar salads, wine and champagne."

"Sounds good." Sophie reached for her book, and then clicked on the overhead light. "We can eat once we take off again."

When we'd first boarded, I'd gone over the jet like a little kid. I found maple galley cabinets, brushed chrome appliances, and a vase of fresh flowers sunk into the granite countertop, in an airplane no less.

I knew I was out of my league when I discovered the china, crystal wine glasses, and expensive silverware. I didn't want to appear conspicuously blown away by the affluence of the privileged few, but I was more than slightly awed.

Monte and Eznik stayed in the rear of the plane, turned off the movie and prepared for our landing, which was flawless. Very cool, Will.

We taxied to the private charter lounge. Once they parked the jet, Will and his co-pilot emerged from the cockpit. "You can stretch your legs while we refuel and file a flight plan. We'll take off in about forty minutes." We followed them off the plane.

Monte and Eznik were right behind us. I heard Eznik mumble to Monte, "We're far enough away now. It'll take them two days to figure it out."

Moments later, I turned to Sophie. "Did you hear that?"

"I did. What do you suppose it means?" she asked, her brow furrowed.

I scowled. "I told you I had serious doubts about bringing them along."

"Let's not jump to conclusions. I'll ask them. You're too intimidating."

I ignored her. My suspicions about these two went to warp speed. They're far enough away from whom? The dreaded masked dry cleaner from Fresno? All their secret agent crap really annoyed me.

We walked into the lounge, which resembled the one in Orange County. The brothers made a beeline for the smoking area. Sophie followed them outside, hunched against the cold as she talked with them. What was it about these two that appealed to her?

I checked my cell. Three calls from Ralph, and six from Maddie. Neither had left a message. Odd. I tried to reach them. No answer. I left voicemails, asking them both to call me. I stared at my phone, wondering if Luke was in trouble. Had Kent blown a fuse?

Will and Travis returned. They gathered at the food cart to graze. Sophie came in and gave me a smile. I couldn't wait to hear what the brothers had said to her.

Everyone sipped mugs of soup and chatted. I stayed on the fringe of the group, watching the brothers. The threat of acid indigestion courtesy of those two prompted me to take my roasted tomato-basil soup on a stroll over to the window. Leaves and trash skittered across the runway and whirled around the gas truck refueling our jet. Ah, brisk, cold Spring weather.

Will followed me, balancing his mug of soup on his clipboard as he nodded at the plane. "Isn't she something? She's fast. Five hundred forty miles an hour. And she can travel up to forty-five hundred miles on one tank."

"I'm impressed." I had a hard time not smiling at him. He sounded like a kid with a new bag of marbles.

He gave me one of those searching looks again. "The minute I laid eyes on her, I knew she'd be the love of my life."

I grinned. Couldn't help myself. Why did Will Graham give me such a thrill?

He turned his attention back to the plane. "She's a fabulous jet. We just bought another Challenger, but we won't take delivery till next year." He leaned nearer, whispering, "The Challenger six-oh-five."

"I'll be sure to alert the media." I kept my eyes on the plane.

He cracked a smile. "So tell me, what's your relationship with Monte and Eznik?"

"No relationship at all. Just met them yesterday. Sophie hired them to help us get to the right places in Istanbul."

"That's right. Sophie's collecting art." He turned, faced the group, and leaned against the steel railing at the window. "Somehow, Monte and Eznik don't seem like the art collecting type."

"They're not. They were hired to help us get to the right places."

"Still. That's an interesting job description." Will pretended to quote an employment ad. "'Must be able to get to the right places in Istanbul.'"

I glanced at him, liking the way his silvery hair caught the overhead light.

"So, how far back do you and Sophie go?"

"Not too far."

"And you jumped at the chance to join your friend in a little weekend buying spree."

"Something like that."

"Your husband doesn't mind?"

I stared at my toes. "No husband." And there was a damned good reason. But I wasn't going to tell him.

"So your boyfriend doesn't mind?"

I laughed. Talk about blatant. "No boyfriend, Will."

"Really? What's a girl like you doing with no husband or boyfriend?"

"Working."

His eyebrows rose. "Okay, I'll bite. And what kind of work do you do, Miss Paletto?"

Time to put his curiosity to rest.

"I'm a private investigator."

I enjoyed watching Will's jaw drop. I nodded. "Yeah. I've had my own business for five years. I've got a great partner. Now, *he* minded this trip to Istanbul, but that's another story."

"No kidding. No kidding. You're really a private eye?"

"Yep."

"Were you a cop before that?"

I looked at him. "As a matter of fact, I was."

He leaned in conspiratorially. "So, are you like, working now on a case, or are you really buying art?"

"I'm just along for the ride. Sophie's the art buyer. I don't know diddly about art."

"Really?"

"Really."

He stepped closer his green eyes alight. "I'll just bet you're full of stories. Stomping out criminal life in the big city. Crushing the bad guys."

I took a small step back, displaying mega mock surprise. "You've been reading my mail."

The gas truck drove off, catching Will's attention as he smiled at me. "Time to go. Since I won't be in the cockpit this flight, would you mind if we continue this later?"

I frowned. "Continue what?"

With a raised eyebrow and a pursed smile, Will shook his head. Then he announced to everyone it was time to board.

My cell rang. My sister, Maddie.

I flipped it open and hit the talk button. "Maddie, what's up?"

"Jenna." She let out a sob. "Where have you been all day? I've been trying to reach you! It's Dad! He's in the hospital... in ICU. He's had a stroke, Jenna. It's bad. Mom wants you to come right away."

Stunned, I sank into the nearest chair and stared out the window. "When?" I steeled myself against family responsibilities that threatened to crush me. I'm thousands of miles away, and my sister manages to stop me in my tracks. I needed to focus on Zach and Sarkis.

"At about five this morning. He got up and told Mom he felt sick. Then, suddenly he couldn't walk or speak. Mom called the paramedics, and they knew right away."

"What do the doctors say?"

"It's too soon to tell the extent of the damage. Mom wants you here."

I translated Maddie's statement: 'I want you here, so my business deals won't be interrupted by long hospital vigils.' Maddie usually handles my dad well, but only in small doses.

I shook my head as I gazed at the vaulted ceiling. How ironic. My tyrannical perfectionist father might be dying, but I'd rather fly half way across the world with two total strangers and a desperate woman. Devoted to dear old dad, I wasn't.

"Listen, Maddie. I'm in the state of Maine. There's no way I can leave my client. Her husband's been kidnapped. I'm boarding a plane for Istanbul right this minute."

"You're in Maine? What about your partner? Can't he take over? Jen-nah! Dad's had a stroke!" My sister wept into the phone. "Mom really wants you here. Can't you get someone else to help them?"

Why am I the only person they call in a crisis? Guilt briefly gnawed, then anger flooded me. I hardened my heart. I refused to allow Maddie to manipulate me. I had to focus on Zach and Sarkis.

I stood and walked to the corner of the lounge. "I'm in Maine, Maddie! I'm leaving for freakin' Istanbul! Haven't you heard a word I've said?" The family would have to take care of itself at least until I was able to get home.

"I can't believe you! You're so selfish! You move away and leave us to deal with Luke, and now Dad. You're infuriating!" She hung up.

I shook my head at my sister. What a jerk. This childish, demanding behavior wasn't really her M.O. I raked my fingers through my hair. The up side was that my paranoia about Monte and Eznik had shifted. Now I could worry about something else. I called Ralph, left him a message, explaining what had happened, and asked him to contact my mother.

TWENTY-TWO

We took off for Prague. I was told it would be about an eight-hour flight. I kept my family news to myself. Across the aisle from Sophie, I whispered, "So, what did Monte and Eznik's covert statement mean? Did you find out?"

Her eyes lit up and she leaned in. "Eznik is getting married in a couple of weeks! He's got a bridezilla on his hands. Monte's convinced him to be secretive, to pull away a little. They think she'll stop all her antics and decide its Eznik she really wants, not the wedding of her mother's dreams."

That actually seemed plausible.

"You seem very distracted. I saw you talking with Will." Sophie studied me, pressing her fingertips together.

"Ah, he was just giving me all the stats on this jet. And they're buying a new one soon." I'd keep my father's illness to myself for the time being.

I worried for my mom, having to deal with my vitriolic father. But if he couldn't speak, wasn't that something to celebrate? It was, trust me.

We dined over the Atlantic. Will heated up portions of lasagna and beef stroganoff, and served them up. Occasionally, I caught him watching me.

Sophie ate a full meal, lowering my worry about a repeat low blood sugar crisis.

Monte and Eznik started another movie. Sophie prepared her bed. She pulled a blanket around her, thumbing through her Bible until she fell asleep. I fished out Professor Takmaz's translations, Morganthau's history of the Turkish Armenians, and began to read.

***

A couple of hours passed. Will came out of the cockpit, he saw that I was awake, and made his way over to me.

I put the translations back into my bag and waved to the seat directly across from me. "How's it going up there?" I whispered.

"Good, so I'm going to try to sleep for a few hours." He buckled up, rubbing his long fingers over his cheeks and temples. "Hey, did you take a sleeping pill? I overheard Sophie talking about it."

"No, I didn't, but I thought once I settled in, I might."

"We've got about six hours left to Prague. Taking a pill and sleeping is a good idea. Once we land, you'll want to be alert. From Prague it's about four and a half hours to Istanbul. Want some hot tea?" Will asked.

"Herbal?"

He nodded. "Sit tight, I'll get it for you since you did the dishes." He made his way to the galley.

I sat there feeling foolish and awkward. No one ever waited on me. It felt good to have Will make tea. Besides, I'm a sucker for nice when I can get it.

Balancing the mugs and teapot on a small tray, he set them down, his hand brushing my fingers as he passed a mug to me. His gaze settled on my face. "You know, I've never been to Istanbul. I'm looking forward to it."

"Me, too." I clasped the mug with both hands.

Will settled back in his seat. "Why aren't you working as a cop? Why a private eye?"

I answered him with a question. "Why did you choose your line of work?"

Will smiled. "I asked you first."

I tucked my legs under me and took a sip of tea. Okay, I thought, it was a dark and stormy night...

"The short version is that I worked as a cop in San Diego for about seven years. I was also married to a cop, and I made detective before my husband. He didn't handle it well." I paused and blew into my steaming mug of tea.

"And?" Will prompted.

I shrugged. "And things went from bad to worse." I looked out the window, thinking about my ex-husband. His jealousy and betrayal had cost me more than anyone would ever know.

"Some men resent their wives advancing ahead of them."

I nodded, remembering how Eric and his buddies had made me look like an inept fool during one important investigation. When my captain offered me a desk job for six months, I quit the force. It still hurt to remember even now.

Will asked. "So, you divorced and moved to Orange County?"

"Yeah, after a while. Eric inherited property when his grandmother passed away. He offered me his grandmother's Victorian house in Orange as part of our divorce settlement." I put down the mug. "Orange seemed far away from him. I drove up there, checked out a city I'd never visited before, and, fell in love with the place."

"Orange isn't San Diego."

"Orange feels like a... sanctuary. I love Old Towne, the quaintness of it. I converted the Victorian into offices."

Will reached over and gave my arm a quick pat.

My heart did a little leap.

"I was married before, too." He spoke in low tones,

leaning in to me with that familiar way of his. "Bottom line, I married the wrong woman."

"How long were you married?"

"Four years. I came home from a charter trip to a wife who accused me of having an affair."

"Did you?"

He blanched. "No, no way!"

I jabbed a finger at him. "She projected her own guilt on to you. This is my line of work. I know this story."

"Bingo. You're good!" He grinned broadly. "She had me running in circles trying to prove my innocence."

"How long's it been?"

"Our divorce was final five years ago. I date casually, but nothing serious so far." Will kept his gaze on me. "I've been busy building the business. I've got a few partners to keep happy. As far as finances are concerned, I took a major hit because of the divorce."

"Isn't that always the case?"

He nodded, his expression reflective. He looked vulnerable, and I felt the urge to comfort him. Good grief.

"Can I ask why you're really traveling to Istanbul?"

I cocked my head to one side. "We told you, Sophie's collecting art."

"Come on, Jenna…"

I leaned back, not saying anything.

Will continued. "This morning Sophie made a comment to me when you were outside. She said, 'I hope we can find Zach and Sarkis.' Then, she looked at me, as if to say, 'Did I just say that?'"

Oh, great. I wondered if Sophie would be upset if Will knew the truth. Hell, she was willing to let Monte and Eznik in on the whole story. Yet, with Zach involved, to a certain extent, it was my call.

He leaned across the table toward me, motioning me closer.

I leaned nearer to him.

He whispered, "Another thing. I know her father. St. James is a powerful businessman through and through. And even though I haven't seen Sophie much lately, I know she lives simply. She's content with a professor husband, and art has never been her thing."

"It hasn't?" I kept my voice as innocent sounding as possible.

"Jenna, I know the rich and famous, and I know how they operate. I don't buy it."

"I can't do much about what you believe."

"And those two guys you're with?" He nodded to the back of the jet. "Personal guides in Istanbul? Doubtful."

"Sophie trusts them."

"But you don't," he countered.

I bit my tongue to keep silent, but I felt like cheering. Will's seeming distrust of those two was satisfying.

"Sophie's acting like she's on a high wire looking down." Will glanced over at her sleeping form. "She's always been a sweetheart. Before her dad bought his own jet, she did her best to make me feel like family." He shook his head. "It's different now."

"A lot's happened to her over the last twelve years." I sat back in my seat. "But she's been happily married for a long time now. Things were going great until she experienced a major disappointment recently."

"Are you going to tell me what's going on?"

I weighed my options. "Let's just say, we're picking up something very dear to Sophie's heart and in fact, to my heart."

His eyes narrowed. "She said she hoped to find Zach and Sarkis in Istanbul."

I shrugged.

Will pressed further. "Is this a business trip?"

"It's an unexpected trip," I clarified.

Will nodded toward the rear of the jet. "And those two?"

"Like I said, we met them yesterday. They're Armenians who speak Turkish, and they know Istanbul. We needed someone who reads and speaks Turkish. I did a background check. They came up legit."

Will whispered, "Does this have anything to do with her father?"

"No." I thought, ah, hell. "The people responsible for our trip know nothing about her father." Why do I trust this guy? "But they think her husband has something they want."

"Does he?"

"It's with us."

"Does it belong to Sophie?"

"It belongs to Sarkis." Why am I telling him this?

Will stared at me and exhaled with a whoosh. "And you're doing this without the help of the police?"

"At my client's insistence."

"I see." Will leaned forward. "And who's Zach?"

"Zach is my nineteen-year-old son."

"Your son!" His eyes lit up. "And what does your son have to do with Sarkis?"

"He tried to help Sarkis the night we tried to do the exchange, and they took Zach too. It was a foolish, impulsive move."

Will registered what I'd said, leaned back, and sunk into his seat. It was a full minute before he spoke again. "Can I help you in any way?"

"Thanks, Will, but I think I've got it covered." I had a sudden inspiration. "But it might be nice if you could stay with us at the same hotel. It'd be good to have a friendly face there."

"I can do that."

Some of my inner tension departed. "That'd be great."

My gut assured me that Will Graham was a good and decent man. I liked that in a guy.

But when I turned in for the night, old fears loomed, I thought about Zach. I recalled his smile, his eagerness for taking notes, his constant questions. He was my son, and I wanted much more than a lousy thirteen hours with him.

And why hadn't I taken a selfie with him?

TWENTY-THREE

A crick in my neck tweaked me out of sleep. I opened my eyes in the semi-dark cabin, and I heard faint sounds behind me. Dim light from the flat screen DVD player cast flickering shadows on the ceiling. Ah. The brothers were probably watching a movie again.

I needed to use the bathroom. I sat up, putting my feet in the aisle. The rustling of papers caught my attention. Groggy, I glanced to the rear of the plane. Monte and Eznik were stuffing papers into a backpack. Eznik shot me a guilty look.

Fear stabbed at my gut. My hackles rose with a flood of adrenalin. I strode to the rear of the plane.

"So, you guys getting enough sleep?"

Monte stared at the screen, refusing eye contact. "I don't sleep well on planes," he mumbled.

Eznik also declined to meet my gaze.

"Did you guys bring any books to read?"

Monte shrugged. "We like movies."

"No books in your backpack?" Bending, I picked up Monte's backpack and opened it in a single smooth motion. Reaching inside, I removed the papers Monte had shoved in.

Neither man tried to stop me, but Eznik cringed and glanced at his brother. Monte stared straight ahead. He didn't utter a word.

I hit the overhead light. The papers in the backpack were our copies of professor Takmaz's translation of the handwritten pages of Sarkis' Bible.

"Oh, look, my client's private property." Anger surged within me. Lowering my voice, I crouched down, leaning in to Monte. "Tell ya what, pal. If you pull another stunt like this again, we drop you and Eznik off in Prague or Istanbul and leave you there. You can find your own way home."

Monte straightened, looked at me, and opened his mouth to speak.

I hissed, "Don't waste your breath."

I included Eznik in my tirade. "You are here to translate for us. Nothing more, got that? You try to make Sophie's business your business, you'll regret it."

Eznik tried to speak.

I held up a hand. "I had a bad feeling about you two from the start, and I was right."

Tucking the papers under my arm, I returned to my seat.

Will was standing in the aisle, awake and cautious. I approached him, and I held my finger to my lips while looking down at Sophie. I motioned for him to sit across from me.

"What happened?" he asked.

I shook my head, my disgust evident, "You just can't trust the hired help these days."

Will looked past me to the two men. "You okay?"

"I'm fine. Now I know I really can't trust them and that scares me."

"What'd they do?" Will looked anxious.

"They took information that is vital to this case out of my backpack while I was asleep. They have no idea what's going on, and they're trying to find out."

"Why did you hire them?"

"I didn't. Sophie thought they'd be our own little tour guides. I can't believe I let her hire these two jerks." I took out the papers checking that I had them all. I did.

"Do you want me to speak to them?" Will asked. "Smooth things over?"

"No, I want them worried and off balance." Glancing behind me, I returned my gaze to Will's emerald eyes. "But feel free to give them the evil eye every once in awhile."

"How did you manage to wake up and catch them?"

"I don't know. I just did. Anyway, go back to sleep, okay? You need your sleep."

"Yeah, well, so do you." He reached out and squeezed my shoulder, then made his way forward to sleep in his seatbed.

I returned to my seatbed, and I watched Sophie, who was still zonked by a sleeping pill. Fear of the unknown niggled at me. Why was I in charge of so many people?

***

The jet engines thrummed, signaling a reduction in speed. A reverberating crack of thunder followed, jolting me awake. I craned my neck to look at the rear of the plane for Monte and Eznik. Blankets shrouded their sleeping forms, the TV finally mute.

Sophie's small Bible lay open on her seat. The light on the bathroom door said occupied.

Groaning at the stomach-churning turbulence, I sat up, gripped the armrest, and brooded over how I came to be aboard a private jet over Europe.

Will lay sprawled on the front seatbed, his eyes shut. He looked handsome, and much too appealing.

Sophie emerged from the bathroom. She'd washed her face, had applied makeup, and arranged her hair. She looked fresh and rested.

I motioned her to sit across from me, and then gave her a quick rundown on Monte and Eznik's snooping.

Sophie shrugged dismissively. "What do you expect, Jenna? We should've told them the whole story from the beginning."

I steeled myself to edit what came out of my mouth. "We agreed on this, Sophie." I kept my voice low. "First, I know you don't care about the treasure, but the lowlifes who do care about it kidnapped your husband. Second, it's obvious Monte and Eznik have a whole different agenda in play here, and that little reality spells trouble. They could endanger your husband's life."

Sophie frowned. "Monte and Eznik simply want to know the whole story. That's fair. Why do you view them as adversaries?"

I exhaled in frustration. "Think about it, Sophie. The day complete strangers from Istanbul kidnap your husband is the same day two more complete strangers, who say they're friendlies, tell us they failed to save your husband. And surprise, they speak Turkish, and they're members of AJA." I leaned forward. "This is not a coincidence."

"Two strangers who risked their lives to save Sarkis."

"That's *their* story. We have no proof of that. You didn't see anything."

Sophie cocked her head, studying me. Then, she seemed to make a decision. "I want you to know, I think the Lord intended Monte and Eznik to help us."

"The Lord?" I repeated, gritting my teeth to avoid saying anything else. I really wondered if logic and reason had a foothold in her universe. Where was God when Sarkis had been kidnapped? And Zach! Had God allowed Zach to act so rashly?

"Yes. I think it's God's plan that they're with us. Monte and Eznik know almost everything, anyway." She reached across the table, picked up her Bible, and held it to her chest.

"You're inviting pirates to assist the rescue party, Sophie. Can't you see that?"

Travis announced from the cockpit, "We'll touch down in Prague in thirty minutes. Please stow your belongings and bring your seats to an upright position."

Will repositioned his seat, jumped to his feet, used the restroom and then made his way to the cockpit, with a quick good morning to both of us.

Kneeling, I pulled out my duffel. Sophie's logic left me unbalanced. Attempting to sort out her half-baked thinking, I paused and stared at her. She looked at me with such sincerity. I decided to appeal to her common sense. "Look, here's the deal. Don't you think rifling through your things makes them suspect? I wanted to keep the whereabouts of the treasure a secret, because they need to focus on one thing, and one thing only. Helping us get our guys back."

I found my travel cosmetic bag. "Another point, good guys don't steal information…"

"They might if they don't have all the facts."

"They're conning you, Sophie. That's the long and short of it."

Shoving my duffel aside with my foot, I went into the bathroom and was surprised at my reflection, not bad for sleeping for just a few hours. I brushed my teeth, washed my face, put on some mostiurizer over the high cheekbones I inherited from my mom. I added some light foundation and blush, took a minute to apply a hint of shadow and mascara, final touch, some lip gloss. I tugged at the jeans I was wearing, now sagging a bit at the knees. I fiddled with my short, dark brown hair, shrugging helplessly at the haphazard way my hair went in every direction. Good enough. Staring back at my reflection, I resolved I wouldn't put up with any bull. My goal: find and rescue my Zach and Sarkis Alexakis and take them home. Alive. Period.

Monte and Eznik made a beeline for the head once I stepped out. Then, we all readied ourselves for the landing.

The plane descended into a rainy Prague morning.

TWENTY-FOUR

The jet emerged from the steel gray clouds. I kept myself occupied by studying the land. The scene below revealed wet pavement and cobblestone roads that glistened under the glow of streetlights. Trees a thousand shades of green contrasted with red roofed buildings. The storm clouds in the sky shadowed the landscape.

The landing was faultless. We taxied to the private jet terminal. Will used the intercom to remind us that we'd need to show our passports.

We bundled up for the short walk to the terminal. The wind, sharp and raw, invigorated me. I felt psyched, ready to drink coffee and do battle—with the brothers, if need be. Inside, we sailed through Customs. In the private terminal, we found tables covered in crisp white linen, matching napkins, and fine china and crystal. Elaborate flower arrangements graced tables that contained an enormous assortment of bagels, cream cheese, chocolate stuffed croissants, hot oatmeal, yogurt, cold cereals and hard-boiled eggs. Thankfully, there was plenty of espresso, tea, and cocoa.

Monte and Eznik passed through Customs, helped themselves to coffee and croissants, and stepped outside to smoke.

Sophie found a restroom in the terminal. Will and Travis left to file a flight plan.

I joined Monte and Eznik.

Monte planted himself in my path, clearly ready for a confrontation. He drew in a breath, and then exhaled. His breath reeked of peppermint and cigarettes. "Jenna, if you're waiting for me to apologize, forget it."

Rankled by his unshaven good looks, I concentrated on his insolent behavior. He leaned in close, his eyes blazing. "Let's talk about what happened last night."

He was all cowboy and no horse. He received zero points for diplomacy, but he garnered my full attention. Eznik seemed nervous, distracted.

I faked cool.

Monte stabbed at the air with his index finger. "Let me tell you how we see this. Sophie hired us, just like she hired you. Our job is to find the bastards who took her husband and your son."

I stood my ground. "No, your job is to interpret for us, and help us get around Istanbul."

"Like the Jews, we Armenians also have a saying, 'never again.' The men we're dealing with aren't confined to Istanbul. They've caused trouble all over Europe and Asia." He punctuated every word with his finger. "We're going to find them and turn them over to proper authorities." Monte glared at me.

I remained silent. I wanted to snap that finger of his just to hear the crunch of bone.

Peering over the rim of his glasses, Eznik studied me.

Encouraged by my silence, Monte continued his roll. "Yeah, you were hired first, which means nothing. Our background and our knowledge of the country and the enemy give us priority."

"Priority?" I mocked as Sophie stepped outside.

Seconds later, she stood beside me. "What's all this?"

I smiled. "Monte here thinks he should be the brains of the operation."

Monte gave a polite chuckle. "No, no. Our only job is to do what you've asked us to do. Actually, we do have many more resources than Jenna does for a situation like this, but we're willing to work with her."

Standing slightly apart from all of us, Eznik stared at his feet. He didn't seem fully onboard with his brother's proclamations.

Sophie's incredulous gaze swept over the three of us. At that moment, Monte reminded me of an agitated hound. I almost snickered.

"Wait just a minute, both of you." Sophie touched my arm. "We work together. I hired Jenna to rescue my husband. You and Eznik will help us get around Turkey. Why is there disagreement on this?"

"I can see you're upset, Jenna." Monte's voice sounded condescending. He gave Sophie one of his 'trust me,' looks. "Last night we read some of those papers, but we didn't have time to read them all. The material contained the stories of how the Armenians lost everything in Turkey during the genocide."

I turned to Sophie. "Ah, screw it. I don't believe anything they say." My worst nightmare would come to life if Monte and Eznik drew the attention of the Turkish authorities.

Monte went very still, abandoning his posturing. "Get off our backs, Jenna. We'll get you around Istanbul. We'll translate for you. And you know what you're gonna discover? That you can't rescue Sarkis or Zach without us."

Sophie spoke quietly, "That may be true, but Jenna is the one who will do the negotiating. She calls the shots."

Monte stepped closer. "All we're asking is that you leave those sons-a-bitches to us."

"Leave them for you? After we get my husband and Zach back, I don't care what you do." Sophie looked frozen, and she started hopping up and down in the cold to warm herself.

I laughed, trying to sound casual. "Unfortunately, I was right about these two. They're vigilantes. Just what are your intentions once you get your hands on the kidnappers? Avenge the deaths of a million and a half people by killing a couple of criminals?" Narrowing my eyes, I stepped into Monte's personal space. "If you don't follow my directions when the time comes, you can swim back to the States." Turning away from him, I walked back into the terminal, surprised to realize that Sophie had followed me.

***

I used the restroom, and then strolled out into the terminal. I spotted Sophie in a small shop across from the executive lounge. Retracing my steps, I returned to the lounge, inhaling the fragrance of coffee, sweet pastries, and cooked oatmeal.

Industrial art-deco metal chairs were set back-to-back in the large room with a wall of floor-to-ceiling windows facing the tarmac. I sat on a cold, gray mesh chair. Partially hidden by a single, large silk tree with its purchase tags still attached, I studied the two brothers, who still stood outside. They were huddled together, deep in conversation. How would I stay one step ahead of those two? And had Sophie finally seen them for what they were?

Will came over with a hot tea and handed it to me. "It's herbal. One pink packet." He followed my gaze outside to the two brothers, now stamping their feet in the cold. Sinking into the seat next to me, he exhaled audibly. "So, you're not over what happened last night."

"Not by a long shot. But they're not over it, either." I took a sip. Perfect. "Thanks for the tea."

He clasped his hands together. "Um, when we get to Istanbul, and things are—" he raised his gaze "—accomplished, can I buy you dinner?"

My pulse quickened. I studied his chiseled features, his silvery white crew cut, and those sea green eyes in that handsome tanned face. "When things are accomplished, I would love that."

"Then, it's a date." He grinned.

I nodded, glancing out the window again at the brothers.

Will sat there and watched me. I felt his curious gaze. I wouldn't cave to female idiocy, so I turned my thoughts to Zach. As I pictured his earnest face, my heart ached.

"This is good. We have a date, then."

"Okay." I gave him the briefest glance.

"Do you always have to have the last word?" he teased.

Giving this some thought, I frowned. "I don't think so."

He rocked back, laughing.

Perplexed, I smiled at his reaction.

Sophie walked up with a container of milk and a package of chocolate covered pretzels. She smiled uncertainly. "Did I miss something?"

"Not a thing." I took a pretzel from Sophie's bag.

Sophie tilted her head to one side. Handing me a magnet with the word, 'Prague' on it, she said, "A souvenir. We'll need to come back and visit in better times."

"Nice. Thanks." I smiled, turning the magnet over. I swiveled to Will. "When are we taking off?"

"We board in ten." Will raised his hand to Travis, who'd just come into the lounge. After a long, lingering look at me, he stood to join his co-pilot.

Sophie looked startled. "That was, well, familiar."

"Don't read anything into it. I'm not." I ate the pretzel. "So, why'd you come outside?"

"I saw Monte shaking his finger in your face." She offered me another pretzel. "I was surprised." She hesitated before qualifying her comment. "Well, it's Monte's behavior. Eznik's guilty by default."

Hallelujah. I popped the pretzel into my mouth.

We boarded the jet for the last leg of our journey. Monte and Eznik put on another movie. The four and a half hour flight passed quickly.

I reread Professor Takmaz's notes, then dozed off for over an hour. I woke to see white clouds on the horizon.

Across the table from me, Sophie, too, had fallen asleep, her Bible at her side.

Will's voice came over the intercom, announcing that we'd entered Istanbul air space.

Sophie opened her eyes and sat up.

"Not too hard to fall asleep in these jets, is it?" I stretched.

She yawned. "It's what I do best when I travel."

Monte walked down the aisle and sat beside Sophie. Eznik plopped down right by me with a nervous smile.

I tried to keep the edge out of my voice. "Can we help you?"

Monte pointed out the window. "Since we're entering Istanbul's air space, we thought you might like to know what you're looking at."

Like an obedient child, Sophie peered out the window. I gave the scene below a churlish glare.

Monte brought out paper and pen and began to sketch the terrain below us. "The two main waterways are the Golden Horn and the Bosphorus River, which flow into the Marmara Sea. Istanbul is divided on two continents, Europe, and Asia. That's Uskudar, way over there in Asia." He waved at the horizon to a land mass separated by the rivers.

I found myself glancing at his map.

Monte stood, pointing out the window. "That's the Bosphorus River."

I watched the ships and small boats that dotted the

immense rivers. Soaring above the vast city of Istanbul gave me a rush.

As we descended to the airport, everything on the ground became more compact. It was as if a decree had been passed that no open land could exist.

Sophie shivered as she met my gaze. "My husband is somewhere in that huge maze."

"And my Zach."

TWENTY-FIVE

We landed hard at Ataturk Airport. It was almost three in the afternoon. The modern architecture of the main terminal was a surprise to me. There was lots of green glass and chrome windows, and polished floors reflected the sun's orange and red rays exploding behind dark clouds. Customs lingered over our passports. After paying a hundred dollars per person for entry, we gathered our luggage and made our way down the corridor of the sleek, massive terminal.

Busy with the arrangements for the jet's fuel and servicing, Will and Travis waved us forward.

An uneasy Sophie suggested that Travis stay at our hotel with all of us. He declined her invitation, opting for a hotel near the airport.

Will tapped my arm, giving me a wink. "I'll be right with you, Jenna. You get the taxi."

Walking through the terminal, I kept an eye on the two brothers. Since we'd landed, Monte and Eznik had been observant and informative. Their good behavior left me feeling guarded.

As a group, we garnered a few curious looks from men, but most ignored us.

Two trim women clad in dark business suits rushed past us, while a few women, covered head-to-toe in loose, black robes, stared openly at us.

"Can you believe all the western clothing?" Sophie asked me. "I thought most of the women would be totally covered in the traditional burkas."

"Me too."

Eznik remarked. "Actually, those were chadors. They're not mandatory, just a religious preference." He tugged at his earring. "Chadors are universally black. Burkas can be colored, and can have floral designs. Nicer than the chador."

Will joined us just as we were leaving the terminal. I appreciated his presence. He and the brothers took care of our luggage after flagging down two taxis.

Monte spoke seemingly perfect Turkish to the taxi drivers. Eznik and Will climbed into one taxi while Monte joined us in the other. The crowded streets rivaled any major city in the United States at rush hour.

I held my breath while our drivers raced each other to our hotel. "Monte, tell the driver to slow down."

Monte laughed. "You're not in control, are you?" He obviously enjoyed my discomfort.

Cars and buses hurtled along narrow roadways. A strange etiquette seemed to exist among Istanbul drivers. Without warning, drivers changed lanes. Others slammed on their brakes in breathtaking near misses.

My uneducated, preconceived notion of Turkey had been of a backward nation, with belly dancers in seedy back alley dives. In the distance, I saw modern high-rise buildings, and up-to-date billboards everywhere.

Sarkis and Zach remained on the edge of my consciousness as Monte explained some of the local history and geography. I took in the scenery. On one side of the road lay the Marmara Sea, a muddy expanse frosted with white caps driven by the wind. Dark grey oil tankers and Turkish Navy ships were silhouetted against the darkening hills.

An ancient granite wall paralleled the road, medieval towers looming at intervals like castle battlements. No castle in sight, though.

"These are the Citadel Walls," Monte explained. "There are about a hundred and ninety towers from the Marmara Sea all the way to the Golden Horn, built during the reign of Theodosius the Second, around the fifth century. These walls kept out invaders for over a thousand years."

Impressive. Our guys might be held behind these shadowy walls. How on earth was I going to get them back?

Decrepit looking houses, apartments and a few restored homes followed, giving birth to the notion that a few industrious souls were trying to fix up the neighborhood.

"Look!" cried Sophie. We all turned to gaze at the beach. There in the semidarkness we saw the remains of a massive blood red, rusted oil tanker lying on its side, Monte asked the taxi driver about the tanker and then filled us in. The tanker had washed ashore in a storm eight years earlier.

I gave considerable thought to that wrecked oil tanker. My expectation of any possible help from the Turkish government plummeted.

We drove on for a couple of miles, the smell of salt water, decaying fish, and foul sewage making my eyes water.

Monte announced, "We're now in the heart of Old Istanbul."

He pointed out the Citadel Hotel, our assigned destination, per the kidnappers. A small French provincial look-alike with curved black ironwork and a rosy pink exterior, the hotel possessed a fabulous view of the Marmara Sea.

Since we believed we'd arrived at least a day ahead of the kidnappers, Monte suggested to Sophie that we stay close by at another hotel to get some rest. I agreed. We needed the break to recover from jet lag and pull ourselves together to face the kidnappers.

We pulled up to the Sultanahamet Palace Hotel. Well-tended plants in massive burnt salmon colored pots lined the outdoor entrance. Monte cast an appraising eye as he stood in front of the hotel. "This is classic Ottoman Empire architecture. See those small Romanesque columns framing the windows and arched doorways? Very indicative of the period."

"Hey, we appreciate the travelogue, but we're tired." My patience was already worn thin, and Sophie looked exhausted. The fear in her eyes spoke of her escalating anxiety for Sarkis.

My own fear for Zach spiked, but I tried to refuse its grip.

Monte and Eznik dragged our suitcases and duffels into the foyer. Monte escorted Sophie to the check-in desk.

"How about we put our luggage in our rooms and go to dinner? There's a little café right around the corner," he said.

I nodded. Sounded like a plan to me. My energy level was abysmal, and I needed food.

While checking in, Sophie changed a thousand dollars into liras. We endured a short lecture by a staff member on the value of each banknote.

Eznik laughed. "I'll teach you the money in five minutes! It's easy, really."

Will stayed by Sophie's side, caring, protective, just keeping watch over her. His stock climbed yet again with me. Then, he walked us to our room. Sophie went in first, but I lingered by the door.

"Be back in two minutes. I'll just put my suitcase in my room." He winked at me before heading down the corridor.

Five minutes later, we took off for the café Monte had recommended.

It was near dusk. As we sat in an upstairs café at a large picture window overlooking the street, Monte and Eznik ordered dinner-lamb stew and roast chicken with all the trimmings, a fantastic meal if only we could have enjoyed it. We ate, watching the weather change before our eyes.

The thick clouds that had hovered on the horizon when we landed arrived in force. The wind kicked up, hurling trash along the street. Shrouded women hurried along the road, their chadors wrapped tight around them.

Our waiter poured hot tea. "I know English." He smiled, patting his chest with his hand. "I want to go to USA."

"You do?" Will asked.

"Yes. Very much, I would like to go."

Monte and Eznik gave him a tolerant smile.

"What would you like to see when you visit?" Sophie asked.

"New York, Disney World, Hollywood..."

We all laughed. Dinner was over in an hour.

Turning my head, I gazed outside again. The wind

sighed and wailed. A tattered banner, torn loose from a market across the street, whirled away. Suddenly my jaw trembled, my thoughts turning to Zach. A wave of anguish slammed into me. Everything seemed surreal.

Taking a steadying breath, I stood. "Come on. It's time to go."

We put on our jackets and coats. We'd grown warm and content in the restaurant. When we emerged onto the street, Sophie and I shrieked in surprise at the harsh cold. In unforgiving fits and spurts, the howling wind pummeled us all the way back to our hotel.

Stumbling into the cozy foyer was welcome relief. I asked the desk clerk, "How long's this weather supposed to last?"

His eyebrows rose dramatically. "Tonight and tomorrow. This is big storm. Very bad."

I returned to our group. "They're expecting wicked weather. Tomorrow could be bad, too."

Monte shrugged. "We're here, and we'll get a good night's sleep."

Everyone was bone weary from traveling so far. We said good night, agreeing to meet in the hotel café at ten o'clock for breakfast.

Will escorted us to our room. "How come you ladies don't have your own rooms?" he asked.

I shrugged. "Security. Gotta stay on my toes."

Sophie turned to Will. "Truth be told, I want Jenna with me. We both have a vested interest in this trip."

Will nodded, his eyes flicking over to me.

She slipped inside our room, leaving me alone in the hallway with Will.

As he stepped closer to me, I looked up at him as I gripped the doorknob.

"You know..." I cleared my throat. "I'm... I'm going to be really honest with you."

He took another step. "I can take it."

"Good. I like that." I placed a hand on his chest and felt the pounding of his heart, in rhythm with my own, fast and hard.

"I swore to myself I wouldn't get, you know, emotionally involved with you. Nothing, not one thing, can come between me and the rescue of my son and Sarkis."

To his credit, he nodded. "Okay."

I studied his eyes. "Then we understand each other."

He cupped my chin. "But after this is over? You've saved Sarkis, you have your son, and Sophie and her husband live happily ever after? I'm serving notice." His green eyes sparkled.

"Look, I'm... complicated."

"Even better. I intend to pursue you. I mean that. I want to know all about you, learn what makes you laugh, what makes you cry." He smiled wryly. "I've already got a good idea of what pisses you off. And I also think you're funny."

"I read you loud and clear. Now, go to bed. 'Night, Will."

"Good night, Jenna." He turned and ambled off.

I stood in the doorway and watched him. I felt elated. Then, a movement caught my eye at the other end of the hall. Monte stood there with an ice bucket in his hand and a smirk on his face. He stared at me. He lifted the bucket as if to say, 'Just getting ice.'

I turned and entered our room, locked the door, and wondered about Monte. I still didn't like or trust him.

After we each took a shower, washed our hair and readied for bed, Sophie and I were in our beds and sound asleep by 8:00.

TWENTY-SIX

Rain pelting the windows woke me. I lay awake for thirty minutes, watching the digital clock on the nightstand. At 2:15 a.m., I sighed, got up, and walked to the window. Trees thrashed around in the roaring wind. Rain hammered the pavement. The top of the Blue Mosque, illuminated by streetlights and huge beacon lamps, looked fuzzy in the downpour. Wide-eyed and hyper-alert, I itched to do something. Anything.

Suddenly, the light clicked on. Sophie stared at me. "You can't sleep, either?"

"Nah. It's probably jet lag. We've had enough sleep, but we're still on California time."

"Jet lag? Gosh, even with all the sleep I got on the plane?" She kicked off the covers.

"That's my diagnosis."

Sophie sat up and crossed her legs Indian style on the bed. Taking a long look around our room, she exhaled. "Now what?"

I noticed a new tension in Sophie's demeanor.

"How are you?" I asked.

"Scared. How are you?"

"I'm scared, too, so you're in good company."

She swiped at the sudden tears spilling onto her cheeks. "And I feel guilty.

I feel guilty about Zach being involved in all this. It's my fault."

"Zach did it to himself, Sophie. His choice. Think how relieved Sarkis will be that you made it to Istanbul. Don't forget, he asked you to come."

"That's right, he did. I miss him so much." She reached for a tissue and blew her nose. "I've been thinking about Sarkis's grandparents. They gave their precious son away to save his life. Can you imagine? My husband wouldn't be alive if it hadn't been for such a selfless act. And they lived here. It's so... so unreal."

I could imagine it; in fact, I lived something akin to what Armen and Varteni Begosian went through when I gave up Zach. But I didn't want to discuss it now with Zach's kidnapping on my heart. "They lived right around here too."

"I'm glad Monte and Eznik know the area. Eznik told me they used to work for a man in a pottery business close to the Grand Bazaar.

"We read about that bazaar in Armen Begosian's entry in the Bible. It's gotta be close by." From the nightstand I took out a brochure on the sights to see in Istanbul. I found directions to the Grand Bazaar; apparently it was quite popular. I studied the map and saw another familiar name, Kum Kapi, right off Kennedy Caddesi, the main highway around the point of Stamboul, but I couldn't quite place its significance.

I dug through the papers Professor Takmaz had translated. There it was. Kum Kapi. "Look, Sophie. Kum Kapi is where Armen Begosian lived. According to this map, it's not far from here."

She gazed at me, her brown eyes narrowed. "What do you suppose the kidnappers think is hidden in that house?"

"They only know what Professor Takmaz told them. A map found in a book gives directions to a buried treasure in Old Istanbul. They came halfway across the world to find the answer."

"Read what it says again. What did Begosian hide?" I pulled out the translations, scanned them, and then read out loud. "'All week long, I've pulled the inventory from my storeroom, and I've chosen the finest, most beautiful pieces. If we can keep this treasure hidden from the police, it will be more than enough for us to buy safe passage and start a new life.'"

I returned the papers to my backpack. "The 'finest and most beautiful pieces.' And he was a jeweler."

Sophie cocked her head. "And the kidnappers have no idea what or where it is."

"No, they don't. Look." I showed her the map. "Kum Kapi is so close, we could hop in a taxi and go check it out."

"Now?" Her eyes grew huge.

I shrugged. "Why not? We're wide awake. Let's check out the neighborhood. We'll just take a look."

"I'm game. I don't want to lie around for the next three hours. Let's go." She rolled off her bed, grabbed the phone, and asked the front desk for a taxi with a driver who spoke English.

I was stoked. We were movin' forward without Monte or Eznik. We dressed in multiple layers for warmth. I topped off with my favorite long trench coat with lots of compartments for lots of things. Armed with our umbrellas, gloves, wool caps and scarves, we left in the dead of night, during a bitter storm.

The foyer was dark. A single lamp glowed at the registration desk. The night clerk sat behind the counter, smoking a cigarette and reading a Turkish newspaper.

A compact yellow taxi arrived, its headlights shimmering on the wet pavement. The driver flicked his lights, obviously not too keen on getting wet.

Sophie and I scuttled forward, hunched against the cold and wet. Between the hotel doors and the cab, we got a good soaking. I handed the taxi driver the written address. The driver cut the motor.

"You want go this?" He waved the slip of paper at us, looking skeptical as he stared at us.

"Yes." I nodded, settling back. I shook the water from my hands.

He shook his head. "Bad place, bad night. Not good."

"Look, just take us there."

"Sure, sure. You want go, I take." He started the car.

I muttered, "Don't go puttin' the kibosh on our adventure."

Sophie shot me a nervous smile.

The taxi whisked us away. A few turns and we sailed down the main highway. No pun intended.

"It's freezing!" Sophie pulled her knit cap down over her ears, and blew on her fingers.

The driver glanced at us in his rear view mirror, gripping the steering wheel with both hands and obviously wary. He set the windshield wipers on high.

Sophie whispered, "He's watching us, not the road."

I nodded. "He's got two crazy Western women going calling in the middle of the night in a raging storm. Anyone in their right mind is not doing what we're doing."

Sophie giggled, the sound a bit too high pitched. I gave her a quelling look, and she clapped her hand over her mouth.

We entered the Kum Kapi area, slowing as the driver

pointed to a shabby sign that hung over a train trestle. He muttered, "Kum Kapi."

I nodded. He raced along the narrow streets, but he took care at intersections. Even though no one was out, I appreciated his caution in the driving rain.

We zipped along a series of roads woven among cramped and crowded hills. The driver finally pulled over and parked, pointing to a large old home.

"This is it?" exclaimed Sophie.

"*Evet! Evet!*" He nodded, gesturing at the decrepit residence. An old wrought iron streetlight across the road cast dim light on the house. Around the block, the homes still standing were in various states of ruin.

I turned to Sophie. "Let's get out and look around."

Tapping the driver on the shoulder, I asked, "You wait? Wait here?"

With a sour look, he cut the engine. Sophie handed him two twenty million-lira notes for the six-minute drive. The smoke from his cigarette curled out the infinitesimal opening above his window. He sighed and shook his head. I'm sure he thought we were certifiable. The bitter cold almost forced me to agree with him.

We stood under our umbrellas in the pouring rain, in front of the abandoned dwelling. I checked the address carved into the side of the building. "Sure enough, this is the place."

Boards covered the windows, adding to the gloom.

We approached the house, tilting our umbrellas as we peered up at the top floor.

"I cannot believe it." Sophie stared at the once fabulous five-story home. Removing one of her gloves, she touched the wall. "This was Sarkis' family home. I wish he could see it."

"Zach would like that, too. We'll bring them back here when they're free."

The house looked dreary with age and neglect. At every level, concrete Greek Ionic columns were paired around each boarded-up window and extended to the top floor. Curved wrought iron window guards had withstood the march of decades. Even with broken windows, the old structure managed to carry itself like an old monarch.

A sudden gust of frigid wind sent twenty feet of lifeless electrical wires whipping against the side of the building walls. The air moving in and out my nose felt like ice cubes.

"I'm going to check the front door." Sophie ran up the steps to the tiny porch.

I looked around. Across the way, I spotted an old couch leaning against a telephone pole in an empty lot. Two abandoned cars sitting on their rims rested on the curb. Broken glass, bits of trash, and plastic bags littered the terrain.

"It's locked. Shall we go around and see if there's a back door?"

Together, we hurried along the sidewalk to the narrow

alleyway. At the rear of the Begosian house, an unlocked gate creaked in the wind. That and the weed-choked bit of earth leading to the back door seemed to be the only thing that prevented us from prying further.

I heard the taxi start up. "Oh, no!"

Sophie and I exchanged a shocked look. We ran to the front of the house just in time to see our taxi round the corner.

TWENTY-SEVEN

"Son of a bitch!"

"We'll have to walk back," Sophie moaned, hugging herself.

"Well, we're here now. We can't just walk away."

"What are you talking about?" Sophie hopped up and down in order to generate warmth. The rain fell steadily, pinging like ice pellets off the tops of our umbrellas.

Shoving my hand deep into my pocket, I shivered. I grinned at Sophie. "It's cold out here. Let's go inside, and check it out."

"Are you serious? We'd have to break in."

I opened my trench coat, and I patted a narrow, inside pocket. "We have tools."

She gasped.

"This will be easier than I expected. I don't want to come back, Sophie. We're here, so let's do it now."

Icy wind swirled around us. The rain intensified even more. A dog wailed in the distance. I knew how he felt.

Sophie nodded. "All right, but let's hurry." We made our way to the rear of the house.

On the small back porch, I closed my umbrella and tucked it into a pocket. I withdrew a slim-jim from my small fold-up tool kit. The pounding rain camouflaged the sound of prying boards. Two good shoves, and the door gave way. Within seconds, we stood inside a tiny room. I handed Sophie my extra miniflashlight.

We crept forward, tiptoeing into an adjacent kitchen. Bone-chilling cold permeated the room. The place smelled God-awful, an unwieldy blend of old dust and neglected cat box. A cracked enamel sink sat abandoned on the floor. All the furniture had been stripped from the dusty room long ago.

We made a silent path to the front door. I directed my flashlight around a large living room. The walls were beige, the wood floors scuffed and scarred. The ceiling resembled a spider web of fractured plaster, and a hole gaped where a light fixture had once hung.

A hissing sound made me stiffen. Sophie lurched against me. I shone my flashlight into the corner. A mangy, skeletal brown cat arched its back. "Damn, that scared me!"

"Me, too!" Sophie stayed close. "That explains the smell."

It was then we noticed four black newborn kittens huddled for warmth in the corner. They lay on a filthy towel. Mama cat paced anxiously, growling warning sounds emerging from her throat.

Sophie breathed, "Oh, look at her babies."

"Don't even think about it."

We crept to the entryway. I froze when I saw the filthy orange and gray geometric patterned, tile floor.

Sophie pulled a copy from her pocket of the diagram drawn by Armen Begosian. She held it up, and I focused my flashlight on it.

"Right over there," she whispered, pointing.

I nodded, quivering with adrenaline and cold. Kneeling in the alcove, I took out a small ball-peen hammer, wrapped it in a hand towel from the hotel, and gave the tiles a few good whacks. The sounds reverberated in the room as dull thuds.

"This isn't my expertise, you know," I whispered. "Breaking and entering, I mean. I do a lot of investigating, but mostly with a computer." I pointed a shaky finger. "Focus your light right there."

Sophie pointed her flashlight. The beam wobbled, kind of like my nerves.

I felt the tiles break apart, giving way after decades of holding their secret. The flashlight illuminated a dull piece of carpet. I shoved it aside And then I saw a satchel.

A dust-covered satchel. I sat back on my heels, stunned. Just like that, there it was.

"Oh, my God, Jenna!" Sophie knelt at my side.

I put my hand over my mouth. "Armen Begosian, you pulled it off! You beat the bastards!"

It was an old-fashioned doctor's satchel, black and trimmed in brown leather. Together, Sophie and I lifted the thing out of its cold tomb, and then we hauled it into the darkened living room.

Sophie knelt down in front of it. "The treasure's real! It's real, Jenna!"

Mama cat had settled uneasily on the grimy towel, still warning us with her low sounds.

I pointed my flashlight into the satchel opening. I tossed aside another small patch of carpet, and we saw leather pouches in deep burgundy, gold, and black. Dozens of them. Picking up a pouch, I handed it to Sophie. I kept the light steady.

She untied the leather cord, and poured the contents into her hand. White, green, and pink stones tumbled into her palm. Sparkling diamonds and other precious stones spilled over into the folds of her coat.

Totally shocked, we stared at one another. A huge grin spread across Sophie's face.

"Put them back," I said. "Let's get out of here."

A creak from the stairs behind made me freeze. My heart leapt into my throat. Whirling around, I stared in alarm at a young girl of about seven or eight. She stared at us, wide-eyed. With one hand, she held a bowl of something, probably for the cat. With the other, she clutched a small, worn blanket around her shoulders.

I heard Sophie exhale as she sank onto the floor. I half rose, ready to flee.

The child didn't utter a sound.

I felt caged. Everything in me screamed: RUN! Get up and get out! Wrong house. Sorry about your floor, we'll get back to you.

"Hello," Sophie whispered.

The little girl shrank back with a whimper.

"Oh, can this get any worse? Sophie, we are so out of here. Now!"

Sophie scooped up the jewels from her lap and handed them to me. Turning back to the girl, she smiled. "Where's your mother? Mamma?" Sophie pointed upstairs.

The dark-eyed girl nodded.

"Jenna. Give her one of those pouches." Sophie hadn't taken her eyes off the girl.

I gave her a sharp look. "Wait a minute. How are they going to trade in these gems?"

Sophie blinked.

I pressed on, "This could lead to trouble for them, especially if the kidnappers find out about the gems. Think about what they might do to them. They've already kidnapped your husband, and took Zach when they were threatened."

The girl scurried behind us and placed the container in front of Mama cat. The creature didn't snarl or bare its teeth once.

Headlights suddenly swept the front of the house. Sophie and I ran to the boarded up window, looking through a crack in the boards. A taxi. I wildly hoped it was our driver. Two figures emerged.

Sophie nearly shrieked, "Monte and Eznik!"

"We've got to get out of here!"

Sophie ran to the satchel, pulled out a burgundy drawstring bag and dumped the contents into her palm.

I watched the brothers approach the house in the torrential downpour. "They're coming!"

Sophie whipped around to the girl, who looked increasingly alarmed.

Abruptly, a woman called out from upstairs, "Kamile? Kamile! Cabok ol!"

The front doorknob wiggled back and forth. The girl and Sophie froze, staring at the doorknob.

I pressed my fingers to my lips. "Shh! Polis!"

Sophie pushed the child toward the stairs. After dropping several gold and sparkling pendants into her palm, she folded her little fingers over it. "For Kamile and Mamma... now run! Go! Shhh!" The girl shot up the stairs.

From my vantage point at the window, I watched Monte and Eznik glance up to the top of the house, confer with one another, and then move around to the rear door. Thank You, God, for the pounding rain.

"They're going around to the back. Give me a hundred lira note." I grabbed the satchel and sped to the front door. I love adrenaline when it kicks in. Opening the front door, I peered out.

Sophie reached into her jacket. She handed me a bill as we stepped outside.

"I only have a five hundred lira bill."

"Whatever. We're stealing their ride." I closed the door. "Hurry."

We ran to the taxi and knocked on the window. Not the same driver as before. I held the note against the window. The man's jaw dropped. He nodded.

"Get in," I told Sophie. She did. I followed, shoving the duffel-sized satchel between us on the seat.

"Go. Go," I ordered, waving the driver forward. Twisting around, I watched the Begosian house fade from view. The Kazarian brothers didn't reappear as we disappeared into the night.

"Well, that explains how much they read last night." I turned to Sophie. "They had the address. I told you we couldn't trust them."

"I can't believe they showed up here in the middle of the night!"

"What are you confused about? They came to find Armen Begosian's treasure." My teeth chattered from the cold and wet. "We cannot trust them, Sophie."

"I was wrong about them." She swiped at her wet hair, pulling it away from her face.

Within ten minutes, we were back to Kennedy Caddesi, the main thoroughfare around the city.

Sophie blew on her hands. "My fingers are numb." She glanced out at the rain-slicked roads. The rain fell in diagonal torrents. Her expression became pensive. "I wish I'd given that little girl money instead of jewelry."

"Me, too, but neither one of us thought to do the smart thing."

She nodded as she met my gaze.

TWENTY-EIGHT

Our driver delivered us safely to the hotel. I handed him the one hundred-lira note, and he thanked us at least seventeen times. He tried to carry the satchel, appearing worried when we refused his offer. He opened the door to the hotel for us and followed us inside.

"You call tomorrow... ask for Nuri. I take you anywhere, anywhere," he promised.

I muttered something rude. Sophie smiled and thanked him.

The front desk clerk was nowhere in sight. I felt relieved that we could slip through the lobby unnoticed.

Once inside our hotel room, I locked our door and then shoved the only chair in the room under the doorknob. We stripped off our cold, wet clothes. Sophie got into her robe and pajamas. I changed into a pair of jeans and a warm sweater, parked myself at the window, and watched for taxis pulling up to the entrance.

Sophie opened the satchel. "Let's see what we've got. One bag at a time?"

"Okay." I must admit, I was eager to see what we'd rescued.

She selected a gold leather pouch, empting the contents onto the bedspread. Out tumbled several beautiful pieces of vintage jewelry. One brooch was twisted into an exquisite, ornate peacock design, encrusted with diamonds and pearls.

"Can you believe this?" She held the peacock up to the light. "This is more than I ever imagined."

"And that's just one bag."

Sophie slid a ring on her finger, turning her hand to admire the sparkle of the stunning deep butterscotch stone. She set aside that bag after tying the drawstrings. She then withdrew a burgundy leather sack, spilling dull, uncut gems onto the bed. She scooped them up and put them aside. Then, she brought out a black leather bag.

I stood by the window, alternately watching the road outside and Sophie's satchel discoveries. Another dazzling display of loose diamonds and gems fell onto the pink bedspread.

"Oh, my gosh!" Sophie looked awestruck as she stared at scarlet, emerald green, yellow and blue polished stones. The dim light from the room lamps gave the stones and jewelry a rich, smoldering glow.

Again, Sophie swept up the loose gems and put them to one side. She pulled out another gold bag, turned it upside down and dumped the jewelry on the bed. Rings, this time. Sophie tried one on, tossed it aside, and picked up another.

As she rummaged through the rings, she handed me a fabulous diamond and sapphire ring. I put it on and gazed at it. It adorned my finger as though it belonged there. I was wearing something I'd never own in ten lifetimes.

Handing it back to Sophie, I returned my attention to the road. Taxis were beginning to venture out in the early morning hours, storm or no storm. I recalled the cut-rate diamond ring my ex had given me. I'd sold it to replumb my house.

"Jenna. This ring is perfect for you. It matches the blue in your eyes. I want you to have it. It's our gift to you." She smiled.

Stunned, I straightened and looked at her. "Are you serious?" My face flushed and I stared at the blue sapphire and diamond ring in the palm of her hand. "You have no idea what that's worth. It could be priceless."

"I'm very serious. And Sarkis would want you to have it, too. In fact, if you don't want that one, then choose another. Take whichever one you want."

My heart pounded. Every impulse I owned urged

me to refuse. She seemed to really mean it. We weren't under stress or duress. Not at this moment, anyway.

"I... I don't know what to say. Truthfully, Soph, I've never been given a gift like this before. Ever." I leaned against the windowsill and thought a moment. "I mean, the nicest thing my ex ever gave me was a treadmill."

Sophie smiled. "Good. I want you to have this. Go ahead."

Without another moment's hesitation, I accepted the ring. I put it on and admired it. "Thank you, Sophie. I'm at a loss for words."

After a few moments, I crossed the room for my makeup bag and brought it over to the window. I removed the ring from my finger, carefully wrapping it in a bed of cotton balls. I placed it into a pocket Kleenex pack and put folded tissues on top. I crammed the Kleenex packet into my makeup bag next to my Tampax and my toothpaste.

Suddenly, we heard the sounds of movement outside our door. Sophie shot me a look of alarm. I put a finger to my lips. Crossing the room, I pressed my ear to the door. The footsteps faded off.

Monte and Eznik? For sure, they'd be pissed. Had they overlooked the child and her mother in that derelict house? I hoped so.

Striding back to the window, I looked out on the night. The rain continued to lash against the glass panes. I wondered about Monte and Eznik, and then I thought about the kidnappers. How would they react to the missing treasure?

Apprehension gripped me. I gnawed on my thumbnail. Sure, I'd trumped the kidnappers, but how would we get the treasure out of the country? And what had I just done to Zach and Sarkis? Sophie actually thought I knew what the hell I was doing. Regret resonated in my skull. Suddenly, I missed Ralph.

Although I felt the press of Sophie's gaze, I kept my eyes on the street below.

"What do we say to Monte and Eznik?"

I turned to her. "Nothing."

"You think they're walking back?"

"Nah. But we left a lot of evidence back there. They're not idiots."

She gave me a helpless shrug. "We're supposed to meet them for breakfast."

"Yeah. Supposed to."

"That's going to be awkward."

"No. We act like nothing's happened."

"I'm not a good liar, Jenna."

"Don't give me that. You were quite the liar with Detective Berhmann."

"I like to think those were little white lies." She'd put the jewels away and shoved the satchel close to her bed.

"How many bags were there?"

"I counted seventy-three. I just can't believe we did this. It seemed almost too easy."

"Yeah." I warned myself not to feel smug. Better to stay cautious. "Everything's easy when you have a map."

"And you follow the directions." She snuggled down into the bed and pulled the covers to her chin. "I heard a pastor say that, if people on this planet followed the directions God gave them, this world would be a different place."

"Oh, yeah? Did God send us a map with those directions?"

She hoisted herself onto one elbow. "Yes. It's called the Bible."

Crap, I walked right into that one. I held my hand up, no more.

She got the hint and spoke to the ceiling. "You know, Jenna, I'm glad we did this. I didn't want to, but now I'm thankful we did it. You're right, the kidnappers shouldn't get one thing of Armen Begosian's. I'd like to be a fly on the wall when the kidnappers break into that house in Kum Kapi, and they find nothing but a hole in the floor."

"Hopefully, we'll be headed home when they do, and we're restoring the treasure to the Begosian family what was rightfully theirs," I reminded her.

"I have to admit you were right about the brothers. I didn't want to believe they were here for the jewels, but now... ."

Would the kidnappers come after us? "We have to find a safe place for all the jewels."

"Any ideas?" Sophie asked.

"After breakfast, let's go to the bazaar. We might find an answer there."

"What about getting through customs? How are we going to smuggle all these jewels out of here?"

"I've got some ideas," I lied. "And Will might have an idea or two. This stuff might be an historic find."

Sophie regarded me, a thoughtful expression on her face. "Do you think the government would fight us on this? We have the Bible as proof of ownership."

"I think they'd put up a fuss. The authorities could confiscate the jewels and make us look like major criminals." What would life be like in a Turkish prison? I didn't want to find out. "You might want to ask God to get involved here. This could turn into a hellava mess."

Sophie gave me a long look, and closed her eyes.

Why did I say these idiotic things? And I'd been sarcastic. Damn.

TWENTY-NINE

We slept for almost four hours. I dozed fitfully, jittery with exhaustion and worry. I toyed with the idea of calling Will to tell him what we'd done. At eight-thirty, I ordered tea, took a shower, and then woke Sophie. "We have to meet the guys at ten. I thought you might like a shower."

She dragged herself off to the bathroom.

I dressed, brought out my makeup case, and managed a fast repair. It helped, but not by much. Nothing I could do about the fine lines under my eyes, and around my lips. Underlying worry over what Zach was going through amped up my anxiety.

Sophie dressed, sat at the desk, and moisturized her face. "Do you think they'll call today?"

"Anything's possible."

The shrill ring of the phone on the nightstand made us both jump. Sophie whirled around, her hands to her mouth.

"Yes? Hello?" I frowned, listening to an operator, who fumbled with her pronunciations. "Yes! I'll hold." I turned to face Sophie. "It's Ralph!" Fear flooded me. Why was he calling? Did he have news about my father?

Sophie approached me, watching my face.

I heard a click, and then Ralph's voice.

"Jenna?" Ralph's voice boomed, sounding like he was calling from the next room.

"Ralph! What's wrong?"

"Nothin'. I told you I'd call. I had a devil of a time tracking you down. Will's charter gave me your location. What time is it there?"

I glanced at my watch. "It's eight forty-five in the morning."

"Did I wake you?"

"No, no. We're wide awake. Sophie's right here. How's my dad?"

"Your mom and I played phone tag, but we finally caught up with one another. Your dad's doing okay; he can't speak, and at the moment, he can't walk. The stroke affected his left side. They start speech therapy today."

"Aw, do they have to?" That ought to be something, my father muted.

"Careful, Jenna. Maddie's on the warpath and your

brother Luke's blaming himself. He thinks it's his fault your dad had the stroke because he called him late that night."

"Crap. Do you know if Francie's been notified?" More than likely, Maddie had called our sister.

"No one said anything to me about it. Anyway, I explained everything to your mom about the case you're working for George St. James's daughter. She's amazed you're involved."

"I'm amazed myself."

Sophie looked up, perplexed.

"Still, at least Maddie's there for Mom."

"That's family, Jen-kins. You get what you get."

"No kidding."

He laughed.

"How did it go with Kent?"

"You're right about that guy not being a happy camper. I told him Zach was pretty firm on staying down here for the time being, and that he said he didn't want to talk to his dad right now. I played Dr. Phil. Told him he needed to give the kid time, and that it was a real shock to learn he was adopted. Told him that I thought Zach was a decent kid, and that time heals."

"Hey. You did great. How'd he take it?"

"I've seen his car around. He keeps looking for the kid. But his car disappeared around seven last night. So, I dunno."

I decided that Kent and Lizabeth could sit tight for the time being.

"How's Lynne?" I asked. "What did the doctor say?"

"She's scheduled for all sorts of tests next week. They're thinkin' its esophageal cancer."

Stunned, I blurted, "I'm so sorry, Ralph! Tell Lynne I send my love. You okay?" Knowing Ralph, he wasn't sleeping.

"Well, this is..." He paused for a few seconds. "Have you heard from the kidnappers?"

He sounded rocky, so I shifted gears with him. "No, but we move to the Hotel Citadel today. They'll probably know we've arrived as soon as we get there."

"So, you got nothing yet."

"Well, we've been successful in other endeavors..."

A pause. "Oh, man, I hope you were careful."

"I can't wait to tell you about it." I shot Sophie a smile. She gave me a thumbs up.

"As long as you're both safe. Listen, we did a full investigation on Monte and Eznik Kazarian. Get this... Monte was with Interpol twelve years ago. Worked in counterfeiting, money laundering, credit card fraud."

"That explains his lame surveillance skills. What else you got?"

"Eznik, as far as I can tell, is his business partner in the six dry cleaning joints. Monte was married, now divorced. Eznik's supposed to get married in five weeks."

Exactly what they'd told Sophie. "Where'd you get your information?"

"I did the old-former-college-friend-looking-up-his-buddy routine. Their Auntie Yeva was very helpful. She filled me in on Monte's life, including his divorce."

"You're good, Ralph."

"And I contacted Detective Berhmann, filled him in on what actually happened outside Sophie's home."

I tightened my grip on the phone. "Berhmann! Oh boy. Okay, how'd it go?"

"Ah, the usual B.S. I reminded him it was Sophie's decision not to contact the police, because of the threat to her husband's life. And I told Berhmann that Sarkis was specifically given the option to contact the police, and he declined. Berhmann still threw a fit, and he threatened to throw the book at us."

"Why am I not surprised?"

"I reminded him that he'd be the one to get all the credit for solving the case, which got his attention."

Sophie nodded as she listened to the one-sided conversation.

"Good. That's a load off." I paused, the brief silence comfortable. Finally, I said, "Ralph, don't forget to tell Lynne I asked about her."

"Will do." Ralph sighed into the phone. "You be sure someone's watching your back."

I felt very humble at that moment. "I will. You know me."

"No heroics."

"No heroics, I promise."

"Okay, then. Keep in touch. Bye."

"Bye, Ralph. Thanks." I was talking to the dial tone by the time I said his name.

I sat for a moment, not trusting myself to speak.

Sophie waited only a moment. "Jenna! What happened with your dad?"

"Don't we need to meet the guys at ten o'clock?" I asked.

"That's in forty-five minutes."

Stretching out on out on my bed, I wedged a pillow under my head, and filled her in on Kent and Lizabeth, my father's situation, Eznik's pending nuptials, Monte's previous career with Interpol, and then I explained about Ralph's Lynne.

Sophie came over and plopped on the bed. I blinked back tears. Were they for my father, or for Ralph and Lynne? Perhaps it was Zach. But sharing with Sophie had lightened the load, I realized.

Sophie dabbed at her eyes after I described Lynne's diagnosis. "Is there anything I can do to help?"

I squinted at her. "Like what?"

"Well, I'm a living, breathing cancer survivor. I know some of the best doctors in the country. Perhaps one of them can steer Ralph and Lynne in the right direction. Give me his phone number."

"That'd be awesome." I sat up, grabbed a pen and paper, and jotted down Ralph's pertinent information. I hesitated. "Sophie, Ralph has basic medical insurance. He can't afford the best."

She took the piece of paper from me. "Let's see who's available first."

I nodded, reality slamming into my chest once again. "The doctors said it doesn't look good."

Sophie grimaced. "Cancer never looks good." She picked up the phone and asked for an international operator.

A knock sounded on the door. Adrenaline surged through me.

"Yeah?" I called out.

"Time for breakfast."

Will. Breathing a sigh of relief, I crossed to the door and removed the chair so I could open it. I looked up and down the hallway. Empty.

"Hi, " I whispered, stepping back to let him inside.

Sophie turned away from us, speaking in a subdued voice.

My spirit lightened. Will looked great. He wore crisp jeans, a black sweater, and a black raincoat. How does he do that while traveling?

He looked around. "Nice room. Whaddya tip the bellhop for this? In my room, I roll over and flush the toilet by accident."

Pulling him into the room, I put a finger to my lips. "Shh, Soph's on the phone. I just had a call from my partner. His wife's been diagnosed with cancer. Sophie is talking to a doctor who might be able to help."

Concern flashed across his face.

"So, listen, I have something to show you and a problem for you to solve."

His green eyes looked hopeful, his smile wide and inviting.

"Hey, Soph," I whispered. "I'm going to bring Will up to date."

She nodded, and then returned to her phone call.

"Remember our conversation about Sarkis when we talked on the jet? The kidnappers took Sarkis and Zach. What I didn't tell you is what they're after. What they want is a map detailing the exact location of a treasure. Last night Sophie and I recovered exactly what the kidnappers want."

He looked puzzled. "Last night?"

I struggled to lift the old satchel. "What time is it?"

Will arched over, grabbed the valise and settled it on the bed. He glanced at his watch. "Nine-forty."

"Okay, I gotta do this fast. We meet the Brothers Grimm in twenty minutes, give or take a few." Reaching past Will, I picked up Armen Begosian's Bible. Opening the book to the first couple of handwritten pages, I held it for him to see. "This is an Armenian Bible." I proceeded to give him a nutshell version of what we'd been through in the last few days. Waving Professor Takmaz's translations in front of Will, I explained how and why Sarkis was kidnapped, why Sophie had hired the brothers, and the reason we were in Turkey. Then I told him about finding the treasure the night before. As

I talked I unwrapped three of the leather bags, one from each color group, and displayed the gems.

Will was aghast. "Last night. You did this last night? You broke into a home..."

"Well, it was abandoned... just a couple of squatters there."

"My God! People actually live there?" His eyes widened with shock.

"If you want to call it living, yeah. They were destitute."

"And in this storm? You went out in the middle of the night in this storm?"

I shrugged. "Jet lag. We couldn't sleep."

He looked incredulous.

My face began to heat up. "It's all good, Will. I just need to know how to get these jewels out of the country."

"Are you out of your mind? You're talking about smuggling." He stared at the impressive layout of gems on the bed. "Do you want to end up in a Turkish prison?"

"Couldn't we say we bought these at a museum?"

"You need a receipt from the seller. The museum would have to issue you a certificate...." his voice trailed off.

"Okay, so that's a no-go. Can you think of anything else?"

Will rubbed the back of his neck. "Just like that? You want answers?" His perfect tan took on a reddish hue.

This wasn't going well. Admittedly, I'd barely considered the legal repercussions. I felt embarrassed, but I asked, "Can you help us?"

He looked as if he wanted to bolt.

"Listen, please," I implored. "Sophie doesn't care about this treasure. God knows she doesn't need the money. What we want is justice. In 1915 Sarkis' grandfather, Armen Begosian, and his wife were rounded up and taken from their home. They disappeared and were never heard from again. The authorities allowed someone to steal his jewelry business. Now, the kidnappers are doing the same thing to Sarkis and Sophie." I took a step toward him. "I refuse to let that happen."

THIRTY

Will looked intently at me. He turned away, running a hand through his thick, silver hair. Then he picked up a gemstone, studied it, and laid it down. He began to pace back and forth between the door and the window as he thought.

After tucking away the jewelry, I fretted over his silence. "Will, you don't have to give us an answer right away. I'd just like you to be thinking about how we can smugg... how we can get these jewels out of the country."

He stopped in front of me. "The authorities enforce strict regulations on antiquities. Yeah, it's a broadly defined term, but I'd say this qualifies." He paced to the door and window again. Suddenly, he stopped dead in his tracks. His furrowed forehead became smooth.

I knew he'd thought of something. "What? What did you come up with?"

His frown transformed into a sly grin. "Charter a boat. Sail to Cyprus, then to Greece. I could meet you in Cyprus." He straightened. "It could work."

He looked at his watch. "We're supposed to meet Eznik and Monte in five minutes. We can't let this out of our sight, not ever."

Man, when he was in, he was *in*, I thought.

"I agree, but right now I'm more stressed about the brothers and raising their suspicions."

Behind us, Sophie hung up the phone. "It's all set. Dr. Maggio is going to make some calls. He'll notify Ralph today about the oncologist's appointment, which might be as soon as tomorrow."

"Tomorrow?" Unbelievable.

She nodded. "That's what I asked for, and I hope it works out."

"Ralph will be blown away." I felt elated until I thought about the cost. "How much do you think they'll charge?"

She shook her head with the tiniest motion. "I took care of it, Jenna. Ralph won't need to concern himself with anything but his wife."

I stood there dumbfounded. What an incredible gift.

Sophie turned to Will who was scanning the professor's translations. "Sorry you slept through our little excursion?"

He tossed the papers on the bed. "Sorry? You should be grateful to God I wasn't there."

"With Jenna, life is never dull."

Will gave a short laugh. "I'm learning that."

I felt embarrassed, but in a good way.

He looked around the room, his gaze snagging on the open closet door. "That small carry-on, empty it."

"Why? What are you going to do?"

"I'm going to take the wheel off. Then we tell Monte and Eznik we need to go shopping for a new carry-on. That way, the jewels are always with us. We'll put the gems inside, and add some clothing so the sacks don't roll around."

Sophie frowned. "Haul that thing all over Istanbul? Why don't I book another room? Monte and Eznik won't ever know the gems are hidden there."

"Brilliant! When we check into the new hotel today, we'll book an extra room."

Sophie removed Sarkis's clothes from the carry-on. Will and I helped her to transfer the stiff, leather sacks.

"Let's see." Will examined the bottom of the small suitcase. "Too bad we don't have a screwdriver."

I dug through the pockets of my raincoat, handing Will a screwdriver. "Ta-da."

Will shook his head as he began to remove a wheel from the suitcase. "What else ya got in there?"

Sophie cracked, "If we told you, we'd have to kill you."

"You two crazies are the ones playing chicken with killers."

He popped off the wheel and tossed it to me. "Tuck that

away, just in case. We'll take the suitcase with us at breakfast, and explain to Monte and Eznik that the wheel broke."

Sophie added Sarkis's sweater and a warm-up suit to the luggage, hiding the bags from view.

Will gave us a decisive nod. "When we get back, we need to arrange to charter a boat."

"Works for me. Thank you, Will."

He leveled those sparkling green eyes at me. "This carry-on never leaves our sight. Right?"

"Right," we chorused.

"Okay, go ahead and lock it. What's the combination?"

Sophie rattled it off.

He turned to me. "Got it?"

"Roger that."

"Time for breakfast." Will locked the suitcase, and used the shoulder strap to carry it. The weight seemed effortless on his broad shoulders. "Think they'll have pancakes?"

It felt good to have a deliberate, energetic ally like Will.

We left the room and headed to the stairs.

Not surprisingly, the brothers were walking ahead of us. They turned to watch us approach. My nerves started to zing.

Monte shot me with his index finger. "Sleep well?"

I shot him back. "Like a rock."

Talk about sleep deprivation. With their red-rimmed eyes, they both looked exhausted. I silently cheered. Couldn't help myself.

Will chimed in. "When you're crossing time zones the trick to a good night's sleep is Melatonin."

The brothers continued down the stairs. They suddenly rushed forward, grabbing a man and shoved him against the wall. Monte and Eznik looked furious. The man they'd cornered turned out to be the taxi driver, Nuri.

Sophie and I froze. I turned to Will. "That's the taxi driver who ditched the brothers for us."

Will paused on the stairs. "Monte's losing it."

"Oh, my gosh!" Sophie clapped a hand over her mouth.

Had he spent the night parked out front? I wondered.

Nuri glanced up at me. I pantomimed zipping my mouth shut. His eyes flicked to Sophie, who pressed a finger to her lips.

The hotel manager moved in, trying to calm the situation.

I approached Monte and Eznik. "What the hell's the matter? Who is this guy?"

Monte ground his teeth. The manager escorted the taxi driver to the door, ushering him outside.

A clerk approached the manager, who hurried to the front desk. Nuri ducked back inside. He looked at me, his expression uncertain.

I played dumb. He went along.

"Stupid taxi driver," Monte spat.

"Why are you treating this man like he ran over your dog? Did you or did you not call for a taxi?" I demanded. But I was enjoying myself immensely.

"No." Monte said, his voice reminding me of ground glass.

"Then what's the problem?"

"It doesn't concern you."

Will smiled at Nuri. "Will you wait for us while we have breakfast? A piece of her luggage broke..." He hefted the suitcase like it was full of cotton balls. My hero. "We need to go to that bazaar nearby so Sophie can buy another one."

"I take you, yes," Nuri said to Will. "I wait."

Will leaned in to me. "Okay with you if he waits?"

"I wait, I wait." Nuri pointed to the driveway in front, and then hotfooted it out to his taxi.

"Sure," I belatedly said.

"Great." Will turned to Monte. "Coffee sounds good."

Monte ignored him.

"Come on, Eznik, let's see what they're serving this morning." Sophie looped her arm in his and dragged him off to the coffee shop.

Pissed, Monte trailed behind them.

I grabbed Will's arm. "What if the taxi driver tells Monte and Eznik we brought a satchel out of the house in Kum Kapi in the middle of the night? Monte's no idiot. The guy might admit he drove us back to the hotel since we gave him that five hundred lira bill."

Will's eyes widened. "Five hundred lira? No wonder he showed up again today. You're a rich American. Look, don't blow this out of proportion. We'll eat breakfast and play it one scene at a time."

Several waiters hurried to our table once we were all seated. We ordered coffee and tea. I checked out the buffet, helping myself to three hard-boiled eggs and some yogurt.

Will squeezed my shoulder as he got up to get his breakfast. I pressed my thigh against the suitcase.

Our table in the coffee shop looked out on to the Marmara Sea. The rain fell with less force, and the wind had settled to a breeze.

Once everyone returned from the buffet and began to eat, I took control. "Today we'll move to the hotel the kidnappers wanted us to check into. First, though, we'll head over to the bazaar, we'll get that new carry-on we need. Then we move out of here and check in at the new place no later than three. Sound like a plan?"

Silence.

"Eznik?" I prompted.

He nodded.

Sophie and Will both nodded.

Three down. One to go. "Monte?"

"Yeah," Monte finally muttered.

"Excellent. At supper tonight, we'll work out a game plan to hand over the Bible and get our guys back, safe and sound."

Sophie focused on her food, but I caught her nod.

"Why wait until the last minute?" Will asked.

"We're pretty much at the mercy of these thugs. Until we know where the exchange will take place, we can't really set up anything. Basically, it will go something like this: Monte goes with me. He has to get me to the right location, and he'll be my translator. When we receive the kidnapper's call, Monte and I will follow their instructions to the letter."

"Ingenious," Monte remarked.

I ignored him.

The taxi driver's head peered around the corner at us as he talked on a cell phone. Alarm shot through me. We made eye contact, and he ducked out of sight. Will saw him, too.

Will whispered, "I'll have Nuri take me to the airport. I'll meet you at the front of the bazaar. If it's still raining, I'll look for you right inside." He stood. "See you all at the bazaar after I take care of some airplane business."

Will brushed my hand before he left.

Suddenly, Monte got to his feet. "If all you're doing is buying luggage, my brother and I will visit some friends."

Eznik looked surprised.

That was fine with me. We'd see them later and the pressure was off for a while.

Monte stormed off with Eznik trailing behind.

THIRTY-ONE

Light drizzle swirled around us as we pulled up to the bazaar. We strolled past outdoor vendors who hawked their wares under large awnings. I dragged the wobbly suitcase behind me.

A couple hundred tourists milled about in the rain. Cold wind scoured the perimeter of the building where we stood.

We entered the market through two normal-sized doors, which opened into a colorful, massive labyrinth filled with tiny shops, some the size of closets. Banners and flags flew everywhere. Updated and trendy ads hung across the expanse of the bazaar. Hundreds and hundreds of people strolled the alleyways under the covered shopping mall. The mingling odors of cologne, tobacco, incense and cigar smoke, body odor, and sour milk smacked us in the face at the door.

Suffocating, I stripped off my coat, crammed my raincoat into the outside pocket of the suitcase, and hoisted its strap over my head, balancing the weight on my shoulder. Sophie took off her coat and carried it. In the chaos, some people negotiated through with the help of tour guides, others went at it alone. Fear shot through me as I realized our vulnerability. All I could think about was protecting Sophie.

"Stay close," I ordered.

She nodded in agreement and moved within inches of me.

Tourists from across the globe worked their way through the marketplace. Gazing up, we studied the detail of forty-foot tall arched ceilings, and the colorful tile work that seemed to go on and on, one style blending with another.

A young man approached Sophie. Clean-shaven, neatly dressed, dark, and handsome, he looked determined to do business.

I casually sidestepped in front of her.

"You American? What you need? Gold? Rugs? I take you."

Another eager Turk ready to help us out.

"No, no thanks." I smiled with a polite shake of my head.

"What you need? I take you." With an expansive sweep of his arm, he indicated the entire labyrinth.

Sophie relented. "Another suitcase. This one's broken."

"Okay! Follow me, I take you."

I grabbed his arm to stop him, shook my head and spoke clearly, "No, sorry! We're waiting for someone. We wait, first."

Another group of tourists flooded the entrance to the bazaar.

Without batting an eye, he walked away, asking the same question he probably asked hundreds of times a day. "What you need?"

Ahead of us, I saw rivers of gold necklaces, pendants, rings, and broaches. I gazed far down the aisle. Gold and silver sparkled like sunlight on water at dawn.

"Jenna." Sophie's voice sounded strange.

I swiveled to face her. "You doin' okay?"

Her eyes welled with tears. Her voice trembled. "I haven't stopped thinking about Sarkis. Or Zach. All this noise and the people, even the smells, it's overwhelming. I can hardly pray... my mind isn't clear." She caught her breath.

"You're in good company, Soph. I haven't stopped thinking about Zach or Sarkis either."

She gripped my hand. "Will they be okay?"

"Everything is going as planned. We'll hear from them tonight. Come on, Soph. Take a deep breath. Your prayers will come to you." I was uncomfortable saying it but it was what she needed to hear.

"I haven't lost faith, but I'm..." Her eyes swept over the bazaar, but she really didn't see. "I'm terrified for my husband, and for Zach, and what they might be going through. I can't seem to take a deep breath, I'm so anxious."

"Sophie, it's almost over. We'll have them soon." I hoped I was right. She whispered, "Promise me, they'll make it."

"They will, even if I have to search every inch of Istanbul for the rest of my life."

She gave me a shaky smile.

I tried to change the subject. "Can you believe it? Armen Begosian had a shop here almost a hundred years ago."

Just then, Will approached us. "There you are."

We huddled together in a tight threesome. He relieved me of the suitcase and shouldered the bag.

"You ditch Nuri?" I asked.

"Yeah, but it took some doing." Will took a good look at Sophie and then put an arm around her. "How are you doing, sweet girl?"

She rested her head on his shoulder for a brief moment, and then she looked at him. "I'm okay, thanks. We were just talking about how this finally might be coming to an end."

Will nodded. "God willing." He gave her a knowing glance.

I looked at him in surprise. *God willing?* A kind of small nudge went through me. Will believed like Sophie believed? I tucked that away for later.

Sophie pulled away. "Let's go buy a suitcase."

I signaled to the handsome guide still greeting anyone who walked through the door. He rushed over.

"Suitcases?"

Sophie pulled out a Turkish lira note. "Will you take us there?"

Our new guide pocketed the money, spoke in rapid-fire Turkish to his friends, and set off. He led us past shops that sold spices, pottery, gauzy shirts, tee shirts, every conceivable leather good, tobacco shops, pipe shops, and toys.

Soon, delicious aromas permeated the air. I smelled mint, honey, roasting lamb, and baking pastries. Waiters darted everywhere, balancing trays high above our heads. I could swear everyone chain-smoked. The crush of people very nearly made me claustrophobic. Which made me worry for Sophie. People ran into us, and brushed up against us. I craved space in the worst way.

Vendors shouted at us, but our guide ignored them and kept us moving. After an attention-grabbing, ten-minute walk directly into the heart of the Grand Bazaar, we rounded a corner and started up a less congested, narrow street.

I glanced to my right at a tiny café with three tables out front, almost stumbling as a bolt of shock and fear hit me. Will and Sophie continued to follow our guide.

Stunned, my thoughts reeled. I turned in slow motion and took another look. Seated alone at a scuffed up table, having tea and smoking a cigarette, a fisherman's cap positioned low on his brow, was one of the kidnappers. The man I'd nicknamed the Skipper.

I hesitated, feigning interest in a shop filled with gauzy blouses. The salesman asked in broken English what color and size I wanted. I glanced around for Sophie and Will, spotting them at a luggage shop at the end of the narrow block. Sophie turned, her eyebrows raised questioningly. Will, too, swiveled and spotted me.

I raised my hand, signaling them to stay put. I cautiously leaned around the corner and took another look at the man. Was it the Skipper?

Same height, same posture, same build. My thoughts raced. Questions flooded my mind. It had been dark and rainy the night when I saw the Skipper. Dare I confront this man? Should I follow him?

Two children and a woman approached him carrying packages. He embraced the boy and girl, as well as the woman accompanying them. I heard him say, "Milda." Was this his family? The woman smiled at the children, and then she looked lovingly at the Skipper. Very likely his family, I decided.

He caught me staring. I sucked in a sharp breath. With a pleasant nod and zero recognition in his gaze, he turned and sauntered off with his family. I watched him walk away.

Sophie came up behind me with her new carry-on. "You're shopping?"

I couldn't tell her I thought I'd just seen her husband's kidnapper. Had I? "Nothing. I just needed to get a pebble out of my shoe."

Will shot me a puzzled, "What's up?" He gave me a close look. I raised my eyebrows and shook my head. Nothing.

That man had seemed calm and normal. I decided I was spooked. I couldn't accuse every man I saw wearing a black fisherman's cap of being a kidnapper.

Our guide led us out of the labyrinth.

Sidestepping strangers, we elbowed our way out of the crowded bazaar. We hailed a taxi, asked to be dropped at a café for lunch, and then returned to our hotel to pack and check out.

***

We arrived at the Hotel Citadel at three o'clock. Will lingered outside to touch base with Travis. Sophie and I walked through the lobby doors to find pandemonium. Musicians were setting up and waiters scurried around food stations. Hotel staff stood on ladders to hang flowered garlands, while others placed silverware and napkins on cream-colored tablecloths. A clerk waved us over to the end of the reception counter. "You have reservations?"

"Yes, for Sophie Alexakis."

He hit a few keys on an antiquated computer, and then he smiled at Sophie. "I have three rooms for Sophie Alexakis."

"What is all this?" asked Sophie, handing the clerk her credit card.

"Wedding tonight." He quickly checked us in and gave us our room keys, and then emphatically told us there were no more rooms for the night.

Monte and Eznik raced up to us, breathless, their duffel bags in tow.

Will followed them at a slower pace. He took the jewel stuffed suitcase from me. "Can I give you a hand?"

We made our way to our rooms on the second floor. In the narrow, ornate hallways, the wood floors under the faded Turkish runners creaked as we pulled our suitcases and duffels behind us. Plants in colorful stands stood near high windows cracked open to let in the cold air. I noted the location farther down the hallway of Monte and Eznik's room.

Will opened our door, revealing a tiny room, a third of the size of our last room. Screaming yellow bedspreads, matching flocked wallpaper, gold carpeting, and sheer golden curtains added insult to injury. My senses rejected the entire color scheme.

"Beggars can't be choosers," I said.

Sophie sighed, "We made it."

"Now, we wait," I said. "A trial, I know, but we'll get through it."

Sophie nodded. "Trials bring perseverance, which is a good thing."

"Humm." I dumped my suitcase on the bed.

Will wheeled the suitcase with the jewels into the closet. "You're right, Sophie. Trials do teach perseverance."

She sat on her bed. "Someone once said that if there were only joy in the world, we would never learn to be brave and patient."

"That from your Bible?" I tried to keep my voice even.

"No, I think it was Helen Keller."

"Oh. Well, she would know."

Will said, "Since we weren't able to book an extra room, and we can't take the piece of luggage we just bought to dinner; we should just order room service, don't you think?

Sophie paled. "Yes. We can't miss that call from the kidnappers!"

I nodded. "Room service makes the most sense. Will, would you tell the guys to order room service? We can all rendezvous here at eight-thirty."

Sophie hefted her suitcase onto the bed. "Will, join us, please. Six thirty sound alright?"

"Love to."

She unzipped the bag, pulling out her robe and

slippers. "I'm exhausted, for no reason. I'm going to lie down."

Will stood. "I'll get out of your way. Actually, a nap sounds good." He left us with a wink.

I sat on the edge of the bed. My first calm moment since leaving California. "I'm calling my mom."

"Good, you should."

It didn't take long for the connection to go through.

"Hello?" My mother sounded wide-awake and alert.

"Mom, it's Jenna."

"Oh, Jenna, thank goodness. I thought it was the hospital." She yawned into the phone. "Ralph called and said you were in Turkey! Are you okay?"

"I'm fine, Mom. Tell me about Dad. How's he doing?"

"He had another stroke last night."

"Oh, no!" I stood and walked to the window. A flood of adrenaline coursed through me.

"They say this one may have caused more damage. It seemed like he was doing so well."

"Which side is affected?"

"His left. He's so angry, Jenna. I see it in his eyes. He's not scared. He's furious. He tries to write things on paper, but his brain won't cooperate." Her voice caught.

I didn't like to hear her so upset. On a good day, Dad was a piece of work.

She yawned again. "I'm exhausted. And after last night, I'm afraid of what he'll be like today."

"What about Maddie? Or Francie?"

"Maddie comes and goes. You know, she's always on the phone with her work. Francie's gonna pop that fourth baby any minute. She can't get down here."

"How are you holding up? You getting any rest?"

"Yes, some." She yawned again. "Uncle Nick and Aunt Paula are flying in today, and that'll help."

"You taking your juices and vitamins?" I'm talking to a woman with her master's in nutrition, for God's sake.

She chuckled. "Of course. I can't possibly get sick when your father needs me. He wouldn't stand for it."

I smiled. "And Luke? How's he holding up?"

"Not well. He blames himself, because he called here late that night. Your dad gave him hell for waking us up. A few hours later, he had the stroke."

"It figures. When it comes to Dad, Luke's always the scapegoat."

An uncomfortable silence extended for a few moments. "Ralph said you were working a kidnapping in Istanbul."

"Yeah. The bad guys got spooked, took the husband to Istanbul." Should I tell her the rest? I weighed my options. Knowing my mom, she'd kill me if I kept my news from her. "Mom, I have something to tell you. It's going to be a shock, so brace yourself." I waited a beat. "Yesterday, my Isaac showed up on my doorstep."

She gasped. "Oh, my gosh! Why didn't you tell me? What's he like?"

"Mom, he never knew he was adopted. Kent and

Lizabeth didn't tell him. He just found out by accident several weeks ago. He took off and decided to find me. He's tall, blond, the spittin' image of Jayson. Mom, and he's a wonderful kid, sweet, smart, you'll love him."

Mom's voice broke with tears. "I'm so happy for you! Where is he now, while you're gone?"

My turn to tear up. "He, he got involved in this case."

"No! What happened?"

Sophie came out of the bathroom clad in her robe.

I turned to the window and looked out. "It was stupid and impulsive. Isaac tried to help rescue Sarkis, and the kidnappers took him, too."

"Oh, my God, Jenna. Who is Sarkis?"

"Sophie St. James' husband."

"Oh, right! Right. Ralph mentioned that. I've read about her father so many times."

"Kent came down from Boise to take Isaac home. This situation's bad, Mom."

"I wish you'd called us."

"It happened so fast. So, Sophie St. James and I jumped on a chartered jet…"

"Alexakis," Sophie corrected me.

"Right. Sophie Alexakis…"

"Is she a nice woman?"

"Absolutely."

"I can't believe you're in Istanbul."

"It's nothing like you'd think. You'd like it. It's old world, but it's modern, too."

"When are you coming home?"

"In two days, if all goes well."

"I hate this business you're in. Are the FBI involved?"

I sighed. "No, Mom, Sophie wanted to obey all of the kidnappers' instructions to make sure she gets her husband back."

"I'm sorry, I just don't understand that, but will you please, please be very careful?"

"I will, Mom. I'm sorry I couldn't be there to help with Dad. I'll be home soon, though."

"I understand, dear. I know you love your dad."

I considered this. "Tell Dad I'll visit him the minute I hit town."

"I'll tell him."

My voice cracked. "And... tell him I love him." I couldn't take anymore. "Bye, Mom. I love you."

THIRTY-TWO

I sat there, holding the phone as I rounded up my emotions. As Sophie dozed off, I took a shower. I put on fresh jeans and layered a black tee under a long gray sweater.

I tossed around a few plans in my head for the exchange. It had to go down perfectly. I do my best while I pace. And so I paced the ten feet to the door and back. At a little before five o'clock, someone shoved a square white envelope under the door. I sucked in my breath, jerked open the door, and looked down the hall. Nothing. I tore open the envelope. 'Contact tonight. Midnight.'

The band in the café below started to rehearse. Raucous laughter filtered up the stairs. Music thrummed and the walls of the hotel vibrated. My stress kicked into overdrive.

I gazed at Sophie. Her mouth slightly open, she looked dead to the world. No sense in disturbing her.

I missed Ralph's direction and his sweet, burly presence. I wondered if he'd been able to contact Sophie's doctors.

Sophie's slim green Bible lay atop the nightstand. On a whim, I picked it up. *The New International Version.* I leafed through it, reading the notes in the margins that Sophie made over the years. She had underlined words, used arrows, and drawn circles around repeated phrases.

My usual resistance to anything 'Christian' stalled, but my questions remained. If the Christians in the world asked for what they wanted from God, then why didn't we have world peace? Jayson had disappeared from the face of the earth. That was God's plan? And what about Zach? Nineteen years without him had been pure hell, thank you very much. And why did we have wars, murder, and terminal illnesses? Why was evil winning over goodness? Surely the good Christians of the world prayed for deliverance from all of these things. My normal argument was that God wasn't living up to His end of the bargain. Yet I was now struggling with feelings that were foreign to me. What if I was wrong?

Sophie began to stir. I closed the Bible and put it back on the nightstand.

After a few minutes, I said quietly, "Soph, we heard from the kidnappers."

Her eyes opened. She struggled to sit up. Still groggy, she frowned at me. "When? What did they say?"

"This was shoved under the door." I handed her the slip of paper.

She grabbed it and scanned the message. "They made it. Thank you, God." She took a pillow and hugged it. "Do you think it's almost over?"

"When we are all on the jet and heading west, it'll be over."

She bent over the pillow and wept.

Quite frankly, I wanted to weep too. Was Zach as exhausted as I was?

"We'll get em'." I managed, patting her shoulder.

She shook her head. "Sorry. I just pictured us on that jet together. Going home. Sorry."

"No need to apologize to me."

Her voice cracked, as she said, "Alright." She frowned, hearing the racket from the lobby. "Is that the wedding?"

"That's the wedding."

I answered a knock at the door, stepping aside as Will entered our room. "Wow. You've got it bad. Sounds like the band's in the next room."

"What's it like upstairs?"

"Well, I can hear myself think." He shook his head in disgust.

I handed him the note we'd received.

He whistled. "Well, now we know." He glanced at Sophie, who dabbed at her eyes with a tissue.

I nodded.

Will called room service and ordered dinner for the three of us. I informed Monte and Eznik that we'd heard from the kidnappers, and reminded them about the eight-thirty meeting in our room.

Dinner arrived, a tasty chicken stew, chock full of vegetables, individual salads and a basket of warm rolls.

Sophie wrinkled her nose. "That smell!" She shuddered. "It's revolting. She picked at her salad and a roll, and meticulously fished tiny pieces of chicken from the stew.

Will devoured every bite on his plate. "Nothing smells bad to me. In fact, it's really good."

I had cleaned my plate, too. "The last time certain smells bothered me, I was pregnant. I couldn't stand the scent of vanilla or the taste of tomatoes." No sooner were the words out of my mouth, a checklist started inside my head. Things fell into place.

The very idea stunned me. But Sophie had claimed she couldn't become pregnant. I leaned in to her. "Soph. Listen to me. Nausea, dizziness, peeing all the time, no energy, taking naps every chance you get." I stopped and opened my hands. "What's that add up to?"

Will sat quietly, watching us like a ping-pong match.

She frowned and shook her head. "I'm not sure what you're getting at."

"When was your last period?" I asked.

She opened her mouth, and then closed it. Seconds later, shock registered on her face. "No. It's not possible…"

"It adds up, Soph." I cleared my throat. "I'd bet on it. And add the emotional roller coaster you've been on…"

"But…" she began as a knock at the door signaled the arrival of the brothers. Right on time.

I patted her shoulder. "Let's finish this later."

Will moved the dinner cart into the hallway before settling into the only chair in the hotel room. Monte and Eznik sat on the bed across from us.

They seemed subdued, contact from the kidnappers seeming to sober them.

I explained the course of action I wanted to take. "I figure they'll have weapons on them when Monte and I arrive…"

"No problem. I've got weapons." He crossed his arms with a satisfied nod.

Alarm coursed through me. Neither brother had weapons on them when we left the States. "Where did you get them? We're not using weapons, Monte. We discussed this."

He shot to his feet. "We must protect ourselves."

"They'll just frisk us and take them. Forget it."

Monte's face reddened. "You're willing to walk into that situation with no weapons?"

"Listen, I'm playing the part of Sophie. Sarkis' wife comes in with a gun strapped to her ankle? Or has a weapon tucked into her purse? No way. No guns."

"Your choice."

"Yes, it is." I leveled a hard look at him and held it for a three count. "We were shot at the last time there was an exchange, thanks to you. No guns."

"Big mistake," he said.

"You picked up guns from the friends you went to visit, didn't you?"

He wouldn't answer me.

I resisted telling him I knew he'd worked at Interpol years before. Instead, I ignored him. "They may not give us much time to get to where we're supposed to meet them. Our sole objective will be to hand over the Bible, get our guys, and leave."

Monte demanded, "What if they tie us up? They might keep us prisoners until they get..." He glared at me. "... whatever it is they're after."

The previous night and the house in Kum Kapi crossed my mind, but I stood my ground in the crowded room. "These criminals have based their actions and their demands on some handwritten directions in a Bible." I shook my head, acting puzzled. "A treasure buried a hundred years ago. We have no idea if someone discovered it decades ago. The kidnappers will get exactly what they're demanding: the Bible."

Monte glowered at me. Eznik stared at his shoes.

Sophie cleared her throat. "Jenna, Eznik, Will and I will follow you at a safe distance. I want to be nearby."

Shocked, I kept my voice level... "No. Absolutely,

categorically, No. Remember what happened the last time? Don't you remember what you said to me after Zach was taken? You felt terrible, guilty. You wept. You said it was your fault he'd been taken."

Add the fact that she might be pregnant. I would not willingly put her at risk.

She was dead serious. "Sorry, I'm not sitting in a hotel room while you rescue Sarkis and Zach. I know what I said back then, but I want to be close by when they release them. Jenna, I promise, we'll stay far enough away to be safe. No one will even know we're there."

"Been there, done that, and got the victims to prove it," I snapped.

Will said, "I think it's a good idea. Sophie, Eznik and I will follow at a distance, like back up. Just in case."

"Back up? How are you going to back us up? Just in case of what? And who told you that you get a vote? I don't care what you think, Will. It's too dangerous."

Monte sat across from Sophie. "Don't worry. If anything goes wrong, Eznik and I know this country, and we have friends."

Blood rushed to my face. "You three are certifiable! This isn't a friggin' movie! The kidnapper's instructions stated no police, which excludes a California support group."

I continued. "Look, we have no authority in this country and I don't even want to know if we break any laws. Can we all agree on our main goal? Rescue Zach and Sarkis and leave Turkey, in that order?" I looked at Sophie. "And what about the possibility we were discussing right before Monte and Eznik arrived?"

Sophie shook her head with a short exclamation. "That's too far fetched to be possible, Jenna. Look, I want to be close by, so we're following you. End of discussion."

My nerves felt raw. The pressure was building. "Fine, do whatever you want to do." I pointed a finger in Monte's face, "No guns. None!"

No one said anything.

I sighed. "Let's get some rest. We'll call you the minute we hear something."

The brothers agreed and left, saying they'd be ready.

Sophie went into the bathroom, which left Will and me alone.

He gave me a quizzical look. "We okay?"

He shouldn't have sided with Sophie. I glared at him.

Will smiled. "Talk to me, Jenna."

"I'm responsible. You're not. This involves my son, his protection, and my client's protection. This thing went south once before because Sophie, Monte and Eznik interfered."

"I'm sorry I upset you. It sounded good that Sophie should see her husband immediately after his release. But now I understand your concern."

"You should've understood ten minutes ago."

"I'll let you get some rest." He paused, then asked again, "Are we okay?"

I shrugged irritably. "What does that even mean,

Will? There is no 'we'. There's no history, hence, no relationship. You're standing in the middle of a kidnapping and you're taking the side of an emotionally distraught wife, and the two idiots who got us into this mess."

I saw the hurt I'd inflicted in his eyes.

After a long moment, he said, "I'll talk to you later, then. Get some rest if you can." He turned and walked out of the room.

THIRTY-THREE

The wedding was going strong downstairs, replete with loud music and boisterous guests.

Sophie lay sprawled on her bed, asleep again.

I was amazed. I was about to meet with her husband's kidnappers, and she's out like a light. She had to be pregnant. When she awakened a little while later, I asked, "How are you?"

She shook her head in wonder. "I just had a crazy dream."

"Yeah?"

She thought a moment. "Sarkis and I were eating that chicken stew we had tonight. You and Will were there, and Dad and Gwen. We were so happy about the stew, we all cried." She shook her head. "Like I said, crazy."

A knock sounded at the door. Scrambling off my bed, I answered it and found a hotel clerk with a note. Sophie stood behind me, trembling.

The clerk held a sealed envelope and a set of car keys. In halting English, he said that a cab driver had requested immediate delivery to Sophie Alexakis' hotel room. I thanked him before I shut the door.

I ripped open the envelope, which contained an address and the time. Twelve midnight. The key was to a car out front. The bedside clock read 11:45.

I called Monte and Eznik's room. "Show time." Then, I called Will. "It's on."

Sophie held the old Begosian Bible close to her chest. From below, I heard the wedding guests as they sang old Turkish songs, ethnic, earthy, and full of passion.

"Are you worried?" Sophie asked.

I pulled on a heavier black turtleneck over my long-sleeved tee shirt.

"Just nervous." I shrugged into my wool coat, shoved my gloves and hat in my pockets.

"I've been praying for you." She looked scared as hell.

"Thanks. You thinking about what we discussed?"

She shook her head. "Come on, Jenna. It's impossible. I can't be pregnant."

I wound a scarf around my neck. "I don't want to get your hopes up, but I think it's very possible."

A soft knock sounded. Will and the brothers filed in when I opened the door.

They saw the car keys and the note. Will called the front desk for a taxi, which would follow the car Monte and I would use. He read the directions aloud and Eznik copied them down.

Monte turned to me. "It's not far. Just a couple of miles." He folded the paper and put it his pocket.

I approached him. "You're not gonna like this, but I need to pat you down." I didn't like it either, but I trusted him as far as I could spit in that wind outside.

The corner of his mouth slid into a smile as he held out his arms. The cigarette smoke on his clothes reeked. Holding my breath, I patted him down. No weapons. "Good, we're ready then."

Eznik said something in Turkish to his brother. "English, Eznik! We all need to be on the same page," I snapped.

Eznik reddened. "It was Armenian. I said, 'Go with God.'"

Monte raised his hands to calm everyone. "We're all jumpy. I'm your interpreter, your guide. I'm here to do the job. Let's do it."

I gritted my teeth, somehow managing not to smack him into next week.

Will reached out and patted his shoulder. "That's appreciated." He gave me a hopeful smile.

Whatever. Slapping around my coat pockets for the room key, I found it.

Sophie buttoned her jacket. Then, almost reverently,

she handed the old Bible to me. "Here." She reached out and took my hands. "Do the right thing, Jenna. If they change the rules, do whatever it takes. Tell them we have money."

I nodded. "Right now, I don't expect problems. The plan is to go in, get Sarkis and Zach, and then get out." Monte waited silently by the door.

Gripping the Bible, I nodded to Will. "Let's go."

Monte nodded. "We're ready." He and Eznik went out the door. Sophie followed.

Will touched my shoulder. "I don't mind telling you how scared I am. Promise me you'll play nice? Be safe?"

"I always play nice." I frowned. "Tell Monte to play nice." Fear had wormed its way into my plans and I wasn't used to this feeling of powerlessness.

Together we traveled down the stairs and through a crowd of wedding guests. We exited the hotel and stepped out onto the street. Monte located the car, a dark blue sedan. The wind blew strong and cold, although nothing like the previous night.

"We'll be behind you." Sophie's voice trembled. Her long black curls whipped around her head in the cold breeze.

Feeling impotent and furious, I rounded on Sophie. "Soph, you and Will stay far back and way out of sight, do you hear me? Out. Of. Sight." My voice shook with anger. I felt weak, defenseless and totally responsible.

"I'll see to it," said Will.

They watched me climb into the sedan. Their taxi pulled up behind us.

I gave them a curt nod as Monte pulled away from the curb.

Oddly enough, I felt comfortable with Monte at the wheel. He drove with deliberate calm.

An uneasy silence fell between us. As he negotiated the streets, I reminded myself of my initial suspicion of him. Distrust kept me sharp and on my game.

Breaking the silence, I asked, "How, after all these years, do you remember what streets to take?"

He gave a slight shrug. "The truth is, our parents didn't send us here, Eznik and I were sent here undercover. We made a game of learning the streets."

"Did you make friends with any of the local Turks when you lived here?"

"Yeah, we have a lot of friends. Most Turks are wonderful people. But, if you bring up the past, they consider you a troublemaker. Most Turks don't believe the Armenian genocide happened. They insist the Turks relocated the Armenians to other countries."

I made a rude sound.

Monte continued, "Some of our friends here are sympathetic to the Armenian point of view, but they feel there is nothing they can do about it. It's old history."

The streets were dark. Either there were no streetlights to illumine the old part of Istanbul, or they were in disrepair.

"Old history," I agreed. "Yeah, even now the Turkish government denies they did anything wrong."

He nodded in agreement. "Eznik and I were stunned to hear the lies the government tells."

Would have been nice if I could've trusted him. "What happened to your hate?"

Monte snorted, "Life has a way of catching up with you. I joined the organization to feed the hate I felt and it's worked for the most part. Lately?" He shook his head. "I've been wondering what good it does. I've been wondering why."

Monte slowed the car and turned into an empty lot full of rocks and weeds. He killed the lights and looked out across the street at an industrial complex that appeared abandoned.

Gray clouds skittered across the black sky, and I saw stars scattered between the clouds. Neighborhood after neighborhood surrounded our location. Up one hill and down the next, the single-family homes reminded me of rows of brownstone apartment buildings.

Monte glanced at me. "You ready?"

"I'm as ready as I'll ever be." My heart hammered in my chest, probably loud enough for him to hear it. "Tell them exactly what I say. Interpret back to me precisely what they say. Be calm. We want to see both Sarkis and Zach before I surrender the Bible. Got it?"

"Got it."

"We're on the same page?"

"Right. The guys first, then hand over the book." He parked the car in front of an old warehouse.

We got out of the car, and I looked around. I saw no sign of Will and Sophie's taxi.

Cold air crept down my neck, and I tightened my scarf. I hugged the Bible close to my body. Strangely, I felt comforted by it.

We stood before a large dilapidated building. The fleeting moonlight made the place look deserted.

Out of nowhere, two men with guns appeared behind us.

Crap. Nervous, I turned and displayed the Bible. One of the men nodded and pointed at the door. Monte and I moved forward. One of the men spoke sharply to Monte. He stopped in his tracks. I hesitated.

Monte said, "I cannot go inside. You are to enter through here."

"Forget it. Tell them I need an interpreter." The guy with the rifle shoved me forward, shouting at me in Turkish.

Monte nodded at me. "Go ahead, Jenna. Tell the man in charge I'm out here."

My mouth went dry. Swallowing hard, I turned to the door, tucking the Bible under an arm and twisted the doorknob.

The door, once painted white, displayed a thousand fingerprint smudges. Another guard with a gun pointed to a door at the end of the hallway. I walked on.

The next door made a low, scraping sound as it opened. The shadowy warehouse resonated each noise.

The storehouse, vast and virtually empty, smelled oddly pungent. Chemicals mixed with a musty sweetness. Two men stood inside the door. From the dim lamp hanging high above us, I observed footprints on the dusty floor. At the rear of the room, two more men guarded the rear door. Looked like the only way out. I scanned around the room, and I spotted another door to the right.

Sarkis and Zach sat side by side on an empty crate, surrounded by three armed men. Zach, sitting straight and alert, watched my every move. Sarkis, his posture slouched, looked tired and uncomfortable. Their wrists and ankles were duct taped. Zach's mouth was duct-taped, but not Sarkis'. I counted ten men, Zach, Sarkis and me. I needed Monte.

"Sarkis," I said softly, playing to the perps. My heart hammered in my chest. "Hey, Zach."

I'd recognized the Skipper at the bazaar, after all, I realized. He still wore the captain's hat he'd worn in California. His phone rang. He answered, glaring at me.

I looked past him and called out, "Sarkis! Are you all right, honey?"

The Skipper demanded in English "Who is outside?"

"My interpreter. He speaks excellent Turkish."

"I said to come alone!" He spat the words.

"I hired him so I could understand you and obey all

of your requests." My hands shook, and I tried to get a grip on my fear.

He nodded at the guards who stood near the door. *Thank God.* Zach and Sarkis made no effort to communicate. I figured they'd been warned.

"Can I talk to my husband?"

"Hayir!" I bet that was a no.

Monte walked into the storeroom and stood next to me, looking around with a casual glance. "Can you imagine heating this place?" His attitude seemed way too confident.

The Skipper studied Monte. Without warning, he started to yell at us, pacing and gesturing wildly.

I hugged the Bible under my sweater. "What's he saying?"

"He said you did not listen the first time. He calls you an imbecile, a stupid shameful wife, and he demands to know why you did not obey him in the first place?"

"Tell him he's right."

Monte gave him my reply.

The Skipper stopped ranting, and smiled, the crow's feet around his eyes deepening.

What an ass.

With an abrupt shout, one of the other men spoke harshly to the Skipper. I shrank back in surprise at the vehemence in his voice. His face contorted with rage as he shouted right into the Skipper's face.

Beside me, Monte made a protesting sound.

"Careful, Monte, careful."

Monte spoke to the shouting man in Turkish.

"Quiet. I told you not to say anything."

"He says I am the man who killed his brother." Monte kept his eyes on the Skipper as he spoke.

Confused, I frowned. "Killed his brother?" Then it hit me. The dead man on Sophie's front lawn. *Double crap.*

The Skipper swung around in a wide arc, shouting at everyone in the room. Spittle flew from his mouth. The other man began to crank up again.

The Skipper roared, "Emre! Emre!"

The man ignored the Skipper. He walked over to Monte and frisked him. Monte muttered words I didn't understand.

Without warning, the angry man spat into Monte's face.

"Monte, shut up!" Terrified, I wanted to shake him.

Monte wiped his face. "I didn't shoot his brother. And it was an accident."

"Shut up!"

"All I did was ask him if he was planning to kill more innocent people to add to the legacy of Turkish barbarianism."

I turned and smacked Monte in the chest. "Keep your mouth shut!"

I stepped back as the man put his gun up to Monte's head. Spewing angry Turkish phrases, he cocked the weapon. I reared back and put my hands up.

The Skipper's cell phone suddenly shrilled. He bellowed. Everyone froze. No one spoke.

The Skipper ended the call and spoke to his men.

Monte paled. "They're bringing in Sophie, Eznik and Will!"

THIRTY-FOUR

I almost keeled over. The warehouse door opened. Armed men led the three into view. Sophie saw Sarkis and cried out his name.

"Enough!" Skipper shouted in English.

Sarkis tried to stand, but one of the guards shoved him back down. Zach's worry showed in his eyes, and my anxiety spiked.

"Quiet, Sophie!" I ordered.

Monte made a sudden grab for the weapon still being held to his head, knocking the gunman off balance. The two men struggled for control of the weapon.

I screamed, "Monte, stop!"

A single shot rang out. Everyone froze.

I caught a movement and looked at Sophie.

Absolute surprise swept across her face as she sank to both knees, her gaze on Sarkis as she went down. Crimson blood seeped through her beige wool coat, forming a large flower-shaped stain.

Trying to catch her, Will cried, "She's been hit!"

"No!" Sarkis stood. "Sophie! Sophie!"

Guards reached out to seize him.

The Skipper shouted orders. Two guards dragged Sarkis toward the rear of the building. A third man walked backwards to the door, pointing his weapon at us. One guard grabbed Zach, who put up a fight.

I watched Zach's forced retreat in horror.

Zach broke free of his captor, running for the side door. Then, he stopped dead, turned to look at Sarkis, the latter kicking at his captors, and screaming Sophie's name. I met my son's gaze. I gasped.

He didn't want to abandon Sarkis.

"Run, Zach!" I roared. "Go!"

Zach darted out the side door. His guard headed for the rear exit. Sarkis' guttural, frantic cries, "Sophie! Sophie! Sophie!" resounded over and over as they pulled him through the back exit.

Sophie lay on her side on the filthy floor. Will crouched next to her, cradling the unconscious woman.

I grabbed Eznik's arm. "Find out where the kidnappers are, see if they left, then get the car."

Monte tossed the keys to Eznik, and he raced off.

"Monte, find Zach. He ran out the side door." For a change, he followed my order.

Will and I peeled off her blood soaked beige jacket. Will kept steady pressure on Sophie's wound to try to stop the bleeding. I unbuttoned her shirt to check the entry wound in her upper left chest. Wild with alarm, I looked around for something to staunch the flow of blood. "We've got to slow down that blood flow."

I leaned Sophie forward and felt along her back and shoulder. There was no exit wound. Not good.

I whipped off my coat, hauled my sweater over my head, took off my gray tee shirt, and handed it to Will. "Here." He folded the small shirt, and pressed it to the wound.

"Give it constant pressure, and don't let up." I hurriedly dressed.

"Sarkis?" Sophie mumbled.

Will made a shushing sound. "It's all right."

"Jenna?"

"Don't worry. Everything's fine, Sophie."

"Fine?" A look of confusion crossed Sophie's face. "I've been shot. Right?"

I nodded. "Right."

Sophie frowned. "It stings..." With that she fainted.

Eznik raced into view. "The car's out front, and our taxi driver is still here."

"Monte's looking for Zach." I pointed to the side door. He took off.

"How bad is this?" Will asked.

"I don't think it's life threatening, but she needs a hospital."

I heard a commotion at the door. I glanced up as Zach walked inside, rubbing his wrists. A rectangular welt of red from the duct tape surrounded his mouth.

"Zach!" I stood as he flew into my arms. I held him tight, overwhelmed with gratitude.

"I'm sorry. I'm so sorry about everything. I thought I could help. I'm so sorry."

"You're alive, that's all I care about. We need to get Sophie out of here."

"Is it bad?"

I nodded. "No exit wound." I turned to Will, Monte, and Eznik. "Monte, you're driving. Zach and Eznik will follow us in the taxi."

Monte and Eznik transported Sophie out to the car with Will maintaining steady pressure against her wound. Will climbed into the back seat, and the brothers shifted Sophie into a position that allowed him to sustain the pressure.

I ran to Zach as he and Eznik were about to get into the taxi and embraced him again. "See you back at the hotel."

"Okay, Mom, Jennmom, Jenna..." it came out as a run-on sentence.

Tears filled my eyes, but I blinked them away. No time for that stuff now.

While Monte drove, I sat shotgun, terrified about Sophie and wanting this entire nightmare to end. Monte spoke as an aside to me, "Best to get all our things, our passports..."

Will made a call on his cell phone. "No questions, Travis. We've got trouble. Get to the airport; file a flight plan to Athens, ASAP. We'll try to make it to the airport within the hour. I'll explain later." He hung up. "He'll be waiting for us."

With obvious care, Monte drove back to the hotel.

"Shouldn't we get her to a hospital first?" I asked Will.

Monte spoke up before Will could answer. "Athens is a better choice if it's not too serious a wound. Fewer questions from the authorities."

Will agreed. "Yes, it's an hour to Athens. Travis is filing the flight plan, and the jet's already been refueled."

I pivoted in my seat to speak to Will. "Okay...once you are in the air, call her father's office. Let her dad know what's happened. Have him call Athens and get the best doctor money can buy to meet you with an ambulance."

"Wait a minute," Will said, genuine alarm in his beautiful eyes. "You're not coming with us?"

"I'm staying here. Sarkis is still out there."

"Jenna."

Monte spoke up. "We will have to pass through security. How do we explain Sophie?"

I cast about for a plausible explanation. "Car accident?" I looked at Will.

Monte vehemently shook his head.

"What?" I demanded, my nerves already frayed.

"She is ill, with food poisoning. With the last name of Alexakis, she can leave for Greece, no question, especially if she has her own charter. A car accident means an investigation and reports." Monte's logic was convincing.

Will nodded his agreement. "That works."

"Okay then, food poisoning it is."

As Monte drove, I stared at the pulse in Sophie's neck, my eyes measuring each beat as I willed Sophie to survive.

I brought out the old Bible, and placed it on my lap.

Sophie murmured, then cried out. Will stroked her forehead with his fingertips and hushed her.

Shaking my head, I looked at my bloody hands. How had everything gone so wrong? What had I been thinking? I'd entered into a foreign country and acted without the help of proper authorities. My own Zach had been at risk, yet I'd tried to do everything on my own, my way. Who did I think I was? And Sarkis. Fear gnawed at me. Where was he now? I felt a lump form in my throat so large and tight I nearly choked on it.

At 1:00 a.m. Monte pulled into the driveway that led to the rear of the hotel. The taxi followed. I got out of our car, ran to the taxi, overpaid the driver, and asked him to wait. I whipped off my coat and struggled to manuver Sophie's arms into it. I buttoned it to the top to hide any blood seepage.

Eznik and Zach rushed to the car to help Will extricate Sophie's inert form from the vehicle. The two brothers, positioned like bookends carried Sophie.

Will removed his coat, draping it over his arm to conceal the blood on his slacks.

"Okay, act like we tied one on," I muttered, barely registering the cold air.

A few staff cleared tables and chairs from the wedding reception. A night clerk at the front desk saw us enter the lobby. A look of uncertainty crossed his face.

Monte and Eznik, Sophie between them, chorused, "Merhaba!" *Hello!* Zach and Will walked on either side of me, our arms intertwined. We staggered and lurched, feigning drunkenness.

Sophie groaned.

Will called out, "Merhaba!" Monte mimed drinking from a glass.

The clerk nodded and waved, all smiles now.

Smiling and singing, Will waved goodnight. I shushed him and giggled as we climbed the stairs.

Monte and Eznik took care not to jar Sophie as they placed her on one of the beds in our hotel room. She resembled a limp, broken doll. Zach dashed into the bathroom for clean towels. Eznik took one, blotting the blood that covered her shoulder and throat. I peeled off her blood-soaked blouse. Blood slowly oozed from the wound.

As I studied the bullet's entry point, I ground my teeth. I turned Sophie over and checked thoroughly for an exit wound. Nothing.

"If you're the praying type, start now." I said. "I think

the bullet hit her collarbone, and it's still somewhere inside her. God, I hope it didn't ricochet near anything vital."

"That explains her not being able to move her left arm." Will placed pillows under her knees and feet. "Hand me that extra blanket."

Zach asked, "How much blood do you think she's lost?"

I shook my head, assuring him, "Not enough to scare me." Obviously, I lied. I hadn't noticed that Sophie wasn't using her left arm. Terror flooded me. I kept my voice even to keep the guys calm. What damage had been done internally? The Bible lay on the bed. The strength I had always depended on, was gone. I had a distinct feeling of unraveling. Have I missed out on something very important? Was God really there? *God, please protect Sophie.* The thought just came out of nowhere in my head. *She believes in You, so help her please.*

Will tore strips of fabric from a clean bed sheet. Together, we fashioned bandages, gently lifting her to wrap them around her wound. Although unconscious, Sophie groaned out her pain.

"We'll be right back." Monte and Eznik left the room.

"Where are they going?" Zach asked.

"I don't know, and I couldn't care less."

Zach gathered the soiled linens and Sophie's blood-soaked blouse, bundling them up and setting them near the door.

I found my black blouse, and then pulled out Sophie's black, knee length, wool coat. Will helped me dress her.

Sophie regained consciousness. She stared as we hovered over her.

Alarmed by her ashen complexion, I rubbed Sophie's cheek.

Sophie swiped at my hand. "Don't. Where's Sarkis?"

"Hold on and I'll tell you everything." Man, shot in the chest and she still had fight left in her.

Monte and Eznik returned with clean towels and sheets from their room.

I handed the bloody bundle to Eznik, "Find a trash bin and toss this stuff. Then, pack your bags and take them down to the car. We leave right away."

Monte started to speak, but he seemed to think better of it. Wise move.

"Five minutes," I said.

They departed as Will hovered over Sophie. I joined him. "Will, go get your things together too? We need to get her to the airport a.s.a.p."

Will nodded. "She's quiet now. I'll be right back."

"Zach, keep an eye on Sophie."

He settled beside her and took her hand.

I checked the suitcase with the gems. Still there. The gems would remain here until Will and I could get them out of the country.

"Jenna," Sophie called out, her voice hoarse. "Where's Sarkis?"

Zach leaned in close. "Try not to speak or move, Sophie."

"I want Sarkis," she said, her voice frail.

I threw her things into her suitcase, found her passport in her purse, and took all of her Turkish lira, stuffing them inside my backpack. "You've been shot and you've lost some blood, Sophie. Will and Zach are taking you to an Athens hospital for surgery. You're going to be all right."

"Sarkis?" Her eyes pleaded.

"I'm meeting Sarkis very soon. Right now, we need to get you on that plane. I won't leave Turkey without him, and I'll bring him back to you."

"Thank you." Sophie closed her eyes in a spasm of pain. "Jesus... protect them." Tears streamed from her eyes, trailing into her hair. "I really messed up, didn't I? We parked three blocks away. But they were waiting for us."

"Come on, that's nothing. I messed up a lot worse." Zach's eyes also swam with tears.

I blotted Sophie's face with a tissue. "You didn't do anything wrong. None of this was your fault, Sophie." It was my fault for not enforcing my own rules. I was beyond demoralized and infuriated with myself.

I put her passport in my coat. Turning to my son, I said, "Zach! Your passport?"

He stood and reached into his back pocket and brought it out. "Sarkis told me we always needed to be ready to escape; and if either one of us ever had the chance, to take it. Our guards kept our passports, but we stole them back yesterday morning while they made breakfast."

I heard a single knock at the door, and I nodded at Zach. He admitted Monte, Eznik and Will.

"Our suitcase is in the taxi," Eznik said.

I handed Zach Sophie's suitcase, and shouldered my backpack with the Bible inside.

Monte and Eznik lifted a conscious, moaning Sophie, shouldering her weight between them.

At the front desk, the night managers were going over the day's receipts. They looked up as we descended the stairs.

The night clerk came out of a back office. He approached us, full of concern. "Can we help?"

Monte spoke in rapid Turkish.

I leaned in to Eznik, "What's he saying?"

Eznik interpreted. "Our friend needs a doctor. We've called and the hospital is expecting us."

The clerk gave Sophie a once over. "One of our guests is a doctor. We'll wake him for you." He gave us a nod.

Monte snorted. "A wedding guest?"

The clerk beamed as he nodded.

Monte said in Turkish, "We're not having a half-drunk doctor examine our friend. We're going to a hospital."

The manager backed off, speaking with deference to Monte.

"He says he hopes our friend will get better."

THIRTY-FIVE

We left the lobby, carefully loading Sophie into the rear of the sedan. Zach and I stayed with her. Will and Eznik followed with the luggage in the taxi.

As we drove, Monte broke the tension-filled silence in the car. "Jenna. I…"

"Monte, please. My only priority is to get Sophie to Athens. You say another word to me, and I swear to God, I'll make your life a living hell."

Monte's jaw tightened. We rode in silence. Zach's eyes looked glazed with tears as he peered out the car window.

As we arrived at the airport, I continued to check for bleeding, which seemed to have stopped for now. Eznik ran for a wheelchair. After being bundled into it, Sophie passed out again.

Will pushed her chair through the airport to Executive Customs. I walked beside him, worried about Sophie, and the authorities we were about to face.

Monte spoke to the two security officials working the midnight shift. Eznik translated quietly.

"Monte's explaining to them that our Greek friend has a charter jet. He's telling them she's ill, and that she wants to meet her husband in Athens."

It was three in the morning. One official gave Sophie a long look. He squatted down in front of her and looked her over. Sophie gave him a faint smile. The official asked Monte what was wrong with her? Monte gave the name of a restaurant, shrugged, and shook his head. The officer stood, nodded sympathetically, walked over to the counter, and stamped everyone's passports. I nearly fell over with relief.

A new official appeared, questioning the guard who'd just stamped their passports. A noisy exchange in Turkish followed. The new guy cast a suspicious look our way. I held my breath as he issued a command into his walkie-talkie and blocked the gate.

"What's going on, Monte?"

"He's playing the hero. He summoned the airport physician."

I knelt down next to Sophie. "Soph, we have a little problem here. They're calling for a doctor to examine you."

She closed her eyes and sighed heavily.

Will approached the two guards, showing them all the documents he was required to carry as the pilot of the charter aircraft.

Sophie looked dreadful, dark circles under her eyes, her skin ashen, and her face contorted with pain.

Two more officers walked up and started asking questions. Heatedly, Eznik, and Monte explained that their friend was ill.

"Jenna."

"What, Soph?"

"The trash can, please."

I heard her gag as I grabbed the small trashcan at the guard's desk and rushed to her side. As all four guards watched, Sophie tossed her cookies. Three of the guards politely turned away, but the fourth one watched her with a steady gaze.

Zach appeared with wet paper towels, God bless him. I took them and cleaned the corners of her mouth. "You barfed at the perfect time. Good girl."

She just moaned and slumped even lower in the wheelchair.

"How long before their doctor gets here?" Zach asked.

"Soon, I hope."

Zach moved the trash can to a less offensive location.

One of the guards approached Monte, and they talked in low tones. Monte glanced at me and nodded.

"Thank you, God," I heard Zach whisper.

A security guard wheeled Sophie to the metal detector and passed a wand over her body. He nodded and waved her through the customs gate.

Travis was out on the tarmac, inspecting the exterior of the jet. Will joined him.

Monte and Eznik looked as relieved as I felt.

"That was close!" said Eznik.

"Thank you for speaking to the guards. You made a difference for Sophie."

They nodded. Then Eznik said to Monte, "I'll be right back, I need to use the restroom."

Monte said, "Me too."

The two brothers strode down the corridor as I turned my attention back to Sophie.

Sophie motioned for me to come near to her. "Jenna."

I crouched next to her. Sophie whispered, "God wants to help you, Jenna. Just ask him."

I raised my eyebrows, leaned over and patted Sophie's arm. "Thanks, Sophie. I mean that. I'm staying until I find Sarkis. I don't intend to leave here without him."

I stood and looked at my son. "Come here." I opened my arms, and he stepped into my embrace. As we hugged, I patted his shoulders. "You've been through a lot."

"I feel so guilty leaving Sarkis."

"You did what he told you to do. You took the chance you were given. I'm proud of you."

"I feel like a coward."

"Look at me." He lifted his sad face and met my gaze. "I have loved you all your life with all my heart, Zach. You're a wonderful young man. You're smart, endearing, and you care about others. You are so much like your father, and nothing could please me more."

Zach's eyes filled with tears. "I love you, too. I know that sounds strange, but I feel it."

Travis strode into the lounge.

I hugged Zach again. "Time to go, honey. You take care of Sophie, and I'll see you very soon, I promise. I love you."

Zach nodded, looking miserable. "You be careful... please, be very careful!"

"I will, I promise."

He took the wheelchair, guiding Sophie towards Travis, who walked with them to the jet. Will stood near the plane with the ground crew.

A few minutes later, Will jogged back to me. "I'll see you back here at seven o'clock! That's in four hours!"

"Okay."

"If you're not here by eight, I'll head to the hotel and wait there for you."

I nodded. "You'd better get going."

Will hugged me so tight I thought he'd break my ribs.

I stood by the security checkpoint, watching the ground crew load food for the Lear's galley. And I waited for Eznik and Monte to return from the men's room.

They never did.

Under the watchful eye of the airport security guards,

I cooled my heels for five minutes, and then I went looking for Monte and Eznik. I stood at the door of the men's restroom and called out their names. Nothing. I couldn't find them anywhere in our area of the terminal. Furious, I walked back to the security checkpoint. Will approached me, an urgent look on his face.

"Where are the brothers? Sophie's bleeding again, and we need to take off."

Fear shot through me. "They've disappeared. Go. Take care of Sophie. I'll meet you back here at seven o'clock."

He gripped my shoulders. "Wait here for me. Don't try to find Sarkis alone. I promise, I'll be back in four hours, and we can do this together."

I hesitated, and then I admitted, "I have to try now, Will. The kidnappers are scared. They've shot an American woman. They looked terrified when they ran off. This is the perfect time. Go! Sophie needs to be in Athens."

"Watch out for yourself, Jenna." He hugged me close again, his lips grazing my forehead, and then ran for the jet.

Sick with worry and marooned in a strange culture, I stood at the window and followed the plane's path. Will taxied the jet. I watched the Challenger hurtle itself upward and into the dark sky. I tracked the aircraft until it disappeared from sight. Again, my thoughts sent a prayer for their safe trip, and for Sophie's well being. Surprised at myself, I added a quick prayer for Sarkis as well.

THIRTY-SIX

I shouldered my backpack, retracing my steps through the airport. It was 3:30 am so I didn't wait long for a taxi. I gave the driver the name of the Citadel Hotel and sat back.

During the drive, I agonized over the events of last two hours. The cab finally pulled up to the hotel. I tossed the driver a hundred lira note. Slamming the door of the cab, I launched myself up the steps.

Approaching the front desk, I nodded at the clerk. "Hello…"

He reached under the counter and withdrew an envelope with the name 'Alexakis' on it.

I tore it open, noting an address and the time. 4:00 a.m. I swore, wheeled around, and dashed back outside.

The taxi still sat at the curb. I ran to the car, jerked open the rear door, and showed him the address on the slip of paper. He floored the accelerator pedal.

I pulled the Bible out of my backpack and held it close. Opening the worn book and smoothing my fingertips over the handwritten pages, I thought about Armen Begosian. Glancing up, I recognized the passing terrain of the Kum Kapi district. Armenian, Greek and Turk families had once lived here, perhaps peacefully.

A million and a half Christian Armenians and perhaps 800 thousand Greeks butchered, and for what? I closed the Bible.

Didn't it all boil down to greed? The Turks coveted the possessions of the Armenians, and they wanted to rid Turkey of Christianity once and for all.

This mess I was in hinged on a treasure trove of gems in a locked carry-on back at the hotel.

My lips narrowed into a thin line. The Turks had already stolen too much from the Armenians and the Greeks, and I'd be damned if they'd harm Sarkis. The kidnappers had done enough damage.

The cab entered a normal looking neighborhood with tree-lined streets. Like most residential areas in Istanbul, it was wall-to-wall apartments or homes. The streetlights even worked. Miracle of miracles!

The driver slowed while he looked for the address. Then, he pointed out a tall apartment building. "Keep going," I said, motioning him further up the street.

The driver continued up the block to the top of the hill. He pulled to the curb, letting the engine idle. I paid him, and then got out.

The quiet street and absence of foot traffic confirmed the early hour.

I jogged to the apartment building and opened the front door, stepping into a dark foyer. I began to climb the stairs, my destination apartment 412. The threadbare carpet runner on the staircase failed to mute the creaking of the wood beneath my feet.

Every so often, I glanced behind me. At last, I reached the fourth floor landing. I walked down the dark hallway, my heart hammering in my chest. An ancient musty odor emanated from the walls and the carpet.

I found apartment 412, but I continued to the end of the hall, searching for an escape route if things went south in a hurry. Nothing. I walked back to stand before 412.

Without warning, incredible fear and panic threatened to overwhelm me. Stunned, I froze. Then, I turned and raced down the corridor, and stopped at the top of the stairs I'd just climbed. I trembled, having never felt such fear in my entire life.

"Oh, God," I thought.

God. Something shifted deep inside my soul. I whispered, "Please, please, God. If you really are there, I need you."

I exhaled shakily as I reoriented myself to my surroundings. Had He heard my plea? Once again, I whispered, "Please, God, be with me. Help me save Sarkis."

Nothing happened, except a quiet stirring within me. I knew something had changed. How can I explain it? I was suddenly filled with an inner assurance I'd never felt before. I turned and walked back down the hallway to 412. I still felt the fear and uncertainty, but I was oddly no longer crippled by it.

I knocked at the door. It flew open. A man clad in a heavy gray sweater reached for my arm and jerked me inside. He smelled unwashed. Didn't anyone bathe in this country? He shoved me at a bearded man, who smacked my head with the back of his hand.

From somewhere in the apartment, I heard the sound of a woman's feeble cry. The man in the gray sweater peered out into the hallway, and then slammed the apartment door. The bearded man spat a few words into a cell phone.

"I have what you want, I have the book." I held the Bible tight against my chest. The bearded man pushed me forward into a large room.

Someone slammed me against the living room wall. My head hit the wall, and I dropped like a stone. Stars exploded across my field of vision, and I nearly blacked out.

Once again, I heard an elderly woman cry out. I struggled to sit up, despite how sick to my stomach I felt.

The Bible lay nearby on the floor.

Slowly turning my head I saw an old woman lying on a divan. Propped up by colorful pillows, she'd witnessed their assault. I felt her concern for me, and I wondered if she was related to one of the kidnappers.

Her eyes, wide with fear, met my gaze. She shook her head, and then began to weep.

One of the men lunged at the old woman, his voice rage-filled. The woman covered her ears. The other men in the room stared at the commotion with passive nonchalance.

I hitched myself up on one elbow, and pointed at her offender, wagging my finger. "Hey! You leave her alone. Pick on someone your own size."

When I got a better look at her, I realized I was gazing at the most ancient-looking woman I'd ever laid eyes on. Bones protruded in sharp angles, accenting her patrician features. Her deep-set eyes were pale and cloudy, the circles under them gave her a haunted look. Even in her obvious distress, she shook her head at what was happening.

The Skipper, still wearing his infernal captain's hat, emerged from another room. He looked irritated. The angry kidnapper whose brother had died followed him. The two men walked over to where I lay.

As they approached me, I flattened myself against the floor. The Skipper leaned down to grab my arm. With all my strength, I kicked him in the crotch. He let out a roar, collapsing onto the floor beside me.

I'd acted on impulse, with no thought to the consequences.

The dead man's brother retaliated, stomping hard on my left arm. I convulsed into a tight ball, intense pain streaking through my upper arm. I cried out, not able to muffle the agony.

My attacker smirked down at me. The Skipper, still writhing on the floor, gripped his damaged parts and groaned.

I inched away from the Skipper, struggled into a seated position against the wall, and shook my head. "Skipper, you and Gilligan here give new meaning to the word vicious."

The Skipper gasped out a single word in Turkish.

His buddy kicked me, and I slammed into the wall yet again. I felt like seven kinds of hell as I blinked back tears and tried not to weep. Suddenly I had difficulty breathing.

The Skipper collected the abandoned Bible as he muttered a sharp command. His friend backed off after the third blow to my side. He thumbed through the first few pages of the Bible; finally reaching the diagram Armen Begosian had drawn one hundred years ago.

The Skipper shut the Bible. He looked triumphant as he summoned his troops. Five men dwarfed the main room of the apartment. All five turned to study me.

I looked back at them, feeling strangely fearless despite my injuries.

The Skipper said a few words, and two of the men hauled me up from the floor and dragged me into a dingy bedroom.

The only light in the room was suspended from the ceiling, its metal lampshade casting an eerie, coppery glow.

I spotted Sarkis, sitting quietly with his back against the far wall. His mouth was covered with duct tape, his ankles and hands also secured with tape.

The men forced me down onto the floor beside Sarkis and taped my wrists and ankles. Pain radiated up my left arm. My vision clouded over, and I fought to stay conscious. A strip of duct tape covered my mouth, with additional tape pasting clumps of my hair to my cheeks. I cast a frustrated glance at Sarkis.

He shook his head at me. He looked furious, but also cold, and calm. His gaze contained so much grief; I sucked in a breath.

It finally dawned on me. *He thinks Sophie's dead!*

The Skipper and his buddy entered the room, displaying the handwritten pages they'd ripped right out of the Bible. The Skipper gave me a contemptuous smile as he waved the pages. "We go... when we back, you go."

I heard the front door of the apartment open and then the sound of it closing. I struggled to sit up. Sarkis made a sharp sound and shook his head. I sank back against the wall. No use. Minutes passed in quiet agony.

Someone fumbled with the doorknob. I froze. The

door swung open. The old woman entered the room gripping a knife. Sarkis uttered a muffled sound of alarm.

The old woman surprised me when she knelt in front of me. She held the knife, speaking in Turkish as she motioned for us to raise our taped wrists. Stunned, I extended my wrists. Surprised by the strength of her grasp, I kept my eyes on the serrated knife as she sawed through the duct tape.

Once my hands were free, I tore at the tape that covered my mouth and cheeks, taking a few strands of hair as I rid myself of the stuff. "Thank you! Thank you!" I took the knife from the old woman and released my ankles from the tape. Turning to Sarkis, I sawed through the tape on his wrists with one hand, as I said, "Sophie's alive! She's in Athens and under a doctor's care, I promise you!"

Sarkis' eyes widened with shock. He pulled at the tape fixed over his mouth, tossing it aside once he removed it.

I handed Sarkis the knife. "Sarkis, I might have a broken rib or two, and my arm's definitely broken. You're gonna have to do the honors."

"Sophie's alive? I thought... I thought she was dead." His voice broke. Overcome, he brought his hands to his face. "She's alive!" he said through his tears.

"Yes, she is. That bullet hit her collarbone, I think!"

Sarkis sucked in a few steadying breaths. "I thought I'd lost her." He swiftly removed the tape from both his ankles.

"Sophie? Nah. She's sturdy. She even prayed for you, right before they flew her out."

Sarkis smiled. "That sounds like my Sophie."

He gingerly climbed to his feet and then helped me to stand. "Let's get out of here."

I turned to the elderly woman, helping her stand, patting her thin shoulders. "God bless you! I have never meant anything more in my entire life!"

I felt so grateful to her, I hugged her with my good arm. "Thank you."

Holding up the roll of duct tape and speaking in Turkish, she made a circular motion with her hands.

"She wants us to tie her up," Sarkis said.

"Smart." I grimaced. "Then they won't blame her for our escape."

Sarkis guided her to the front room. I limped along behind them.

Chattering away, the woman pointed to a stained wall in the living room. Her family history hung there, a series of heirloom portraits in outdated frames.

Sarkis acknowledged the pictures and made polite noises before he whispered to me, "Can you get my duffel bag? It's over there." Then, he helped the woman back onto the sofa, tucking the blanket around her fragile body and adjusting the cushions.

I found my backpack in the living room on the floor near the sofa. I found Sarkis' duffel near the front door. I also spotted the old Armenian Bible on the floor, now stripped of its handwritten pages. I retrieved it, and shoved it into Sarkis' duffel.

He wrapped a small kitchen towel around her narrow wrists, and then gently secured her hands.

She motioned Sarkis forward, reached up to him despite her bonds, and kissed his forehead.

Sarkis stroked her cheek. "I can't understand a thing she's saying, but she's beautiful, isn't she?"

I nodded, too choked up to say anything.

Then the old woman motioned me forward. Despite the pain, I eased down and she kissed my cheek.

"Oh, Lord, bless and protect this dear lady," Sarkis said. Then he looked at me. "We're outta here."

THIRTY-SEVEN

As the old woman looked on, we left the apartment, shutting the door behind us. We made our way down the hallway to the landing, pausing there to listen for any movement on the stairs. With a quick nod, Sarkis scooped up both the duffle and my backpack and then slid his free arm around my waist. We descended the flights of stairs to the building's entrance.

While I caught my breath, he looked out the windows. "We need to get as far from here as we can in a very short time."

I gritted my teeth against the pain, then said, "Let's do it then."

Sarkis put his arm around me again, and we exited

the building. We walked as quickly as I could manage for nearly ten minutes. Every step I took jarred my broken arm and damaged ribs, but I refused to stop until Sarkis slowed his footsteps and paused at the end of an alley.

I glanced at my watch as I gasped for breath. 5:15.

"I'm afraid to ask you about your injuries," he said.

I grimaced. "I'll give you the list later."

He chuckled. "You're a tough one, aren't you?"

"No, just very bruised at the moment." I breathed slowly in and out. "Sophie's going to be all right," I managed to assure Sarkis, as we set off again, his arm looped around my waist.

We walked for several silent minutes, zigzagging our way through a dreary-looking neighborhood.

"I couldn't believe what I was seeing." Sarkis glanced over his shoulder, checking for any sign of the kidnappers. "When I saw all that blood, I thought she was dead, or close to it. I'm amazed, amazed and so thankful she survived."

We stopped again, giving me time to breathe carefully as Sarkis looked for landmarks and kept a watch for the Skipper and his crew.

I managed to say, "Thank you for looking out for Zach."

"He's a very nice young man."

I spotted the Citadel Walls, pointing them out to Sarkis, as I said, "Head east, toward the sea."

Sarkis changed course several times, pulling me into

dark doorways to avoid car headlights or the occasional pedestrian. We reached a boulevard and stepped out of the shadows.

A taxi spotted us, nosing in our direction as he flashed his headlights. Sarkis raised his hand. The driver stopped.

We climbed into the taxi. To take my mind off how bad I felt, I explained the events following his kidnapping. "After Sophie found the dead guy on your front lawn, she called me. Since the brothers screwed up the first attempt to exchange the Bible for you, she hired a chartered jet. We arrived in Istanbul ahead of you and the kidnappers."

We hit a pothole, and I winced as I cradled my arm against my torso. "We holed up in a different hotel, and Sophie and I managed to locate Begosian's treasure. We transferred it to our hotel."

Sarkis looked at me, astonished.

Pausing for a steadying breath, I added, "We need to be at the airport in a few hours. Will is flying back from Athens to pick us up."

"That was Will Graham from Pacific Moon?"

I nodded.

Sarkis said, "He's a good one. And Zach was remarkably helpful. He told me what you both had discovered. He encouraged me not to lose faith, and he prayed with me. I think the world of that young man."

I smiled faintly. "So do I."

Sarkis asked, "Who were those two guys?"

I filled him in on Monte and Eznik Kazarian and the Armenian Justice Alliance. I also let him know I was none too happy that they'd ditched me at the airport.

Sarkis shook his head. "I didn't know what to think when I found out about the old Bible and some hidden jewelry." He paused. "I guess it's all part of my grandfather's estate."

"Sarkis, we're talking about seventy-three bags of precious gems. It's worth millions. And yes, it's your grandfather Armen's estate."

"My grandfather Armen." He seemed to test the phrase.

Our taxi braked sharply in front of the Hotel Citadel. After I paid the driver, Sarkis helped me out of the vehicle, and we climbed the steps to the lobby. I nodded to the clerk, but I kept walking. Sarkis followed me.

Sophie, I figured, was probably in surgery by now. With a good surgeon and a bit of luck, she'd enjoy a reunion with her husband in a few hours. For that, I felt overwhelming relief.

Sarkis dug through my backpack for the room key. He pushed open the door and waited for me to enter the room first.

I whispered over my shoulder, "Sophie packed a bag of clean clothes for you. It's in the closet." I approached the closet, pointing to the carry-on bag on the floor. "Will you put it on the bed, please?"

Sarkis transferred the luggage and then stepped aside as I joined him.

I fumbled around the zipper, searching for the lock. The lock was gone! My heart sank as I unzipped the suitcase, opened it, and found nothing. Not one of the jewelry bags remained in the carry-on.

Gasping for breath, I stood at the foot of the bed. Despair overwhelmed me. "Monte and Eznik! They've stolen the jewels." I swore.

Sarkis, unshaven, his eyes bloodshot, and his exhaustion evident on the heels of four days and nights as a kidnap victim, stood quietly in front of me. "Look at me, Jenna."

I met his gaze, still furious and ready to scream.

"Jenna, I don't care about the jewels. Sophie's all that matters to me. Now, we need to get to the airport and meet Will."

I opened my mouth to protest. Monte and Eznik won. They got what they were after. I hated that.

Sarkis shook his head. "Priorities, Jenna. Sophie is mine."

I exhaled, air gusting out of me, and reluctantly nodded.

He hurriedly jammed the few clothes I'd put in the closet into my duffel bag, zipped it closed, and looked around the room. "Anything else?"

"Just my coat."

Sarkis draped it over my shoulders.

"Boy, do I feel stupid. I should never have let Sophie hire those two."

Sarkis handed me four Advil and an uncapped bottle of water. "Forget it. I have."

"But I knew better. Those two never felt right." I popped the tablets into my mouth and chugged the water, still mentally cursing Monte and Eznik.

He picked up our bags. "Let's go."

Sarkis dropped the room keys onto the front desk counter, when we reached the vacant lobby. He flagged down a passing taxi, and we climbed in after he stowed our duffels.

A few blocks from the hotel, I spotted a speeding taxi full of men traveling in the opposite direction.

"The Skipper!" I exclaimed.

"The Skipper?" Sarkis turned to look at me.

"The head honcho of the crew that grabbed you."

"His name is Duman." Sarkis glanced at the road behind us. "They don't know where we are or where we're headed. Sit tight. We'll be fine."

I wanted to believe him, so I watched the passing landscape.

Dawn spilled across the sky. As the sun edged into view, I caught glimpses of pale clouds and hints of diffused blue light. Perhaps the storm had passed.

***

After a hard ride to the airport, the taxi driver skidded to a stop at the main terminal.

Sarkis muttered, "They hand out driver's licenses to anyone here."

I pulled myself out of the vehicle, biting back a volley of swear words. It was all I could do to stand up straight.

We did a slow hustle into the airport terminal. Sarkis and I headed for the VIP customs area. As vendors began to open shops and cafés, I noticed the time on an overhead clock. Six o'clock am.

We stopped twice so that I could take in deeper breaths. The black dots dancing before my eyes faded each time I stopped. The sparse crowd seemed to thicken with each minute.

As we approached the security checkpoint, a guard motioned for us to place our bags on the x-ray trolley.

Then, I heard a sudden commotion behind us. The hairs on the back of my neck lifted in alarm. I whispered, "Oh, please, we're so close to blowing outta here."

Sarkis glanced back, and then he stumbled to a stop. "Oh, no."

I looked over my shoulder, registering the threat.

The Skipper, followed by four of his gang, including his buddy with the boots stood a dozen feet from us. Sarkis and I were poised to enter the V.I.P. area. A stand off if I'd ever seen one.

They appeared outraged as they glared at us. If looks could have killed, Sarkis and I would have been dead meat. I glared right back at them.

The Skipper, his face purple with rage, pointed at us and shouted something in Turkish.

"He just can't help himself, can he?" I said, out of the side of my mouth to Sarkis. "What a total jerk." Sarkis straightened to his full height. He glowered at his kidnappers, looking like a very displeased professor in front of a class of unruly students. "They're thugs. They won't try anything here in airport."

Two armed guards approached the kidnappers. The two men spoke heatedly to the guards, gesturing all the while at us.

I whispered, "Should we mention those two clowns kidnapped you?"

Sarkis shook his head. "Just follow my lead."

The two guards walked over to us and ordered us in Turkish to place our bags on the counter.

"No problem." Sarkis did as instructed, an expression of faint confusion on his face.

Two airport officials, one of them a woman, joined our gathering. They commanded the guards to start searching our luggage.

THIRTY-EIGHT

I turned, donning the most confused facial expression I could manage, and stared at the two kidnappers.

The female official, whose nametag said, 'N. Zengin,' asked Sarkis in excellent English to produce his passport, which he did. He included my passport.

"And your airline tickets," she said.

He smiled. "A private jet will arrive for us at 7:00. It will take us to Athens to pick up my wife. From there," he explained, "we will return to the United States."

The guards thoroughly examined our luggage. The woman spoke into her walkie-talkie, her tone no-nonsense. Turning to us, she politely asked us to take seats in a nearby bank of plastic chairs.

Sarkis and I sat side by side, pleasant expressions on our faces as the officials did what officials the world over do and the Skipper and his four comrades paced angrily nearby.

"I think she's the one in control," I said quietly.

"I agree."

"In case anyone asks, I took a header down a flight of stairs at our hotel."

Sarkis met my gaze.

"You didn't see me fall. You found me afterwards."

"Okay." He shot me a worried look.

"I want to get out of here, Sarkis, and I'll smile while I lie to accomplish it."

I kept my eyes on the kidnappers, who began to show signs of nervousness. The Skipper treated the guards like they were drinking buddies, but his Mr. Congeniality act bombed. The guards regarded the kidnappers with obvious reserve as they also kept a watchful eye on us.

Officer Zengin gave the guards instructions before she departed the security area. The head guard spoke firmly in Turkish, and the Skipper and his men produced their identification.

A cranky baby wailed and two kids played tag in the waiting area. My head pounded.

Shop owners opened their airport retail shops, passengers roamed the concourse, and porters pushed heavy carts laden with luggage to the x-ray area.

The Skipper and his cohorts still lingered. For the life of me, I couldn't see the point. This was a classic checkmate, unless, of course, the Turkish authorities refused to allow us to board the charter when it arrived. Not a pleasant thought.

Movement among the five kidnappers made me blink and refocus. I bit back a triumphant smile as three of the men began to back away from the Skipper and his booted friend. They soon disappeared into the crowds of passengers searching for their departure gates.

I slowly, and very carefully, pushed up to my feet. "I'll be right back."

Sarkis said, "Jenna, what are..."

I walked slowly over to the Skipper and his buddy. I waited until I had their undivided attention. "Duman, please tell Milda I so enjoyed seeing her and the kids this visit. I will remember you all forever."

The Skipper looked shell shocked. If that didn't get him out of the airport, I figured nothing would. Me? I was just fed up with those two glowering at me. And a little payback feels good. I sat painfully next to Sarkis and continued the waiting game.

Officer Zengin returned, accompanied by two members of her Canine Unit. One uniformed guard, and one leashed beagle. Time to sniff our luggage.

The beagle inspected our open duffels, trotting in circles around the bags. The handler spoke in a normal voice as he gave commands to the dog. The beagle, after waddling amidst the bags, sat down and yawned, his eyes on his handler.

Officer Zengin dismissed the dog handler and the beagle. Then she personally conducted a thorough inspection of my backpack after emptying the contents onto the counter. She picked up four packs of bubble gum. "You must like it."

I smiled. "I do."

Officer Zengin turned her attention to the two remaining kidnappers. She approached them and a heated conversation ensued.

Zengin returned to us looking irritated. "They accuse you of stealing a large quantity of jewels. What have you to say about this?"

"Jewels?" I exclaimed.

"That's crazy," Sarkis said, looking genuinely shocked.

Officer Zengin nodded to us. "You may proceed to your waiting area. Thank you for your cooperation."

"Thank you, Officer. Thank you very much." I struggled to keep my composure. I hurt all over, and I knew I couldn't keep up this innocent act much longer.

"Miss Paletto, do not thank me yet. I have instructed the guards to thoroughly inspect your aircraft before you will receive clearance to depart Istanbul."

Nodding, I replied, "Of course. We have nothing to hide."

"Very well. You may proceed." She smiled at us and walked away.

Sarkis said under his breath, "Thank God, we didn't have those jewels."

As we made our way to the lounge, I glanced over my shoulder in time to see the guards confiscate the identification of the two kidnappers and escort them under guard from the security area.

"They're taking them into custody," I reported to Sarkis.

"Eyes forward and non-committal," he ordered.

The guard at the checkpoint had witnessed the entire incident. He waved us through without asking for our papers.

I sat pensively in one of the upholstered chairs in the executive lounge. Sophie's face, her look of absolute shock at being shot lingered in my mind.

Sarkis gave me one of the two cups of hot coffee he'd gotten at the kiosk in the VIP lounge.

I held the cup in my right hand, relishing its warmth. Slowly, I began to feel as though we might get out of Turkey intact, my injuries not withstanding.

My thoughts returned yet again to Sophie, who'd displayed incredible strength in the face of adversity. I admired and respected her. And I felt no small amount of awe when I thought about her total faith in God.

I'd lost my faith when Jayson had disappeared all those years ago. And I'd lost it once again when I'd given up Zach for adoption. Now, I knew that I needed to rethink every aspect of my life, especially how I felt about

God and my ability to believe. I wanted to trust and to believe, but how does one start? Perhaps I had already taken the first step when I pleaded for God to help me.

***

"Hey, beautiful."

I blinked, registered a pair of navy blue trousers, and looked up into Will's smiling face. Clad in his uniform and captain's hat, the crow's feet around his eyes deepened as he grinned at me.

Tears stung my eyes, and I almost fell into his arms as I leaned forward. "Oh, you're a sight for sore eyes," I whispered.

Sarkis gently restrained Will before he enveloped me in a bear hug. "She's pretty banged up, and she needs a doctor's immediate attention as soon as we get to Athens."

Will stared at both of us, his shock apparent. "What happened?"

"Got an aspirin?" I managed with a strained smile.

"Oh, babe. What did they do to you?"

Sarkis replied. "A broken arm and a few cracked or broken ribs. Maybe even a concussion."

"I'll live," I said. "Can we leave now?"

"As soon as security gives us the okay, we're outta

here. Can I get you anything at all?" Will asked as he searched my face.

"Anesthesia?" I croaked, as I cradled my bad arm against my body.

Will cupped my cheek with his hand, his eyes expressing emotions that knocked me even more off-balance. Then he straightened, extending his hand to Sarkis. "Sophie's in surgery right now."

"Can we find out how she's doing?" Sarkis asked.

Will nodded. "As soon as we're in the air. Her father and Gwen are with her. They met our plane."

"They're in Athens? Thank God."

I listened to them talk through the dull haze of pain. On the tarmac, security guards inspected the jet.

"Did Monte and Eznik ever turn up?" Will asked.

I refocused on him, frowning at the mention of those two thieves.

"Jenna thinks they took the jewels."

Will knelt down in front of me. "That's exactly what you were afraid they'd do."

I scowled, not at all happy that I'd been proven right.

Will stood, glancing out the window. "Looks like they're almost done." He turned to Sarkis and me. "The good news here is that you two are in one piece. The rest of it is unimportant. I just thank God you're both safe."

"I thank God for Jenna," Sarkis said. "She saved my life."

"I'm not surprised. She was a woman on a mission when we left for Athens."

A guard approached us with a clipboard. Will signed all of the documents. The official waved us forward to the plane. Will gathered our luggage and we left the VIP lounge and boarded the aircraft.

He closed and secured the door as Sarkis helped me into a seat and fastened my seatbelt.

"How did George know you'd taken Sophie to Athens?" Sarkis asked Will as he settled into his own seat.

"I decided Mr. St. James needed to know what had happened to Sophie. I contacted him through our company. But St James and his new wife had already heard Sophie had left for Istanbul."

"How did they know?"

"From his secretary, because Sophie had asked to borrow their jet. Then St. James knew something had happened. They were an hour from Istanbul when I contacted him. He arranged for an ambulance and emergency doctors to meet us at the Athen's airport. They're with her now. She went into surgery as we headed back to Istanbul for you two."

I silently grappled with the guilt I felt.

"What can I get for you? Hot tea?" Will stroked my cheek as he spoke.

With the warmth of his touch and the care I heard in his voice, I began to relax a little. "I've taken four Advil, I think I can get through the flight to Athens."

"We're on our way." Will stood and walked to the cockpit.

Sarkis said, "I'll be right back." He followed Will to the cockpit. "Please call Athens the minute we reach altitude."

"You got it."

At 7:30, the plane vaulted into the morning sky. I looked out the window at the sprawling city below us. The storm was gone. The sun's rays bathed the city in a golden glow as the residents of Istanbul greeted a new day.

THIRTY-NINE

As the jet reached cruising altitude, I stared sightlessly out the small window. What if Sophie died because of my carelessness? Why hadn't I insisted that she remain at the hotel? I felt helpless. I couldn't save Sophie. God, please save her. Please God.

With sudden clarity I realized all the help I had received from God every step of the way on this harrowing journey. He had provided me with countless bits of knowledge, my intuition, and He'd touched the heart of that old woman who'd freed us. He'd also given me the strength to flee with Sarkis.

Sophie's words, "Ask God to help you," resonated in my head. I closed my eyes and remembered. In that dark hallway in the apartment building, I had asked for and received help.

Would it have made any difference if I'd asked God to help me find Jayson twenty years ago? Perhaps. Back then I'd interpreted advice, words of wisdom, or support of any kind as foolish. I'd wanted concrete answers, not prayers. Because I couldn't find Jayson, I'd erected barriers so impenetrable, I couldn't let myself need anyone.

I sighed out loud, accepting my foolishness for what it was, a need to control my world.

The sound of conversation rose above the drone of the jet engines. I opened my eyes, spotting Sarkis near the cockpit as he listened to Will on the headset. Will shook his head at Sarkis. Fear knifed through my heart.

Sarkis made his way to his seat across from me, and slumped into it. He adjusted his safety belt. "No word yet on Sophie. She's still in surgery." He refocused on me. "Will you pray with me?"

I nodded. "You'll have to lead. I haven't prayed since grade school."

Sarkis gripped my right hand and leaned close so that I could hear him.

"Lord, please help us. We are in such a time of need. We know Sophie's in Your hands. Guide the surgeon in his work, Lord, may she heal right and be good as new. And thank You for bringing Jenna into our lives. Thank You for her strength and her persistence. Whatever the outcome, Lord, I praise You and thank You for Your goodness and mercy."

My respect for Sarkis climbed several notches. I'd never heard a man praise God in the midst of his worry and fear.

The pressure and fatigue I felt from being beaten, the betrayal of the brothers, and losing the jewels had been demoralizing. Now, an idea took hold in my mind. Asking God into my life and giving Him control made me feel less alone and frightened.

I opened my eyes and gazed at Sarkis. He looked like the weight of the world was off his shoulders. He appeared to be downright happy.

He said, "I don't know how to thank you for everything you've done, Jenna."

I shook my head. "It was God who touched that old woman's heart."

Sarkis studied me. "Indeed He did." He reached over and patted my good arm. "I'm going to fix you some hot tea."

As Sarkis made his way to the galley, I felt an intangible lightness that lifted my nearly crushing anxiety over Sophie. It was the oddest thing, but somehow I felt certain she'd survive.

FORTY

We landed in Athens without any difficulty at 8:45 that morning. I looked and felt like ten miles of bad road, and every step I took proved to be a major challenge.

We navigated Executive Customs without any trouble. Will stayed by my side, supporting me while Sarkis went in search of a wheelchair for me. I gratefully sank into it when he returned.

A driver stood outside of Executive Customs, holding a neatly-printed sign that read "Alexakis and Paletto." Zach appeared at the man's side, his wide smile quickly replaced by a look of concern. "What happened?"

Sarkis explained, "Your mom had a run in with the kidnappers. She may have a few broken bones."

Zach gripped my good hand.

I said, "I'll be fine once my arm's in a cast."

He nodded miserably.

Our driver glanced in the rearview mirror. "I take you to Hotel Grande Bretagne."

"She needs a hospital!" Sarkis insisted.

Zach said, "No, Sophie's at the hotel with tons of equipment and more doctors and nurses than you can imagine. They'll have everything you'll need."

The driver said, "I have instruction. Hotel Grande Bretagne. Mr. St. James tells me." And then he asked in a thick Greek accent, "Is first trip to Athens?"

We all nodded. The driver gestured to the windows of the limo. "Then, drink coffee, enjoy scenery! Nikolaos Dimitraki will drive you to Hotel Grande Bretagne."

Every so often, our driver pointed out famous landmarks. Like obedient children, Will, Sarkis and Zach looked at the famous memorials and monuments, as well as the ruins that seemed to be everywhere.

With my eyes closed, I listened to the driver as I rested.

"How are you?" Zach asked quietly. I opened my eyes. He looked so concerned my heart nearly broke.

"I was so worried for you, I prayed you'd be safe."

He'd prayed for me! I smiled, certain that we'd be having some interesting conversations in the not too distant future. "I'm so thankful you're here," I whispered.

"Constitution Square!" informed the driver, pointing

off to the left. Even I obliged him, gazing at the beautiful open area filled with people walking to work or sitting on benches with their morning coffee as they read the paper.

The driver brought the limo to a stop. "This your hotel!" Dimitraki declared. "Most expensive hotel in all of Athens!"

After Will helped me out of the limousine, I stared up at the massive seven-story hotel, which dominated the entire right side of the square. Black and gold Greek mythological characters made up the railings on the balconies, and pale blue-green curtains draped every window.

The doorman brought a wheelchair that Will requested, and he and my Zach tenderly helped me into it.

I took in the elegant furnishings that complemented our surroundings as Zach guided my wheelchair into the lobby. Large, roomy claret-colored velvet ottomans sat atop exquisite oriental area rugs.

"Wow," I croaked, as two fashionably dressed women crossed the lobby. I felt out of place, and overwhelmed by my surroundings.

Zach said, "There's a private elevator for suite 745. It's the Presidential Suite."

Will commented, "Talk about being a stranger in a strange land."

Sarkis laughed. "You are a stranger in a strange land."

Zach grinned. "I could definitely get used to this."

As the elevator doors opened, I spotted an armed

guard stationed just outside the penthouse. Other guards were in evidence as well.

Sarkis addressed the guard at the penthouse double-doors. "You know Zach Carpenter, I'm Sarkis Alexakis, and this is Jenna Paletto. The gentleman beside her is Will Graham."

"Passports?" the guard asked.

Sarkis fished our passports from my backpack, and handed them over. Will added his. Just then, the door swung open. With a shout of surprise, a large, powerfully built man pulled Sarkis into his arms.

"Sarkis!" George St. James exclaimed. The resemblance between Sophie and her father was quite evident.

"Sarkis! Thank God!" St. James wrapped his son-in-law in a gigantic bear hug, tears glittering in his eyes.

Sarkis stepped back. "George! Where's Sophie? Zach says you've set up your own surgical unit here."

"I certainly did!" he boomed. "Sophie's inside. The doctors are with her now. We'll know soon how she's doing." He paused and looked down at me. "You must be Jenna! Why the wheelchair?" St. James bent down, reaching out to hug me.

Sarkis grabbed St. James as Will said, "Sir, she has a broken arm and the possibility of fractured ribs, courtesy of the kidnappers, and she needs immediate attention."

Clearly shocked, George St. James straightened.

"Jenna, we have best doctors in Athens right here for

Sophie. Let's get you inside so we can get you patched up."

Will pushed my wheelchair into the penthouse, Zach at my side every step of the way.

As we entered the nearly palatial Presidential Suite, Sarkis said to Sophie's father, "Jenna saved my life, George, but she suffered a nasty beating to do it."

St. James summoned one of the nurses. "Miss Paletto needs immediate attention."

Feeling bemused, I willingly surrendered to the benevolence of George St. James and the medical staff he'd assembled.

The woman took one look at me and nodded, quickly commanding my wheelchair and whisking me into one of the adjacent rooms.

FORTY-ONE

The nurse helped me out of the wheelchair and onto a gurney in a room that reminded me of a mini-ER. She took my vitals before rolling a portable x-ray machine into position beside the gurney. After x-raying my arm and upper body, she disappeared into another part of the suite with the films. I closed my eyes, grateful for a few minutes of quiet.

Ten minutes later, a man entered the room. He clipped several of the x-rays he carried into a lighted viewing box before meeting my gaze. Although he was Greek, he spoke excellent English. "Miss Paletto, I'm Dr. Makridis."

"Call me Jenna, please."

"Jenna, what happened to you?"

I sighed. "I had a run-in with some bad guys. Got kicked in the chest, and one of them stomped on my arm."

"Bad guys, huh?"

I nodded. "'Fraid, so."

He pushed his glasses up higher on the bridge of his nose as he studied me. "What's that they say? You got the bad end of the deal."

"The raw end of the deal. But they didn't get what they wanted. I did." Sarkis was free, Sophie was alive, and Zach was safe. It was all I cared about.

"You actually sound pleased," the doctor observed.

"If Sophie is going to be all right, I'll be very happy."

"Then be happy, Jenna. Sophie will recover."

Relief flooded me, and tears slid down my cheeks. "That's great news. Thank you, Doctor."

"You have a broken humerous. We'll set that for you."

"Yeah, I figured. What about my ribs?"

"You have two fractured ribs." He gently applied pressure against my sternum and side with his fingertips.

I sucked in a sharp breath. "Man, it feels like every rib on the left side of my body is cracked."

"I imagine it does."

He placed his stethoscope to my chest, instructing me to breathe in and out, slowly and deeply. I did, but it hurt like the devil.

"Your somewhat labored breathing and the pain you're experiencing are because of the multiple hairline fractures. Fortunately, your ribcage protects your internal organs. The x-rays reveal no internal damage."

"You gonna wrap them up?"

"That's no longer standard practice. Fractured ribs generally heal by themselves. You'll want to begin an aspirin or ibuprofen regimen for the pain, and you'll need to rest and allow your body time to heal."

"I've got the time."

I studied the ceiling while Dr. Makridis gave the nurse her instructions. She quickly hooked me up to an I.V. line, and I began to drift off. I remained vaguely aware of Dr. Makridis and his nurse as they set my arm in a cast, but I dozed on and off through most of it. The doctor placed his hand on my shoulder to rouse me when he finished, and I opened my eyes to focus on him.

"Jenna, your arm is set. The nurses will remove the I.V., clean you up, and then they'll take you into another room so that you can sleep for a while."

"Thank you, Doctor." At that point, I felt zero pain, and I was too groggy to say anything more.

***

Later, I wakened to the sight of Will and Zach sprawled on chairs positioned on both sides of the bed I occupied. Both appeared to be sound asleep.

I stretched my neck from side to side. As I stirred, I realized that my arm cast had hardened to granite. I tried to test my range of movement, discovering that it was minimal. The next few months would be a real treat, I thought.

"Are you supposed to be doing that?" Zach whispered as he leaned close to me.

I smiled at my worrywart of a son. "Hi. What time is it?"

Will answered my question. "It's almost 5:00. You've been asleep since noon." He hefted himself from his chair and stood at the side of the bed.

"Hi, there." I suddenly felt shy.

"Nice cast, girlfriend."

Girlfriend! I blinked with surprise. When had that happened? "Any more news about Sophie?" I asked.

Will nodded. "The docs removed the bullet. She'll need physical therapy, but she'll be fine."

"No internal injuries?"

"None," said Zach.

"That's wonderful news."

"Sure is. You're doing great, too, despite the broken arm and a couple of fractured ribs. You should be right as rain in no time."

"I'd like to try to get up."

"I'll go get the nurse," Zach offered.

Alone with Will, I asked, "Where are Mr. St. James and Sarkis?"

"Sarkis hasn't left Sophie's side all afternoon. Mr. St. James and his wife are in the suite next door. Once things settled down, they decided to give Sarkis and Sophie some time alone." He laced his fingers through mine. "I'm relieved you're all right, Jenna."

"Me, too," I whispered. "I had some bad moments in Istanbul."

Will nodded, his usually sunny expression becoming more sober than I'd ever seen it.

Zach returned in short order with one of the nurses, and then he and Will excused themselves. I used the bathroom, groaning when I saw my reflection. My nurse joined me, steadying me at the sink as I washed my face and brushed my teeth.

"Oh! What a beautiful ring," she exclaimed as it slipped out of the tissue pack and rolled onto the counter.

I caught my breath as I picked up the ring Sophie had given to me in our room at the Istanbul hotel. How had the security in Istanbul missed this? They'd gone over all our things with extreme care. I couldn't believe it was still in my possession. "Isn't it?" I said, admiring the only remaining evidence of the cache of jewels hidden so long ago by Armen Begosian.

I knew I couldn't keep it, not when it represented the last sign of Sarkis' heritage. I slipped the ring into the pocket of the plush robe the nurse draped over my shoulders.

She asked, "Shall I wheel you into the living room now?"

"I'm ready."

The nurse did the honors, pushing my wheelchair into a spacious sitting room adjacent to my bedroom. She parked me between Will and Zach, set the chair's brake, and then left the room.

Sarkis emerged from an adjacent bedroom a few minutes later. He grinned from ear to ear when he spotted me. "Ah, how's our patient?"

"No complaints. How's Sophie holding up?" I asked.

"She's feeling very feisty, and she insists on seeing you. Since you're awake, I'll get her into a wheelchair and bring her out. Be right back."

Mr. St. James and his wife arrived as Sarkis disappeared into Sophie's room. I listened while Will and Zach updated them on my medical situation. A few minutes later, the door to Sophie's room opened and Sarkis wheeled her into view. Zach shot up from his seat to help with Sophie's mobile IV pole. Despite her obvious post-surgical fragility and the surgical wrappings that encased the upper part of her body, she looked wonderful.

"Jenna! I'm so glad to see you."

As Sarkis positioned her in front of me, I clasped her extended hand and squeezed her fingers. "How do you feel?"

"Exhausted. What about you?" she asked, her eyes skimming over the cast that covered my left arm from shoulder to fingertips. Tears flooded her eyes. "They hurt you, Jenna."

"Hey, they shot you! I think you got the worst part of the deal. Besides, we'll both be as good as new in no time."

"I certainly hope so. Right now, though, I'm starving!" she announced.

"Sounds like it's time for some of that famous Greek room service!" boomed St. James.

Everyone laughed.

"Darling, I'll see to it," volunteered his new bride.

"Gwen, wait, please," Sarkis said, as he wheeled Sophie into the center of the room and turned her chair so that she faced everyone. "Dad, Sophie and I want to tell you about a discovery the doctor made today."

I held my breath, even though I thought I knew what was coming. Sophie's bright eyes and broad smile confirmed my suspicions.

St. James sank onto the nearest chair. It hit me then that years of dealing with his cancer patient daughter's health issues probably made him expect the worst when doctors were mentioned.

"Sophie's pregnant," Sarkis quickly said, as if sensing St. James's distress. "She's more than three months along, and we didn't even know it."

St. James sat there for a few seconds, obviously stunned. As he gazed at his daughter, tears streamed down his face. Pushing up to his feet, he crossed the short space that separated them, and leaned down to gently embrace her.

"Daddy," she managed before she began to smile and weep.

He clasped her hands in his larger ones. "Sophia Catherine, this is what you've wanted for so long. I am so happy for you."

A beaming Gwen joined St. James. They both gazed down at Sophie, who blotted her tears with a tissue.

St. James turned to Sarkis, hugged him, and then shook his hand. "It's another miracle."

I motioned for Will to push me forward to Sophie. "I'm thrilled for you, Sophie."

"Jenna, you promised you'd bring Sarkis back to me, and you did it. Thank you from the bottom of my heart."

I met her gaze, and said quietly, "I had help, Sophie. Do you remember what you said to me just before you flew out of Istanbul?"

Her eyes widened. "I do. I urged you to ask God for help."

I nodded. "And when I did, He delivered. In fact, He was there with me every step of the way."

Her eyes glittered with new tears. "I didn't think you really heard me."

Sarkis leaned down and handed his pregnant wife a box of tissues. I fished the ring out of the pocket of my robe, handing it to Sarkis. When she saw it, Sophie gasped.

"Since all of the jewels were stolen, I think you should have the last surviving piece of Begosian's treasure," I whispered. "Sophie gave me the ring as a gift, and I hid it. I think its rightful place is with you, Sarkis, since it's a part of your grandfather's legacy."

Sarkis studied the extraordinary ring.

"Thank you, Jenna. I'm honored that you would want me to have this." He glanced at his smiling wife. "However, I would be more honored if you would keep the ring. Consider it a token of our gratitude for all that you've done for Sophie and me. Besides, I have Armen Begosian's Bible as our legacy." With that, he returned the ring to me.

Speechless, I stared in shock at the ring now resting in the palm of my hand.

Will teased, "Just so we're clear. Jenna's still going to send you a bill."

"Nah," I said. "If you have a daughter, just name her Jenna."

To my surprise, both Sophie and Sarkis nodded. They looked totally serious.

EPILOGUE

Eighteen months later.
Hundreds of guests and the national media attended the grand opening of the new Armenian Museum. Suspended above the entrance to the museum, the year "1915" had been rendered in distressed gold on a massive scale. Politicians and celebrities offered brief speeches. Waiters circulated among the attendees carrying trays of food and crystal goblets filled with champagne.

Jenna, Will and Zach strolled the grounds. Paparazzi swarmed around George St. James, who displayed his grandson like a trophy. Even as they answered questions from reporters, Sophie and Sarkis looked amused by the antics of the elder St. James.

Will located a table. The trio settled into their chairs, sipping drinks and enjoying a selection of appetizers.

After a trusted nanny relieved St. James of cranky baby Armen, Sophie and Sarkis made their way toward Jenna, Will and Zach.

They found seats and joined the group.

Jenna spotted a familiar figure. "Oh, good, Ralph made it."

Zach groaned. "Rats. I bet him he wouldn't show up. Now I owe him a twenty."

"This is his first outing since Lynne passed away." Jenna waved him over.

Ralph lumbered in their direction. He ruffled Zach's hair with a swipe of his beefy fingers before he sat down. He accepted a glass of champagne from a passing waiter as he glanced around. "Nice place."

Jenna reached over and hugged him. "I'm glad you decided to join us."

"Me too." He shrugged and took a sip of champagne.

Will reached out and held Jenna's hand while they watched multiple generations of Armenian families as they wandered about. Some of them read the framed historical documents affixed to the walls. Others followed the signs directing them to the new exhibit in a wing that had taken a little over a year to construct.

As a few small groups of people began to depart the museum's main hall, Jenna nudged Will's attention in the direction of a frail-looking couple. They clung to each other, drying their tears and speaking quietly. They approached museum workers, holding hands, appearing to thank them. Composing themselves, they walked away with obvious pride.

Will and Jenna exchanged a thoughtful, sweet glance. Will raised her hand to his lips and kissed it.

Sophie caught them then gasped. "What is that on your ring finger?" she demanded.

"Told you it would take her less than 30 minutes." Jenna smiled and lifted the ring for Sophie to see. "Will proposed last night."

"Man, am I glad that's over!" Zach said. "It took everything in me not to spill the beans!"

"Oh! Congratulations, congratulations! I'm so happy for you!" Sophie exclaimed. "We have to get together and discuss the wedding!"

As they all bent forward to see the ring, Will drew Jenna close to his side and accepted the warm accolades.

"Shall we go see the exhibits now?" Sarkis asked. They rose together and walked toward the entrance to the exhibit hall.

Sophie greeted Zach with a side bump as she hugged him. "How are all your classes going, Zach? Is Astronomy really your favorite subject?"

Zached grinned. "My math classes are easy. I'm handling all my physics classes. The hardest thing I have to conquer is my Chinese professor's accent! I find myself parking at his office, grilling him on things

I don't understand. But yeah, astronomy is one of my favorite classes."

With Will on one side of her, listening to Zach and Sophie chat, Jenna leaned in to Sarkis, "I hardly get to see him. He's always studying. But we're managing."

Sarkis nodded. "I think physics would be a tough major. But, how are his parents? How are they handling Zach's change of university and that he is living with you?"

"You know," Jenna mused. "Oddly enough, they've backed off and have been quiet for the most part. They call him once a week and he's fine with that. Personally, if it were me, I'd be outraged. But I don't see that happening with them, and I can't help wondering why." She pulled Will close who was gazing up at the exhibit. He wrapped his arm around her waist and pulled her in for a kiss.

"Count it as a blessing," Sarkis advised.

As a group they approached the entrance to the exhibit, crossing the threshold and stepping into the semi-dark hall. They heard the faint strains of the traditional music of an ancient culture. The melancholy and somewhat magnetic melodies accompanied them as they walked through the history of the 1915 Armenian genocide in Turkey. A pre-recorded narration eloquently recounted the years leading up to the brutal massacre of over a million and a half Armenian souls. The loss of over a half million Greeks was also given a prominent place.

They exited the exhibit a somber group. Jenna

stopped a moment later, and signaled hello to Monte and Eznik Kazarian as they stood in the lobby. Both were wearing tuxedos and carried filled champagne flutes as they confidently walked over to their group.

George St. James smiled broadly as he also approached. "Ah, Monte, and Eznik. It's a terrific turnout! Better than we expcted!

"It's a great crowd! " Monte motioned behind him with his champagne glass. "There's this reporter from the Times who wants a quick interview with all of us."

St. James looked at Monte. "Perhaps a little later. Remember what we all talked about. And agreed on. We don't divulge a word about where the money came from."

Monte nodded, "People are already assuming you donated most of the funds. But the truth is a good story too, how while Jenna and Sophie were still in physical therapy, Eznik and I managed to smuggle the entire Begosian family fortune out of Turkey."

"With the help of our Turkish friends who live there," Eznik added.

Jenna couldn't help herself. "Yes, it's a good story, but the Turkish authorities might not like hearing they had 70 million dollars in gems taken from their country. Would they demand they had legal claim over the jewels? Even though you and Eznik returned it all to Sarkis, that's the one part of the story that's just for us."

Sophie added, "The saving grace is that Sarkis decided the money from all those gems could be used for a truly good purpose. That the treasure could be used to build a museum that would showcase the truth about the Armenian Genocide."

Jenna shook her head as she gazed around the museum. "Armen Begosian knew his stuff. He collected only the best and rarest of gems."

A waiter appeared with a tray of champagne flutes. Zach and Ralph passed them around to the small group. A photographer asked them to pose while he took shots of them toasting.

Sarkis raised his glass. "To Armen and Varteni Begosian." The photographer clicked away.

George St. James waved off the photographer, and then raised his glass. "And to Jenna Paletto. Who rescued my daughter in her terrible time of need..." he choked back his emotions, paused to regain his composure and went on, "and saved Sarkis, my son-in-law and father of my granson, Armen. None of this would have happened had it not been for you, Jenna. You were fearless. I thank you from the bottom of my heart. "

They all joined in with cries of "hear, hear!" St. James gave Jenna a crushing bear hug.

Beet red, and suddenly self-conscious, Jenna shook her head and turned to Monte and Eznik. "I have to hand it to you! Burying those gems in cheap pottery and painting and glazing over it, and then shipping it all to Fresno. Brilliant. Better than our idea, smuggling them out on a rented boat to Cyprus!"

Sophie joined in. "That was Will's idea."

Will shot them a look of mock outrage. "Hey, I was asked for a solution in the space of five minutes!"

Jenna looked around. "Monte, this museum is spectacular. You and Eznik did a wonderful job here."

Together, Eznik and Monte drew close to her. Monte gave his brother a sheepish glance. Then with a nod, he said to Jenna. "To tell you the truth, our time in Istanbul with you and Sophie changed me. I had a lot of, ah, personal history that I allowed to rule my emotions. It got us off on the wrong foot. And I've never told you how sorry I am for how I acted. I could have done things a lot differently."

Jenna tipped her champagne flute in their direction. "Apology accepted. I think that trip changed us all."

A grinning Eznik threw an arm around Monte's shoulders and gave him a bear hug. "And it helps that Monte met a nice woman who actually likes him."

"You can stop talking now," Monte warned.

At their invitation, St. James and Sarkis escorted the brothers into the lobby to introduce them to the rich and famous.

A few hours later, it was time to leave. Sophie's nanny packed up the baby gear. Sarkis pushed their son's stroller, while Sophie carried baby Armen.

"Don't you feel a sense of satisfaction, Jenna?" Sophie asked as they all departed the museum. "I've felt it all day! To use that treasure in the hopes of preventing genocide from ever happening again."

"Monte was the creative force, and I'm very impressed with what he did," said Sarkis.

"I do feel it, Sophie. This museum and its new foundation are a great way to teach their history." Jenna slipped her arm through Will's, the other through Zach's. "Hopefully, the world will always remember what happened." The friends walked through the massive doors of the museum.

It was a beautiful day.

ACKNOWLEDGEMENTS

I wish to acknowledge the following people:

Special thanks for the loving teaching style of Lou Nelson who opened my eyes to what *Saving Sarkis* could be. Laura Taylor was a whiz at editing during the early stages of the manuscript.

Those friends from my writing group, especially Judy Whitmore, Dennis Phinney, and Janet Simcic, who taught me to critique in love and kindness, and who gave me consummate hope.

Dave Baccitich, who volunteered many details on private jets, airports, security and loads of information only a pilot would know.

My sister Naomi Moon, who was willing to join me on a research trip to Istanbul and Athens, Greece.

The many patient, loving, kind friends and family members who read endless pages for me and gave me their feedback, especially my late mother, Mary Patricia Alex, who loved reading every page as only a mother would!

Kristin Lindstrom at Flying Pig Media for handling every inch of publishing production for *Saving Sarkis*. You're a dream!

My sweet and wonderful husband Armen, whose family legacy provided the seeds from which *Saving Sarkis* grew.

I thank you all from the bottom of my heart.

About the Author

Although born in Minneapolis, Minnesota, Mary Guleserian is a bona fide California girl with a degree in Theatre Arts.

An experienced public speaker, she has spent many years on the speaking circuit for Christian Women's Clubs and Church groups. She is a women's Bible Study teacher at her church, and is also a children's Sunday School teacher and is currently a member of Community Bible Study.

Her writing credentials include a non-fiction work, *The Baby-Sitter's Survival Guide*, which was first published by Focus On the Family in 1996.

Mary resides in the quaint city of Orange, California, with her husband Armen. She is the mother of three grown sons, and stepmother to two sons and a daughter.

Contact the author at: www.maryguleserian.com.

47451532R00227

Made in the USA
San Bernardino, CA
30 March 2017